Lord Roworth's Reward

Carola Dunn

THORNDIKE
CHIVERS

This Large Print edition is published by Thorndike Press, Waterville, Maine, USA and by AudioGO Ltd, Bath, England.
Thorndike Press, a part of Gale, Cengage Learning.

LIBRARY OF CONGRESS CATALOGING-IN-PUBLICATION DATA

Dunn, Carola.
    [His lordship's reward]
    Lord Roworth's reward / by Carola Dunn.
        p. cm. — (Thorndike Press large print gentle romance)
    Previously published under title: His lordship's reward.
    ISBN-13: 978-1-4104-2862-2 (hardcover)
    ISBN-10: 1-4104-2862-1 (hardcover)
    1. Large type books. I. Title.
PR6054.U537H57 2010
823'.914—dc22   2010014473

BRITISH LIBRARY CATALOGUING-IN-PUBLICATION DATA AVAILABLE
Published in 2010 in the U.S. by arrangement with Carola Dunn.
Published in 2010 in the U.K. by arrangement with Carola Dunn.

U.K. Hardcover: 978 1 408 49118 8 (Chivers Large Print)
U.K. Softcover: 978 1 408 49119 5 (Camden Large Print)

Printed and bound in Great Britain by the MPG Books Group
1 2 3 4 5 6 7 14 13 12 11 10

LORD ROWORTH'S
REWARD

CHAPTER 1

The parlour door-latch clicked. Felix glanced up, on the verge of embarrassment at being discovered on his hands and knees on the worn brown drugget carpet, but of course it was only Fanny.

His little rider slid off his back and ran to her, black ringlets flying. "*Tía,* have you buyed me a great big sugar plum?"

"Bought," Fanny corrected automatically, setting down her basket on the table. As Felix sprang to his feet and dusted the knees of his buckskin breeches, he saw that she was hot and tired, her brown curls limp under the jaunty straw hat with its single sagging plume. Though it was still May, Brussels sweltered under a cloudless sky.

"Did you bought me one?" Anita repeated obediently.

Fanny's round face dimpled in a smile at Felix. "Yes," she assured the child, "you shall have a sugar plum but you must eat

7

your bread and milk first. Did you thank *Tío* Felix for giving you a ride?"

"Not yet." Spreading her skirts with two tiny hands, Anita wobbled a curtsy, the tip of her tongue protruding from the corner of her mouth in her concentration. "There," she said with a beam of triumph. "Thank you, Tío Felix, my lord. You are a good horse."

Laughing, Felix swept her up in his arms and kissed her soft cheek. "And you are a good rider."

"She should be. She started on a Spanish mule before she was two." Fanny took off her hat, crossed to the tarnished looking-glass over the mantel, and did her best with deft fingers to set her curls in order. "Thank you for taking care of her, my lord," she said over one slim shoulder. "The marketing took longer than I expected, I'm afraid. There are more and more soldiers in the streets every day, which I daresay we should be glad of."

"Certainly, since sooner or later it is bound to come to a battle. According to all reports, Boney is still drawing troops to his Eagles."

"But half of ours are raw recruits, or Belgian farm lads of doubtful allegiance. Many of them are mere boys, and of the

8

Brunswickers, too, however impressive they look in their black with those horrid skulls and crossbones on their shakos! Still, today you will see the flower of the British Army. I trust I have not made you late for your appointment with Lady Sophia — or is it Madame Lisle you are taking to the Review?" she added with a quizzing look.

"Lady Sophia," Felix answered curtly. Miss Fanny Ingram should not even be aware of his Belgian *chère-amie,* let alone mention her. But then, one could not expect the delicacy of a well-bred, sheltered young lady, the exquisite sensibilities of a Lady Sophia, in a female who had followed the drum from birth.

Now what had she said to make him poker up? Fanny wondered. Lord Roworth usually took her teasing in good part. Of course: she ought not to have mentioned his mistress. Mama would have been equally shocked at her daughter's frankness, but Mama was buried somewhere in the Spanish mountains south of Coruña. After six years, it was difficult to remember all her lessons.

Still, if Fanny should not have spoken so, Lord Roworth ought not to have set up a mistress when he was assiduously courting a noble beauty. Frank had told her about

Katrina Lisle, and they had shaken their heads together over the peculiar ways of the nobility.

Felix Roworth was handsome enough to keep any number of females happy, with his dark-gold locks, ruffled now by Anita's clasp, his brilliant blue eyes, his tall, broad-shouldered form. But Fanny had no intention of being numbered among those languishing females. Nor had she any intention of letting his disapproval abash her.

"Then you had best be on your way, sir," she said tranquilly.

He grinned, his momentary stiffness vanished. "Lady Sophia does not care for tardiness in her suitors, true, but I'm not late. Wellington is not to arrive until two, I understand."

"Well, you should know, intimate with Old Hookey as you are. Poor Frank and Captain Mercer have been out there with their guns since early this morning. They have to see that the men polish the barrels, as well as their buttons, buckles and boots. Though the Duke never has a good word for the Artillery, Colonel Frazer insists that today they shine as brightly as the rest of the Cavalry."

"Do you go?"

"Not I. Twenty miles, in this heat, to see

10

our fellows dressed up in their fancy coats?"
She spoke lightly, with scorn, to hide her
wistful desire to see the Review. Her brother's Horse Artillery battery was seldom on
parade.

Though usually less than perceptive, Lord
Roworth saw through her pretense of indifference. "I wish I might offer to take you,
but Lady Sophia is expecting my escort and
I've borrowed a curricle which will only
hold two, with her groom up behind."

Even if he had a spacious barouche, Lady
Sophia would hardly appreciate the presence of a dowdy stranger and a small child
on her excursion, Fanny thought sardonically. Just as well it was impossible, but it
was a kind notion, typical of his good
nature. Whatever his faults, he was a dear.

"Never mind," she said, turning to practical matters, "I really must finish Anita's new
dress. She grows shockingly fast."

"My new dress is blue and it has scarlet
ribbons," Anita announced with pride.
"That's the same colours like Tío Frank's
best coat."

"*As* Tío Frank's coat. Come, Anita, we
must take the basket to Henriette in the
kitchen."

"I'll carry it," Felix offered, picking it up.
"It's heavy! What a deuced nuisance that

11

Henriette will not go to market."

"She is far too busy, not to mention too fat. Madame Vilvoorde used to go herself, I collect, but now she is a landlady and above such things."

"Landlady! She lets out a few shabby rooms at an exorbitant rent!" he snorted. "You ought not to have to shop for provisions."

"I don't mind. Believe me, it is easy compared to foraging in the Peninsula!"

"That I can believe. I'd send Trevor, but he would quit me on the instant, though he's been with me for years. Already he's sorely tried by having to refurbish my old clothes to make them fit for the company I must keep."

"And the company you choose to keep," she said tartly. After all, the pursuit of Lady Sophia was no part of his duties. "No, it would never do to send a gentleman's gentleman to purchase onions and a leg of mutton. Hoskins, being a mere trooper, helps when he can, as indeed he did in Spain."

"I like Hoxins," Anita observed. "He made my so'jers for me."

"Your brother's batman? I suppose he is on parade today with the rest."

"Yes, and you will miss the parade — or

12

at least vex Lady Sophia — if you do not go now. Thank you for your offer, Lord Roworth, but I'll take the basket to Henriette; it is not so very heavy."

"I'll help you," Anita piped up.

Felix went out with them into the cramped entrance hall and paused at the bottom of the stairs to watch them go down the passage to the kitchen. The basket was heavy, but she bore it with an ease that belied her slight frame, despite the drag of Anita hanging onto the handle and trotting alongside.

He smiled at the sight. The Ingrams' three-year-old ward was an obliging child, and she bid fair to become a raging beauty, endowed as she was with the black hair and eyes of her Spanish mother.

He lost his smile as the door on the other side of the hall clicked shut. That damn woman spying again! Not only did Madame Vilvoorde overcharge for her paltry chambers and refuse to do the marketing, she kept vigil over her lodgers' every move. Doubtless she was now listening for the creak of the uncarpeted stairs as he took them two at a time on his way to his bedchamber.

Still, rooms were hard to come by in Brussels at present, and even if he found them, pleasanter lodgings in a better part of town would cost more than he could afford.

Nor could he hope for more agreeable fellow-tenants than Captain Frank Ingram of the Royal Horse Artillery, his twin sister, and their small charge. The captain had been among the first troops sent out from England. Felix had arrived in Brussels earlier, after following Wellington from Vienna, but he then made a quick visit to London. On his return to Madame Vilvoorde's he found the Ingrams just moved in. Accustomed to the free and easy interchange of army life, they had welcomed him with unpretentious friendliness.

As they shared a common dining parlour, he had perforce seen a good deal of them in the six weeks since. His habitual reserve was not proof against their good-natured cheerfulness. Now they were among the select few who knew that he had a purpose in Brussels beyond the social round.

Lady Sophia Gerrold would be scandalized if she ever discovered that Felix, Viscount Roworth, heir to the Earl of Westwood, was employed by the Jewish banker, Nathan Rothschild of London. The daughter of a marquis was entitled to hold herself on high form.

Fortunately, Lady Sophia need never know. As far as she and most others were concerned, he was in Brussels to enjoy the entertainments of the transplanted Season, as she was. Half the Ton had deserted London.

"My lord, your hair! My lord, your cravat!" Trevor's wail of outrage broke in upon his thoughts.

Felix glanced at the mirror on his dressing table and grinned. Anita had used his elegantly tied neckcloth as reins. He looked as if he had been dragged backwards through a bramble bush. Thank heaven only Fanny had seen him.

"I rely upon you to make me fit for Lady Sophia's eyes within ten minutes," he drawled.

Ten minutes later, a fresh cravat in a Waterfall about his neck, his hair brushed into the fashionable Windswept style, his coat creaseless across his broad shoulders, he ran downstairs. His friend Lord Fitzroy Somerset had lent his curricle since, as Wellington's Military Secretary, he would be riding with his commander today. After all, Felix thought, Rothschild had hired him because of his connections in the ton, so he might as well make use of those connections.

He drove through the busy, sultry streets, between the stepped façades of the Flemish burghers' houses, to the Rue de Belle Vue. Here Lady Sophia's parents, the Marquis and Marchioness of Daventry, had rented a splendid *hôtel.* When the butler showed Felix into the ornately rococo drawing room, he was met by a masculine chorus of groans.

"You're late, Roworth," cried a large young man with luxuriant whiskers, dressed in the scarlet and gold of the Life Guards. "Lady Sophia, punish the wretch by coming to the Review with me."

An older officer in Rifleman's green pressed his claim to the Goddess's exclusive company.

"Milady will be more comfortable in my barouche," suggested a dark, suave gentleman in impeccable morning dress. A large diamond flashed in the folds of his neckcloth. Felix recognized the Comte de St Gérard, a Belgian civilian of reputedly enormous wealth.

"I am promised to Lord Roworth, gentlemen," said Lady Sophia with unruffled calm as she rose gracefully to her feet and offered him her gloved hand. He bowed over it, drinking in the refreshing sight of her cool beauty.

From ash-blond ringlets to dainty foot clad in blue kid, Lady Sophia was perfec-

16

tion. Long-lashed eyes the pale blue of a winter sky, a delicate oval face touched with the blush of wild roses, straight little nose, willowy figure, thirty thousand pounds . . . but of course it was not for her dowry that Felix wanted her.

If her beauty were not enough to explain his devotion, he admired her grace and elegance, and above all her unshakeable dignity. The Goddess was the very pattern-card of what a high-born young lady should be.

He sighed. Pride forbade his offering for her while his family's fortunes were at low ebb, though his birth matched her own. Yet he could dream of his parents' unqualified approbation — denied him since he went to work for Rothschild — if he took her home to Westwood as his bride. He could dream of the triumph of carrying her off under the noses of his rivals.

She handled her many importunate suitors with well-bred composure. Felix watched her depress the pretensions of an enamoured youth with a blank stare of feigned incomprehension. Rumour had it that in the three years since her come-out, she had dashed the hopes of a full score. Lady Daventry was said to despair of her fastidious daughter. Her younger, plainer sister had

17

already contracted a respectable match and had stayed at home in England with her betrothed's family.

"Sorry, fellows," Felix said smugly, content for the moment with a small victory. "Shall we be off, ma'am?"

Though he had, in fact, kept Lady Sophia waiting for a few minutes, it was beneath her dignity to take him to task, let alone to tease him, as Fanny would have. As he escorted her from the room under the jealous gaze of his rivals, she spoke sedately of the unseasonable weather and the necessity of always carrying a parasol to protect the complexion.

"Your complexion is worth protecting," he assured her with fervour. She looked a trifle displeased at so personal a compliment, so he went on to praise her parasol, an elaborate affair of blue silk trimmed with Ghent lace.

"I purchased it yesterday," she told him complacently. "It is shocking how quickly colours fade in the sun, I vow. None of my others is fit to be seen."

One of Lord Daventry's grooms was waiting with the curricle. Handing Lady Sophia in, Felix said, "I have borrowed Lord Fitzroy's carriage. I trust you will find it as comfortable as St Gérard's barouche." He joined her on the seat, the groom swung up behind, and they set off.

"In general I consider the curricle to be an unsuitable vehicle for a female of delicate principles — even a trifle fast. However, Mama assures me that I am a deal too nice in my notions. After all, we are abroad and cannot expect the same attention to the details of propriety as in England."

"Very true."

"You will not drive too rapidly. Major Peters drove me in his phaeton at great speed last week. I was forced to point out to him that haste is vulgar and unseemly."

"We shall not go above a trot," promised Felix, who had hired the best horses he could afford in the hope of impressing the Goddess with his skill in handling the ribbons.

As a result of their sloth on the road, they reached the parade ground, a natural amphitheatre on the banks of a river, considerably after the Duke and his entourage. The rim of the declivity was crowded with the carriages of fashionable ladies in pastel gauzes, elegant gentlemen in swallowtail coats and polished top boots. All the world had driven out from Brussels and from the French king's temporary court at Ghent to view the splendour of the British Cavalry.

In the carnival atmosphere, Felix had to remind himself that the serried ranks of gaudy-uniformed Dragoons and Hussars, rigid on their magnificent chargers, were preparing for war.

The gleaming guns of the Horse Artillery were an ominous confirmation. Shading his eyes against the sun, Felix gazed at each battery in turn, hoping to catch sight of Captain Ingram so that he could tell Fanny he had seen her brother. In the mass of men, no individuals were distinguishable.

He could pick out some members of Wellington's entourage, though, as they proceeded slowly through the lines, inspecting the troops. "There is the Duke," he pointed out to Lady Sophia, "as always the plainest dressed among all the glittering foreign dignitaries. That's Lord Uxbridge in the Hussar uniform. The stout old chap with the white whiskers is Marshal Prince von Blücher, the Prussian commander."

"I see the Duchess of Richmond and Lady Georgiana," she said. "Pray take me to their carriage. I simply must ask Lady Georgiana where she bought that delightful hat. Is it not charming? Something like a Villager hat but with a subtle difference of shape, I fancy."

Helping her down from the curricle, Felix

mentally kicked himself for attempting to draw her attention to the armed might drawn up before them. Fanny might knowledgeably discuss military matters, but delicate young ladies could not be expected to take an interest, he thought with fond indulgence. Thank heaven! If Lady Sophia read the message of those howitzers and 9-pounders, she'd take fright and persuade her parents to flee the country. In that case, months might pass before he saw her again.

The Duchess of Richmond was acquainted with Felix's mother, Lady Westwood, and asked Felix for news of his family. While he chatted with her, Georgiana, a lively damsel of seventeen, laughingly dismissed her court of admirers and invited Sophia to join her in the barouche for a comfortable cose.

Felix caught some of their discussion of the delectable hat, of high crowns and low crowns, plumes and silk flowers. He was recalling with pity Fanny's only headgear, garnished with its single drooping feather, when Georgiana said, "Mama is planning a grand ball, you know. You will receive your invitation as soon as we have settled upon a date. And you too, my lord. I trust you will still be in Brussels?" She smiled up at him with a flirtatious twinkle.

"Now how can he possibly know that," the duchess protested, "when we have not yet set the date, Georgy? I mean to consult Wellington first."

"Oh yes," cried her unrepentant daughter. "How shocking if he could not come!" She turned back to Lady Sophia.

"I was thinking more of the military situation, Roworth," said her grace in a low voice. "Have you any news from Paris? You have connections there, I collect." She was one of the few who had some notion of his position, her husband being an intimate of Wellington's.

Felix passed on the most recent word he had received from Jakob Rothschild in Paris, information he had given to Wellington yesterday. "Napoleon's grand gathering of his supporters — the *Champ de Mai,* he calls it — is now planned for the first of June. I believe the Duke expects him to be disappointed in the numbers, but whether that will dissuade him from marching on Belgium, who can guess?"

"The whole affair is sadly unsettling. I should take the girls home if it were not for Richmond's insistence on staying. William, too, is determined to be in the middle of things, though he is far from recovered from his fall. And of course March cannot leave.

Indeed, he is very happy with his position on the Prince of Orange's staff."

"Slender Billy is an congenial young man, and it is to be hoped that your son will act as a steadying influence upon his volatility!"

The duchess laughed. "Yes, March is a serious boy, compared to the prince at least, though they are both no more than three-and-twenty. And if he fails to restrain the prince, why, I daresay the more experienced officers on his staff will manage it."

"I understand that Prince Bernhard, despite his youth, also has a head on his shoulders."

"Poor Orange must feel quite hemmed in, I vow."

Felix and Lady Sophia strolled on to exchange greetings with a number of other spectators. They moved in the same circles and knew many of the same people.

Lady Sophia remained cool and gracious in the scorching heat, while all around ladies fanned themselves vigorously and gentlemen's starched neckcloths wilted. Proud to have her on his arm, Felix noted the many envious glances cast at him by the officers of foot regiments who mingled with the crowds. Those confounded Life Guards in their flashy scarlet and gold were used to having things all their own way with the ladies. "The Gentlemen's Sons," they called themselves; "Hyde Park soldiers" was the contemptuous name given them by Peninsular veterans like Fanny's brother.

Down on the parade ground, the Review continued. The faces of the Hussars, sweating in fur caps and fur-trimmed pelisses, shone almost as bright as their silver lace. At one of the artillery batteries flanking their precise squadrons, Marshal Blücher had paused and appeared to be inspecting every horse. An occasional guttural exclamation of "*Mein Gott,* fery goot," floated up.

"This looks as if it could go on for ever," said Felix. "Do you care to leave now?"

"If you wish, sir," Lady Sophia agreed obligingly. "I see that several carriages are departing already."

They made their way back to the curricle. Waiting beside it was Major Sir Henry Bissell of the 95th Rifles. Felix greeted him with annoyance. He had thought the fellow routed at the Daventrys' hôtel.

"How kind in you to come to meet us, Sir Henry," said Lady Sophia, sounding indifferent, "but we are just about to leave, you know."

"I shall ride beside you," declared the major, bowing. "Beauty cannot have too many escorts."

As they returned towards Brussels, Lady Sophia politely divided her attention between the two men. She gave no particular encouragement to the soldier in his smart green regimentals, but nor could Felix flatter himself that she favoured him.

The Goddess's preferences, if any, were a mystery. He was the more determined to win her hand.

CHAPTER 2

As Felix reached for Madame Vilvoorde's front door knob, a small man in a frieze coat and catskin waistcoat darted from the shade of a nearby doorway. He doffed a hat that appeared to have been sat upon at some point in its history, then bashed back into shape with questionable success.

" 'Ere, guv, you live in this 'ouse?" he queried in unmistakably Cockney tones.

"What of it?" Felix assumed his haughtiest manner.

"It's like this, guv: Oi'm looking fer summun by name of Ingram."

Frank and Fanny must have left debts in England, Felix guessed at once. Well, it was none of his affair and he'd be damned if he'd assist the bailiffs. Fanny and Anita in debtors' prison didn't bear thinking of. What was more, come to think of it, he rather doubted that an English writ could be enforced in Belgium.

26

"Young chap, army orficer," the man went on urgently. "There'll be a sister, too, if me hinformation's correct. Oi needs ter know their ages, precise-loike, and where they was born, and . . ."

"My good man, even if I happened to be acquainted with the people you are looking for, such personal details cannot possibly be of any concern to either of us. Be off with you, or I'll call a gendarme."

However legitimate his business, the man must have had qualms about tangling with foreign officials for he looked round nervously. Felix made his escape.

Closing the front door firmly behind him, he went into the parlour. Anita knelt on a chair at the scarred deal table, playing with the toy soldiers, made by Corporal Hoskins, that she much preferred to her doll. Fanny sat nearby, sewing a wristband onto a shirt.

" 'Lo, Tío Felix."

"Back already, Lord Roworth? I daresay Lady Sophia was drooping from the heat."

"Not at all, but I was. Ingram will be late home tonight, will he?"

"Yes, he'll have to see his men and guns safely back to their cantonment. The company is at Braine-le-Comte with Slender Billy now, you know. Frank may even spend the night there."

Captain Ingram probably had a pretty Flemish farm girl in starched white cap and wide, full skirts waiting for him. In his absence, Felix was in two minds whether to tell Fanny about the inquisitive Cockney. He didn't want to alarm her — but after her adventurous life she was not easily overset.

His unusual enquiry after her brother alerted Fanny. "Did you wish to speak to Frank?" she asked. Her busy hands stilled as she saw his uncertainty. Fear clutched her heart. "News of Napoleon?"

"No, no, it's probably nothing. I met an odd little man on the doorstep just now, enquiring about you and Frank, your birthdates and so on. I sent him off with a flea in his ear but I thought you ought to know."

"Madame Vilvoorde said someone asked after us," she told him, puzzled, yet more aware of a flood of relief that a battle was not imminent. "She refused to speak to him. I cannot imagine who he is, or why he is asking such strange questions. If she understood him aright, he wanted to know Mama's maiden name, and what we were christened!"

"Now that is something I have long wished for an excuse to pry into. Fanny and Frank

— Frances and Francis?"

Her peal of laughter made Anita look round, beaming. She had always loved to hear Fanny laugh. Knocking her soldiers in a heap, she announced, "All fall down," jumped down from her chair and ran to her. "Tell me what's funny, Tía."

"A grown-up joke, darling." She set down her sewing and pulled the little girl onto her lap, where Anita settled contentedly. "Yes, Roworth, Frances and Francis."

"You were born in India, I think you said, when your father was stationed there?"

"In the monsoon season, and baptised in the middle of a flood. I was supposed to be christened first, being the elder by two hours. Mama was unwell, and Papa was too worried about her — and about his beloved guns! — to notice when the chaplain picked up the wrong baby. Asked for a name he just said 'Frances'. When the mistake was discovered, the chaplain refused to revoke the sacrament, though he did change the spelling of Frank's first name. Papa couldn't think of any girl's name he liked other than his wife's, so we were both christened after Mama." She sighed, recalling how, every time their birthday came round, her father had told the tale as a joke on himself.

"Frank inherited your mother's middle

name, too, I collect?" Lord Roworth enquired. "Dare I ask what it is?"

"I am sworn on pain of death never to reveal it to a living soul."

He grinned. "Like that, is it?"

"Ask him and he'll deny possessing a middle name. Did you see him at the Review?"

"No, though I looked. In the mass of uniforms any one face was impossible to make out."

She nodded her understanding. "Did Lady Sophia enjoy the outing?"

"I believe so. She is not given to effusions."

"Did she not thank you?" Fanny demanded, indignant on his behalf.

"Of course. Her manners are perfection. However, I cannot pretend that the troops interested her. Fortunately it was something of a social occasion, also, so among the spectators we met many mutual friends and acquaintances."

"It must be fun to make one's come-out and spend one's time in fashionable entertainments," she said with regret. Lady Sophia did not realize how lucky she was to be able to dismiss the war preparations from her mind and think only of pleasure. "We do have our own dinner parties and informal

30

hops in the army, but Wellington only invites officers of good family to his formal balls."

He looked vaguely guilty, and she guessed that some grand party was planned to which he was invited. She was grateful when he did not proceed to tell her all about it. Instead, to her surprise, he consulted her.

"Lady Sophia made her début three years ago. Would you not expect her to grow weary of constant social engagements, to long to settle down with a family? I cannot understand why she is not married. I know she has had dozens of offers."

"Who can blame her if she prefers to be single, spoiled by indulgent parents, rather than taking on the responsibilities of married life!" Afraid he might think her irony due to envy, she added, "But perhaps she simply has not yet found a gentleman she cares for enough to choose to wed."

"I must hope she continues particular until I am in a position to offer for her. I wish I could be sure what her feelings are for me," he groaned. "Surely she must care for me a little, since she permits me to squire her although she's aware that my pockets are to let."

"You have told her you work for a living?" No doubt the high-and-mighty Lady Sophia would despise his employment. The more

Fanny heard of her, the less she liked her.

"Not in so many words, I admit, but she knows where I lodge." He glanced around the dingy room with distaste.

To Fanny the parlour seemed comfortable, if not cheerful. Trying to see it through his eyes, she said, "I suppose she considers this the wrong side of town! Will not your employer pay for better lodgings and smarter clothes, since he requires you to mingle with the best society?"

"I daresay Mr Rothschild might count the expenditure justified, but I cannot. My personal expenses must come from my own pocket." Obviously pride forbade his living in clover at the banker's expense, the sort of pride Fanny appreciated. "I've made no secret of being purse-pinched," he went on. "Today, for instance, I pointed out that I'd borrowed the curricle I drove. Her only objection was that a curricle is too sporting a vehicle for a lady to ride in with perfect decorum."

She giggled. "I wonder what she'd have thought if she had seen me crossing the Spanish mountains astride a mule!"

Though he smiled, he said seriously, "She is, perhaps, a trifle over-fastidious, but she always conducts herself with the utmost propriety and I honour her for it. After all, she is the daughter of a marquis. Rank brings obligations as well as pleasures."

"No doubt." She was by no means convinced of any connection between a sense of duty and a disposition to make a fuss over trifles. "Well, I must go and see how Henriette is getting on with our dinner." Setting Anita on the floor, she stood up.

"I'll dine out tomorrow, by the way. I'm going to a café outside the ramparts."

"One of those places where the Belgian bourgeoisie make merry? Not with Lady Sophia, I assume!" She couldn't resist the dig. "Are you coming to the kitchen with me, Anita?"

"I want Tío Felix to play so'jers with me." An admonitory glance made her change her words. "Please, dear Tío Felix, my lord, will you play so'jers with me? Which do you like bestest, infantly or calvary?"

"Artillery," said Felix promptly. Like Frank Ingram, her father had been an artillery officer.

"Me too, but I can't say it," Anita confessed, and tugged him over to the table to set up her fallen troops.

Fanny watched them with a smile before turning to go to the kitchen. Lady Sophia might appear immune to his charm, but Anita adored him. If only she could prevent herself succumbing!

Katrina Lisle had reasons other than Lord Roworth's charm for appreciating him. A voluptuous, red-headed Fleming, she was the widow of a Walloon soldier who had fought for the French emperor. He had died during Napoleon's abortive invasion of Russia and she hated armies in general, Bonaparte in particular, with a passion unusual in the phlegmatic Flemish race.

That passion spilled over into her relationship with Felix. Unattached to the army yet doing his part to overthrow the usurper, he was to her mind the ideal lover, as she told him often. He didn't mind that, but it was a trifle embarrassing when she expatiated on his height and strength; his handsome, aristocratic face; his blue eyes and golden hair; his superior performance in bed.

"Ach, those who say the English are cold-blooded know nothing!" she would exclaim.

Fortunately she kept such effusions for her chamber. They spent a pleasant evening at a café just outside the Namur gate and then repaired to her house for a night of superior performances.

Felix returned to Madame Vilvoorde's after a late breakfast the next day, to find awaiting him a courier from London. Fanny had invited Moses Solomon into the parlour and was plying him with tea. Anita was plying the slight, dark young man with questions, for he was a regular visitor and therefore a friend of hers.

"Was there big waves when you went on the boat? Did you see lots of seagulls? Did you throw bread for them? I did, when I went on a boat. They catched it in the air. Did you see fishes? Tío Frank says there's lots of fishes in the sea, but I didn't see them," she lamented.

"Come along, chatterbox." Fanny smiled at Felix as he entered the room, her irresistible dimples as always bringing an answering smile to his face. "We'll leave you to do your business in peace, Lord Roworth. If you'd like some tea I'll send Henriette with a fresh pot. She has learned how to brew it quite respectably. Mr Solomon, I hope you will take a luncheon with us?"

"Th-thank you, Miss Ingram, I'll be happy to." He turned to Felix as Fanny departed, and said with enthusiasm, "W-what a splendid person she is! P-pretty and gay and always w-welcoming. I haven't the least claim on her hospitality. If she weren't a Goy . . ."

"What, thinking of marriage?" Felix was

surprised and displeased.

"No, no, my mother would drop dead if I brought home a Gentile w-wife," he said regretfully.

"Besides which, Miss Ingram must be four or five years older than you are. Come now, to business."

"Yes, my lord. I've brought another load of g-gold for the Duke of Wellington. As usual, Mr Rothschild wants you to check it, before I deliver it to Mr Herries at the Commissariat, and to personally report its arrival to General Wellington. There's a letter, too — here you are. I think it's about the subsidy for Hanover."

Felix groaned. "Not that business still!" He took the letter, broke the seal, and read it. "All right, I'll have to discuss this with the Duke. We'd best go right away and check the gold. The army's appetite for the stuff is inexhaustible."

At a nearby mews, the carriage that had brought the gold from Ostend was guarded by a stalwart coachman with horse-pistols and a burly guard with a shotgun. Though the Rothschilds owned several carriages with hidden compartments, Felix recognized the shabby black vehicle at once.

Four years ago he and Isaac Cohen had driven it from Paris to the Pyrenees through the very heart of the enemy's country, loaded then, too, with gold for Wellington. They had had no guards with them, only the brave young woman who was now Isaac's wife.

Felix sighed. He still carried Miriam's image in his heart, though no doubt she had been right and a marriage between them would never have worked. Certainly his parents would never have approved of her, he reminded himself, as he knew they would of Lady Sophia Gerrold.

This consignment of gold was mostly in ingots and was soon counted. Sending young Solomon on to the Commissary-General with a reminder to have the receipt signed by Herries himself, Felix walked to the Duke's Headquarters.

As always the hôtel in the Rue Royale, overlooking the park, was aswarm with Wellington's personal staff. Young men of noble birth, equally at home in the ballroom or the saddle — Felix might have been one of them had his father not lost a fortune. They referred to themselves as the Duke's "family," and in fact Lord Fitzroy Somerset was married to his commander's niece.

The older officers, Felix had known during his years on the Town. As the Rothschilds' liaison with Wellington, he had met others in Paris when the Duke was ambassador, or in Vienna during the Congress. As heir to an earldom he was always welcome, especially as most knew something of his unconventional part in the struggle against Napoleon.

"What news, Roworth?" a plump gentleman in the white net pantaloons, blue frock coat, and fringed sash of the Staff greeted Felix. Colonel Sir Alexander Gordon had been one of Wellington's aides since Portugal.

"None for your ears," Felix responded firmly. "Is Fitzroy around?"

"Gordon's 'a round'," teased Lord March, the Richmonds' eldest son. "Fitzroy's on the slim side. He's with the Duke at present, Roworth, consulting with my lord and master."

"Slender Billy's here? I suspect my news will make the Duke speak words about King William that his majesty's royal heir ought not to hear."

"The Hanoverian subsidies?" The youthful Lieutenant the Honourable George Cathcart, lounging by the window, was promptly frowned down by Canning and Percy. Such delicate matters of diplomacy and finance were not to be bandied about by very junior officers.

"They shouldn't be long now," said Gordon, "and Fitzroy hasn't mentioned anything in particular on the schedule that might interrupt you. You'll want to see the Duke himself, I expect?"

"If there's trouble with King William, I suppose he'll be in a devilish mood for the rest of the day," moaned Cathcart.

"I've good news too," Felix assured him with a grin. A shipment of gold was always welcome.

Five minutes later, the Prince of Orange erupted into the room, with Lord Fitzroy following at a more sober pace. The young heir to the throne of the Netherlands, despite the glory of a General's uniform, was an unimpressive figure. He was very thin, with protuberant eyes and a wide mouth that gave rise to his other nickname, the Young Frog, his stout father being known to the irreverent as the Old Frog.

However, the prince's irrepressible gaiety and lack of condescension made him generally popular with the Staff, of which he had once been a member. "March!" he cried, "the Beau wants to see you. It's my belief he'll repeat everything to you in case I wasn't listening."

"And were you listening, sir?" Gordon enquired as Lord March departed.

"To every word that falls from the Great Man's lips, *je vous assure!* Tell them, Fitzroy, that I was most attentive."

"His Highness was most attentive," said Fitzroy gravely, a twinkle lurking in his eyes. "Sir, are you acquainted with Lord Roworth?"

"We've met," said the prince with a friendly smile as Felix bowed. "At some ball or other, was it not?" They exchanged a few words, and then Slender Billy said, "I expect you have business with Fitzroy — don't let me keep you from it."

He went over to Percy and Cathcart by the window, whence laughter soon arose.

"How is Lady Fitzroy?" Felix asked. "And your daughter, of course?"

"Both very well, but I can't help wishing the Duke hadn't persuaded Emily not to go home for the birth. Perhaps her staying reassured waverers, but with the baby she cannot easily travel now, should it become necessary. Do you have further news from Paris?"

"No, from London. You think Brussels will be unsafe for women and children?"

Fitzroy shrugged. "I wouldn't worry about Lady Sophia, if I were you. Daventry's no Richmond. He'll whisk the ladies away at the first sign of trouble."

40

"I wasn't thinking of them. There's a little charmer at my lodgings . . ."

"What! Unfaithful to the fair Belgian, Felix? Not to mention the Goddess."

"This particular charmer is three years old. Three and a half, as she would have it. There's a young woman too, her guardian, but she is far too intrepid to desert her soldier brother." He wished he were in a position to insist that Fanny take Anita out of danger. He could not even offer to accompany them, since his duty to Rothschild required his presence within easy reach of the Commander-in-Chief. War was coming, and victory or defeat, his employer demanded immediate news. "Oh, here's March. Is the Duke free now?"

Fitzroy looked round. "As far as I know. I'll stick my head in and ask."

"Into the lion's den," said Lord March ruefully. "I've been properly raked over the coals."

When Fitzroy beckoned Felix into Wellington's office a moment later, he was glad, for once, that he was not under the irascible Duke's command.

The Commander-in-Chief of the Allied forces, seated at his desk, favoured him with a hard stare of his light-blue eyes and demanded, "Well?"

41

"A consignment of gold has arrived from England, sir. The courier is delivering it to Mr Herries."

"Excellent. If I can rely upon anyone in this business it is Mr Rothschild. Make a note, Fitzroy, to let De Lancey know. Take a seat, Roworth. What's the news from London?"

"Here's a letter for you, sir. I can tell you the gist of it. Mr Rothschild is prepared to advance the entire sum for the Hanover subsidy immediately, but the Government wishes you to make another effort to persuade King William to pay his agreed share."

"It is impossible to persuade the King to anything," snapped the Duke impatiently. He rose and began to pace the room. Though he wore plain morning dress, every vigorous movement of that trim figure exuded authority. The piercing gaze and famous hook nose swung back towards Felix. "And every delay brings new demands from those avaricious Hanoverians! How am I to carry the day against Napoleon without cooperation from my allies and my Government?"

"Mr Rothschild cannot proceed without authorization from the Government, sir," Felix ventured to point out.

"No." The Duke dropped into his chair,

tore open the letter, and scanned it rapidly. "Fitzroy, a letter to King William. You'll put in all that ceremonious fustian for me. Thank you, Roworth, I'll let you know when I have an answer," he added absently, and began to dictate.

Felix slipped out, returning to the less stressful atmosphere of the staff room. "One of you glorified errand-boys will shortly be on his way to Antwerp," he announced.

A united groan answered him. They all enjoyed escaping from Headquarters for a wild cross-country ride, but the stuffy Dutch court was not a popular destination.

De Lancey, the harrassed-looking Quartermaster-General, and Captain Lord Arthur Hill, who was even stouter than Gordon, had joined the others. Felix chatted with them until Moses Solomon arrived with the receipt signed by Herries, and then walked back with him to Madame Vilvoorde's.

He told Solomon that the Duke was writing to King William. "This afternoon I'll add a word about that business to my report for Mr Rothschild," he said, "and then you can be on your way home."

Moses looked less than pleased. "Hadn't I b-best wait until the Duke receives a reply?"

"That may take days." Noting his disappointment, Felix wondered again about the young man's infatuation with Fanny. Somehow he had never envisaged her as "splendid." A pleasant companion, certainly, and pretty, too, but compared to Lady Sophia all other females paled.

CHAPTER 3

Fanny had set the parlour table with fresh-baked bread and butter, Dutch cheeses from Gouda, Edam, and Limbourg, cold mutton, and a small dish of early strawberries. When Felix and Moses Solomon arrived, Anita was eyeing the ripe red berries hopefully.

"Tía Fanny says I liked strawbies last year when I was two," she explained.

"Frank brought them as a treat," said Fanny.

"M-miss Ingram, I'm sure the captain meant the b-berries for you and the child."

"There are plenty for everyone, Mr Solomon," she assured him untruthfully. "Frank's upstairs. I'll call him down to eat."

As she went out to the hall, Solomon's gaze of fervent devotion followed her. He glanced at Felix, his dark eyes demanding, "Is she not wonderful?"

Amused, Felix sat down at the table and

took Anita on his knee. Such a small matter to excite such admiration! No fashionable picnic or supper was complete without mountains of strawberries and lakes of cream. He'd not deprive the others now by eating any.

Fanny returned, with her brother. At twenty-five, Frank Ingram appeared older, a sturdy figure in a well-worn uniform jacket, dark blue with scarlet facings. He had his sister's brown eyes and curly brown hair but his face was more square than round, with a look of steadfast — perhaps a trifle obstinate — determination softened by his friendly smile. Though Felix had always considered him short of stature, he was taller than Moses Solomon by half a head.

Shaking the young Jew's hand with a hearty greeting, Frank said, "I hope your arrival means more gold for the army. Our pay is overdue again."

Solomon looked to Felix for permission, then assured him, "Yes, I brought gold from Mr Rothschild."

"Good. Take a seat and help yourself. Carting bullion about must give you a good appetite."

"That was how I first came into contact with the Rothschilds," Felix remarked as they sat down. "I worked for the Treasury then. My superiors didn't yet trust Nathan Rothschild, so they sent me to escort his first shipment of gold to Wellington in the Peninsula, right across France." He buttered a slice of bread, removed the crusts, and cut it into fingers for Anita, who was still sitting on his knee.

"I remember when news of that gold's arrival spread," Frank said, filling glasses with beer from a pitcher. "Just before Fuentes de Oñoro, it was. I can tell you, the men went into battle with a better heart for knowing they'd be paid. But it was rumoured that two Jews brought the gold down out of the mountains," he added, puzzled.

"I never reached Spain," Felix confessed. "When Isaac Cohen and I were reconnoitering the border, in the Pyrenees, I was stupidly careless. I had a bad fall. Isaac went on to meet Kalmann Rothschild and deliver the gold, while Miriam Jacobson — she was our guide — had to stay behind and nurse me."

He was unaware of his change of tone when he spoke Miriam's name until Fanny cast him a shrewd glance, with a hint of compassion. To the devil with the woman, she was too knowing by half! He concentrated on slivering a slice of cheese and feeding a piece to Anita.

What Lady Sophia would have thought if she'd seen him cuddling a nobody's by-blow didn't bear thinking of. If she ever heard about Rothschild — yet the Duke and his staff respected him no less for his employment. As Isaac and Miriam had pointed out to him, he performed a necessary task, vital to Napoleon's defeat, which was more than most members of the aristocracy could claim.

Anita whispered in his ear, pointing, "Please, Tío Felix, my lord, may I have some strawbies? If I eat all my cheese first I'll be too full."

He reached for the dish of berries. What did he care what anyone thought? His little charmer was worth a dozen Lady . . . ladies.

"Yet Rothschild hired you despite your making a cake of yourself," Frank commented, peeling the red wax from a large chunk of Edam. "Do you like working for him, my lord?"

"The work is interesting. I respect him enormously, both his ability and his integrity, and I have no qualms about giving him my loyalty, second only to my family and my country. Equally important, he pays well, and on time."

"Better than a captain's pay, I wager. Besides, once we've put Boney to bed with a shovel, I shall be on half pay, I daresay. Any chance of a position with Mr Rothschild, do you suppose?"

"I honestly couldn't say. He hired me because I have an entrée to Society which is useful to him." And on Isaac's recommendation. Felix didn't mention that he would have been prepared to recommend Frank to the banker if the mystery of the inquisitive Cockney had not cast a shadow of doubt on his seeming respectability.

"I can't offer any friends in Society," said Frank, crestfallen. "I'm a simple soldier."

Fanny sprang to her brother's defense. "Mama's father was a peer." At once she wished the words unsaid, as Felix turned on her an incredulous gaze.

"He was? You have never mentioned that before."

She shrugged her shoulders. "He cast her off when she ran away with Papa, so it cannot signify. She used to tell us the story as a fairy tale, ending with her living happily ever after with her soldier husband." She sighed.

"We don't know which lord, not even his rank," Frank explained. "So he'd be of no use for obtaining a position with Rothschild."

"He's of no use for anything practical," said Fanny caustically. "I cannot imagine why I brought him into the conversation."

"So you are the granddaughter of a peer! You're right, I fear, the relationship alters nothing since the family doesn't acknowledge it."

She tried to turn it into a whimsical joke. "We can't even boast of him, alas, since we don't know his name or rank."

"A pity!" he said with smile. "I'm glad you are too sensible to repine, Miss Ingram."

Though grateful for his sympathy, Fanny had had enough of the subject. "Frank, pray pour some more beer for Mr Solomon. Lord Roworth, you have been so busy spoiling Anita, you haven't eaten a bite."

"I had a late breakfast, and a hearty one."

Fanny gave him a mocking look. She was very well aware of where and why he had breakfasted late.

Frank pushed back his chair and stood up. "I have to get back to Braine-le-Comte," he said. "Slender Billy wants to march us around a bit this afternoon."

"I met the prince at Headquarters this morning," said Felix, as Anita slipped down from his knee, her mouth all stained with strawberry juice, and ran to hug Tío Frank. "He's an engaging young man, full of fire and enthusiasm."

"I've heard Old Hookey was terrified,

50

while Slender Billy was in charge alone here, that he'd start the war without waiting for his allies. It's to be hoped his enthusiasm don't rush us into calamity," said Frank dryly, swinging the little girl up for a kiss.

The silence that followed this reminder of the perils of war was broken by Anita's piping voice. "Where's Clamity? Don't you want to go there, Tío?"

Frank laughed, his face suddenly younger. "No, sweetheart, I most certainly don't. I must be off; duty calls. You be a good girl and mind your Tía while I'm gone."

"I awways do," said Anita with dignity.

Fanny had errands to run, and Solomon begged the privilege of accompanying her. He was a bank courier and a Jew, but he reminded her strongly of the young officers she knew so well, and she was perfectly at ease with him. She found his evident admiration mildly flattering. Not for the world would she let him see that it also amused her.

"I shall be glad of your company," she assured him cordially.

They took Anita, so Felix was left in peace to finish his report. He ended with a verbatim account of a conversation in the park between Wellington and Mr Creevey, which that inveterate gossip had repeated to all

51

and sundry.

"Now then, will you let me ask you, Duke, what you think you will make of it?"

"By God! I think Blücher and myself can do the thing."

"Do you calculate upon any desertion in Bonaparte's army?" Mr Creevey had persisted.

"Not upon a man," the Duke assured him, "from the colonel to the private, inclusive. We may pick up a marshal or two, perhaps, but not worth a damn."

"Do you reckon upon any support from the French king's troops?"

"Oh! don't mention such fellows!" Wellington's braying laugh rang out. "No, I think Blücher and I can do the business." He pointed at a British infantryman, a private, strolling by in his scarlet tunic with a girl on his arm. "There, it all depends upon that article whether we do the business or not. Give me enough of it and I am sure."

That ought to please Nathan Rothschild, who supplied the gold to pay "that article," and whose family had loaned Louis XVIII hundreds of thousands of pounds, the fate of which hung in the balance.

Felix blotted, folded, and sealed his missive. Impatient now to call upon Lady

Sophia, he waited for the others to return, then sent Moses Solomon on his way.

"But he only just arrived!" Fanny protested.

"Rothschilds' couriers are the fastest by land or sea," said Solomon importantly, and dashed off.

Fanny smiled at Felix. "A nice boy."

"And much taken with your charms," he teased.

"A little," she conceded. "It is just as well he takes such pride in the speed of his journey. I'd hate to see him hurt."

It was typical of her to be more concerned for the young man's feelings than complacent at discovering an admirer, Felix decided as he walked towards the Rue de Belle Vue. She was a thoroughly kindhearted person.

Passing through the Marché aux Fleurs, he stopped and spent more than he could afford on an armful of gladiolus. When he reached the Daventrys' hôtel, he carried the sheaf into the drawing room, where Lady Sophia was holding court. The Comte de St Gérard was there, and Major Sir Henry Bissell in his Rifle green hovered discontentedly on the outskirts of the group. The major's place at the Goddess's side had been usurped by an officer of the Light

Dragoons uniformed in blue with silver lace and yellow facings.

"That's Viscount Garforth," Bissell muttered to Felix. "I'm a mere baronet, and infantry at that. The ladies always go for the cavalry."

Lady Sophia greeted Felix briefly, murmured "Very pretty," when he offered her the flowers, and directed him to hand them to the butler. Then she turned back to Garforth and St Gérard and continued planning a picnic in the forest of Soignes.

She did not realize, of course, that buying the flowers had been a sacrifice, however small. All the same Felix wished he had taken the unappreciated blooms to Fanny, who would have been thrilled.

He crossed the room to talk to Lady Daventry, a thin, anxious matron who was chatting with a friend. He amused the ladies with a lively description of the Prince of Orange's eruption into the staff room at Headquarters, then made his excuses and returned to Lady Sophia.

A pair of Guards had joined the group. Feeling drab in his morning coat beside their gold and scarlet resplendence, Felix took his leave, claiming an engagement elsewhere.

"You will come to my picnic, will you not,

my lord?" said the Goddess, pouting a little.

"I should not miss it for the world, ma'am," he vowed, elated that she desired his attendance. Dared he hope that her neglect of him this afternoon was an attempt to make him jealous?

He called at the Richmonds' hôtel in the Rue de la Blanchisserie, and found the young Lennoxes also planning a picnic.

"We want to go to Tournai," Georgiana told him.

"Or Lille," said Lady Jane eagerly, "just across the border, to snap our fingers in Boney's face."

"It's too far," Lady Sarah protested.

"William cannot go so far," Lady Mary seconded her.

Their fifteen-year-old brother, still pale and weak from his fall, said stoutly, "If you will only wait a week, Georgy, I shall be able to go."

"Of course we will wait," cried Lady Jane. "Mama, say we may go if we wait for William to be better."

The duchess looked dubious.

"You'd best see what Wellington has to say, Mama," put in Lord George, one of the Duke's youthful aides-de-camp. "Do you not agree, Lord Roworth?"

"Certainly. A fine thing it would be if the

Duke had to send out the Dragoons especially to rescue you from Boney's advance guard."

The duchess's offspring laughed, and she sent Felix a glance of gratitude. She had enough on her hands keeping a rein on her husband, who would have given a fortune to be allowed to join Wellington's staff.

Felix spent an entertaining half hour with the lively Lennoxes before returning to Madame Vilvoorde's. He found Fanny, in a faded pink muslin walking dress and her straw hat, about to take Anita to the park to feed the swans.

"May I join you?" he requested.

Fanny was taken aback. Companionable as he was at home, she'd never expected the aristocratic Lord Roworth to choose to be seen in public with the shabby sister of an obscure Artillery officer. After all, his wish to take her to the Cavalry Review had been voiced in the knowledge that it was impossible.

"Yes, you come wiv us, Tío Felix," said Anita decidedly, and took his hand.

He smiled down at the little girl with real affection. Fanny decided it was not her company he sought, but Anita's. What a splendid father he would make! Walking along together, she could almost pretend they were a family, only that would mean she was married to him, an inconceivable notion.

But not altogether a disagreeable notion.

Alarmed by the trend of her thoughts, she caught up his mention of the Richmonds and asked him about that family. His tales of the exploits of the spirited Lennoxes made her regret that she would never meet them. They sounded delightful. Lady Georgiana's vivacity, in particular, sounded utterly unlike Lady Sophia's refined impassivity.

The sun had turned westwards and the streets had cooled a little. Anita trotted happily along between them, holding a hand of each, until they reached the cathedral of St Gudule, where she stopped dead.

"Pigeons," she said, pointing at the indolent birds perched on the steps. "Pigeons like bread, too. Be they hungry, Tía, like the swans?"

"Pigeons are always hungry," Felix told her.

"Poor pigeons! Can I give them some bread, Tía?"

Felix took the bread from Fanny and broke it into small pieces for Anita to throw. The birds speedily awoke from their torpor and flocked about their feet, pecking and squabbling. Anita laughed in delight.

"That's the last of it," said Fanny. "The swans will have to go without today."

Anita's expressive mouth drooped and tears welled in her dark eyes. "They will be hungry," she wailed.

"I'll get some crumbs from the pavilion by the pond," Felix hastened to promise. "Do you think swans like cake crumbs, Anita?"

"Cake's much nicer than bread," she assured him, sweetly earnest.

"I ought to scold you for spoiling her," Fanny said in a low voice, "but there were times on campaign when we all went hungry, and she remembers, though she was very young. Thank you, sir."

"I daresay you have had little opportunity to spoil her. If I do so, it's purely for my own benefit, since a tear in those eyes is enough to pierce the most hardened villain to the heart."

She matched his joking tone. "Then, for heaven's sake, don't let her learn of her power!"

Anita's short legs grew tired as they went on towards the park. Willing to compromise his dignity for her, Felix set her on his shoulders, to the imminent danger of his top hat. He took it off and gave it to Fanny

58

to carry.

"A shocking breach of propriety to be seen in the streets bare-headed," she quizzed him to hide how deeply his gesture touched her.

"I be Tío Felix's hat," said Anita, and laid her little head on his. Her ankles looked tiny and fragile in his strong, well-kept hands, but Fanny trusted him to keep her safe in a firm yet gentle grip.

Reaching the park, they strolled between beds of iris, blue, yellow, white, purple, and bronze. "If ever we settle in England," said Fanny passionately, "I shall have a flower garden. I shall grow mignonette and speedwell and sweet williams and love-in-a-mist . . ."

"And forget-me-nots, no doubt. For all your practicality, I believe you are a secret romantic, Miss Ingram."

". . . and candytuft and honesty," she finished with a reproachful look, and sighed. "But if Frank has to live on half pay or sell out, I daresay we shall have to find work in a city and live in some horrid tenement. I shall grow geraniums in a window-box," she added, defying fate.

"You would have appreciated the flowers I took Lady Sophia more than she did," he said ruefully.

"Put me down," commanded Anita.

"Please. I want to smell the flowers."

His hat restored to its proper place, Felix returned with equanimity the greetings of a pair of youthful ladies of his acquaintance who passed on the arms of two officers. "Mr Creevey's stepdaughters, the Misses Ord," he told Fanny. "One of the two is betrothed to one of those fellows, but I can never remember which."

She retrieved Anita from the flowerbed, just in time to stop her picking a bouquet, and they continued towards the pavilion. The cool of the early evening had attracted both citizens of Brussels and English visitors to the park. The sober dress of the burghers mingled with pastel muslins and bright regimentals in a constantly shifting spectacle.

"Tío Cav!" shouted Anita, letting go of Fanny's and Felix's hands. She dashed after a trio of dark blue uniforms with scarlet facings. The Horse Artillery officers turned and the eldest of the three caught her up, laughing, swinging her high into the air.

"Good day, Miss Fanny," he said, setting the child down and saluting. His companions echoed him. One of them, a tall, fair lad, gazed at Fanny with such yearning that Felix had to suppress a smile.

"Lord Roworth, you've met Captain Cavalié Mercer at our house, have you not?" she said. "These two are Lieutenants Farrow and Barnstaple."

Felix shook hands with the abashed young men. He guessed that his title awed them, for the sons of the nobility rarely chose to enter the Artillery. Yet as Fanny's friends, her brother's colleagues, and Napoleon's enemies, they deserved his respect.

They walked on together for a few minutes. Fanny asked the captain whether he had yet succeeded in having his guns and his horses accommodated in the same quarters.

"No, and Colonel Frazer's breathing fire over the business. It's those damned inexperienced staff of De Lancey's. Lord, what a mess it'll be when we're suddenly called to arms and there are no horses to move the guns."

"At least Frank has his all gathered together at Braine-le-Comte."

"A devil of a lot of use if we're attacked in the west. The colonel says Old Hookey expects Boney to try to cut us off from the ports." Mercer looked enquiringly at Felix.

"So I have heard," he confirmed shortly. The man's freedom in swearing before Fanny annoyed him, and her lack of reaction annoyed him more.

"The Duke likes to keep his back door open," put in Lieutenant Barnstaple, turning crimson as everyone looked at him. "I mean . . . his escape routes . . ."

Anita tugged on Fanny's sleeve. "The swans," she reminded her.

The two groups parted, the swans were fed, and they turned homeward. Anita trudged wearily along. Felix was about to lift her to his shoulders again when he saw the Goddess riding towards them on her dainty bay mare, flanked by Lord Garforth and one of the Life Guards. She was superb in a black-frogged habit à la militaire, with a shako-style cockaded hat setting off her blonde ringlets.

He raised his hat to her. She looked straight through him and trotted onward without betraying by the slightest sign that she had seen him.

"Here, carry my hat, will you, Miss Ingram?" he requested, trying to hide his chagrin. "Anita is about to fall asleep on her feet."

"I'm not!" said the child crossly.

In the ensuing fuss, as Fanny persuaded her to ride, he recovered his countenance. They walked on a little, then Fanny said in a constrained voice, "I am sorry that Lady Sophia cut you because you are with us."

He thought of suggesting that Lady Sophia had not recognized him, but she would have had to be blind as a bat. "It wasn't your fault," he said.

"Not in the least," she agreed with asperity. "You must not suppose that I was apologising. I simply expressed my regret, for your sake."

Felix was inclined to take umbrage, then he realized that hers was an eminently sensible, and generous, point of view. She, after all, had been more insulted than he had. He was suddenly furious with Lady Sophia.

"She does not know you," he attempted to excuse the Goddess. "The Fashionable World is all too apt to judge people by their clothes." He wished he had chosen his words with more care when she glanced down ruefully at her dress. "Lady Sophia did not mean to be rude," he hurried on. "She is gently bred and her manners are beyond reproach."

Fanny's snort of disbelief was as *sotto voce* as a snort can be. If Felix heard he had the good sense to ignore it, or she might have been tempted to give voice to her feelings. Lady Sophia was elegant and she was beautiful, but she was ill-mannered and she was utterly heartless. Even if she didn't care for him, how could she treat him so? And how could he defend her?

They walked on for some way in silence.

Having encountered Lady Sophia, Fanny found herself suddenly curious about the woman who had travelled with Felix and his friend across France. There had been a definite note of yearning in his voice when he spoke of her, yet surely she had been nothing like the Goddess. Impossible to imagine Lady Sophia doing anything so outrageous!

"I gained the impression," she said at last, tentatively, "that you were fond of Miriam . . . Jacobson, was it?"

"Cohen now. She married Isaac. 'Fond' is not the word. I was madly in love with her and asked her to marry me, but I suppose even then I knew it was an impossible dream. I'd have brought a hornets' nest about my ears if I'd taken a Jewish bride, however well-dowered, home to Westwood. It's my duty to the family to marry someone my parents can like and approve, someone of rank and wealth and good breeding. Lady Sophia is ideal in every respect."

Fanny was thoroughly disheartened. Even Lady Sophia's rudeness had not made him look beyond her beauty, elegance, wealth, and noble family. If he won her hand, Fanny could not believe he'd ever be happy. He deserved better.

"She'll relent," he said hopefully. "Her temper is too equable to continue out of humour. Why, I wager she will waltz with me tonight."

CHAPTER 4

At the Marquise d'Assche's soirée, Lady Sophia did indeed waltz with Felix. Ethereally beautiful in a gown of silver net over white satin sewn with seed pearls, she was a superb dancer, graceful and light on her feet. Felix himself was no greenhorn on the floor, and the skills learned in youth had been honed in the ballrooms of Paris and Vienna. As they circled the room together, he was aware of admiring and envious glances.

However, Lady Sophia refused absolutely to grant him a second dance.

"My card is already full," she pointed out.

He took it and scanned it. "You cannot wish to dance with Ensign Faversham. He's a mere boy, however impressive he looks in his Guards uniform. Give me his set."

"It would be most improper to cry off when I have promised to stand up with him. Besides, Lord Albert Faversham is the son of one of Mama's dearest friends."

"What about your second dance with Garforth? He is the clumsiest fellow in the room. I wager your toes are black and blue after the first."

"Lord Garforth is an agreeable gentleman. We shall sit out the set."

Determined not to let the Dragoon officer best him, he demanded, "Then may I beg you to grant me a waltz and the supper dance at Lord Stuart's ball on Saturday?"

"A waltz, certainly, sir. I am already engaged for the supper dance but if you wish, a country dance?"

Better than nothing. "Thank you. Will you ride with me tomorrow in the Allée Verte?"

"The park is more fashionable."

But less private. "The park, then. I shall call for you at two, if that is convenient?"

"That will be delightful." With a cool smile, she left him to take her place in the next set with his civilian rival, the Comte de St Gérard.

He watched them for a few minutes, spoke briefly to one or two friends, then departed in search of Katrina Lisle. His mistress's uncomplicated pleasure in his company was balm to his self-esteem.

Inevitably, the ride in the park next day was far from a tête-à-tête. Not only did young Lord Albert accompany them, his showy Thoroughbred and gold-braided scarlet tunic outshining Felix's well-worn riding coat and hired hack, they were constantly stopping to greet acquaintances. After seeing Lady Sophia home, Felix returned to Madame Vilvoorde's in a mood of thorough dissatisfaction.

Fanny was entertaining a couple of artillery officers' wives to tea, so he went straight up to his chamber to change out of his riding clothes. When he stepped out onto the landing a little later, Anita was standing there in her chemise, bare-footed and sleepy-eyed.

"I did wake up."

"Were you taking a nap?" He heard below the leave-taking of the women. "I expect you can come down with me now." Picking her up, he carried her down to the parlour, watched through the crack in the door by Madame Vilvoorde.

Having seen her guests out, Fanny returned to the parlour. Felix was sitting on the sofa with Anita on his lap, sprawled back against his chest.

"You're still half asleep, lovie," she said, smiling at the sight. "Lord Roworth, while you were out, the smartest footman I've ever seen called with a gilt-edged card for you.

The Duke of Richmond's livery, I think, and I couldn't help seeing it's an invitation to a ball. I put it on the mantelpiece — here it is."

He took it from her with a casual glance. "The Richmonds are holding a ball on the fifteenth."

She concentrated on collecting the heavy white china tea cups. "So I've heard. It is to be a grand gala, is it not? People say only Wellington's ball will eclipse it, since the King and Queen of the Netherlands will attend that, and a dozen or so royal princes. What a spectacle that will be! But it will surely be very stiff and formal." Despite her efforts to match his casualness, a hint of wistfulness crept into her voice. "The duchess's will be more fun, I expect."

"I wish you could go!"

"There's no sense repining over what cannot be altered," she said with resolute cheerfulness. "Indeed, it is entirely your fault if I fret for fashionable frivolities! Before we shared lodgings with you, I never spared a thought for such unreachable heights."

He smiled at the tart accusation. "My humble apologies, Miss Ingram. May I redeem myself by escorting you to the Review on Saturday?"

"In the Allée Verte? Thank you, but I have an escort already." And how she wished she had not! She would have loved to go with him, especially as his frown even suggested that he was piqued, not relieved, at her rejection. "Doubtless there will be many more reviews," she said soothingly.

"Then consider yourself engaged for the next!"

"I will," she promised, laughing.

"Would you like me to take care of Anita for you that afternoon?"

"It's kind of you, but Mrs Major Prynne will have her. Now, shall I make a fresh pot of tea? This is quite cold and I daresay you will like a cup?"

"Can I have a bixit, please, Tía?" asked Anita, wide awake now and studying the tea tray greedily.

"Yes, but heavens! we must go and put on your frock and shoes first."

"I'll get Henriette to make tea," offered Felix. "I trust you appreciate how domesticated I am becoming."

"I shall hold my applause until you learn how to make tea for yourself!" Grinning, he carried the tray out to the kitchen.

Saturday, the 3rd June, began with a light, cooling rain that washed the dusty streets and left cobbles gleaming, but boded ill for the afternoon's Review. Fanny kept peeking out of the window and Felix hoped she was not to be disappointed of her treat. However, by midday the sun was shining. She left to take Anita to the Prynnes.

The English, Scottish and Hanoverian regiments quartered in Brussels and its immediate environs were to march in the Allée Verte, just outside the city walls. Though Lady Sophia had said she would not attend, Felix thought he might as well go. He was bound to see acquaintances there, and he might even meet up with Fanny and discover the identity of her unnamed escort.

Spectators were beginning to gather as he walked without haste along the wide avenue of lime trees, paralleling the canal. Plumply pretty Bruxelloises clucked at swarms of children while their solid burgher husbands gathered in groups to discuss matters of import.

Felix knew Wellington intended the display of the crack troops of his Reserve to reassure the faint-hearted. The Duke also wanted to show French sympathizers among the Belgians that the Corsican usurper would not find smooth sailing if he decided to march on Brussels.

The opinions of the Belgians would

doubtless be of interest to Rothschild. Felix decided to mingle with the crowd and listen to what the man in the street was saying — the French-speaking man in the street at least. Miriam had taught him to speak French; now doubtless hers was rusty with disuse while his had been polished by constant exercise.

He caught odd phrases: "What's to choose between a Dutch King and a French . . . ?" "They say the Russians . . ." "Milord Wellington has never faced the Emperor in . . ." "Milord does not worry: balls, horse races, le cricket . . ." "And the English pay in good gold, and besides . . ." He grinned at the notion that Rothschild gold had won more allegiance among the Belgians than their own King William.

Listening and strolling, Felix watched out for Fanny and her unknown escort, but he wasn't surprised to miss them. He stopped when he reached the bridge over the canal and leaned against the parapet. Slow barges, painted red and yellow and green, slid past on the still water, neither bargees nor their plodding, be-tasselled horses paying much attention to the crowds on land.

A commotion at the far end of the Allée Verte resolved itself, as it drew closer, into cheers and the stirring, martial clamour of bagpipes. Whatever their feelings about the Allies, the Belgians adored the Scots. Small boys jumped up and down in an ecstasy of excitement as the Cameron Highlanders marched past with swinging kilts, followed by the Royal Scots, then the Gay Gordons. Between them came a battalion of Riflemen in their dark green, their caps set at a jaunty angle. Felix recognized Major Sir Henry Bissell riding alongside his men. At least, at this precise moment, one of his rivals was not busy fixing his interest with Lady Sophia.

The Belgians lost interest and began to head for home as a Hanoverian regiment brought up the rear. Felix strolled back along the alley, wondering whether the Duke had heard yet from King William about the Hanover subsidy. He would mention the matter tonight, to Lord Fitzroy if not to Wellington himself. The Duke had invited him to dine before the British Ambassador's ball.

A pair of riders, waiting in the shade of a tree for the crowds to pass, caught his attention. Their horses were no Thoroughbred hacks but heavy troopers, dwarfing one of the mounted figures.

It was Fanny, in a brown habit and practical black hat, perched high above the ground on a side saddle, looking perfectly at ease. She was smiling at her companion. Felix switched his gaze to the other rider and scowled as he noted the Horse Artillery blue and scarlet.

Was it Captain Mercer who dared to risk her life on a brute far too powerful for any female? Or that young lieutenant who had gazed at her like a mooncalf when they met in the park? Aghast at the risk she was taking, furious with her careless escort, he pushed through the leisurely throng towards them, his heart in his mouth.

By the time he was close enough to recognize Lieutenant Farrow — not the adoring mooncalf — three more mounted artillerymen had joined them. Two were strangers, the third was Frank. He said something to his sister and she laughed. Handling the reins with unselfconscious competence, she turned her monstrous mount towards the Allée.

Felix felt foolish. He found it difficult to remember that Miss Fanny Ingram's slight, delicate-seeming frame had endured hardships at which he could only guess. He wondered which of the officers was the escort she had mentioned. All of them, perhaps. But if so, why had she not invited him to join them? Did she consider him too high in the instep? He was about to slip away, hiding himself in the crowd, when she saw him. Her round face, with its engagingly tip-tilted little nose, lit with pleasure and she waved to him. He changed his mind and approached the group.

"Are the Highlanders not splendid, Lord Roworth?" she said, smiling down at him. "I have been telling our fellows they ought to try wearing kilts."

"To please you, Miss Fanny, I'd consider wearing kilts," declared one of the strangers, a dark, stocky man with captain's insignia, "if only it weren't for the bagpipes. They give me indigestion."

Fanny shook her head at him with a mocking expression, and Felix at once took him in dislike. "Indigestion?" he queried skeptically. "A headache, perhaps, or even nightmares . . ."

"Gerald has a delicate stomach," Fanny explained. "You have not met? Roworth, allow me to present Captain Gerald Lloyd, and — oh dear, I expect I ought to have introduced you first — Major Prynne."

Felix nodded as the two officers bowed awkwardly in the saddle, then he recognized the major's name and decided he liked the look of the tall, thin man with the mournful face. "Your wife is looking after Anita, Major?"

"Aye, m'lord. She don't care for this kind of do and the child's no trouble. We've three of our own."

"She will be wondering where I have got to," Fanny put in. "Frank, it is time I was going home. With so many people about, it might be quicker on foot."

"If you want to take the horses back to their stable, Ingram," Felix suggested, "I'll be happy to escort Miss Ingram home."

The twins accepted this offer and Felix gave Fanny his hand to dismount, which she did with more energy than elegance. Standing next to the huge beast she looked more fragile than ever. No female could have dismounted from the brute gracefully, Felix decided.

"Drat, I forgot the train," she said, looping the extra length of skirt over her arm. "I have scarce worn riding dress since we arrived in Brussels. I'll see you later, Frank. Thank you, gentlemen, for a delightful afternoon." Gaily she blew them a collective kiss.

"Entirely our pleasure, Miss Fanny," said Captain Lloyd with altogether too much warmth.

The riders turned their horses' heads toward the bridge, while Felix and Fanny set off in the opposite direction.

"Is every officer in the artillery a close friend of yours?" Felix asked, carefully casual.

"In the Horse Artillery, at least, they are more like family than friends. How do you suppose we survived when my father was killed at Vimeira? Frank was an ensign; Mama had a tiny pension, until she died on the retreat to Corunna. If it were not for them, all of them, I'd probably be struggling in some back slum to earn a living as a washerwoman, or on the streets. They are the only family I have."

Felix thought of his parents, retired from the social whirl — to the family mansion at Westwood; of his sisters, deprived of their London Seasons, to be sure, but never doubting that there would be food on the table. He had bitterly resented having to earn his own living while his friends sparred at Gentleman Jackson's, gambled at White's, strolled down Bond Street, or raced their curricles to Brighton. Yet always he had known that one day the mortgages would be paid off, one day Westwood would be his.

"I have shocked you," said Fanny in a small voice.

"No!" He pressed the little hand resting on his arm. "No, if I'm shocked it's at the way I have always taken for granted the support of my own family."

"How gratifying to think that I have taught you a salutary lesson," she exclaimed with a smile, restored to teasing cheerfulness.

They fetched Anita from Mrs Prynne's and returned to Madame Vilvoorde's. As they approached the house, a man darted out from the shade of a nearby doorway. For a moment Felix was certain the inquisitive Cockney had come back, then he realized that the fellow was much younger, and clad in a respectable coat of old-fashioned German cut.

"Milord Rovort?"

He recognized the mangled mess most foreigners made of his name. "Yes?"

"*Ich komme aus Frankfurt,* milord, on my way to London. The old woman would not let me wait in the house."

A courier from Amschel Rothschild. "Come in," he invited. "I hope you haven't been waiting long."

Fanny had already opened the front door and taken Anita inside. Madame Vilvoorde emerged from her den and began to complain in her fractured French about the constant disturbance of her lodgers' and their visitors' coming and going.

"I'll deal with her," Fanny said.

Anita was hiding behind her, afraid of the sharp-tongued, sharp-faced woman in her black dress and starched white cap. Felix picked her up and took her with him into the parlour, followed by the mystified courier.

"Milord's daughter?" he asked as Anita settled on Felix's lap and promptly fell asleep, exhausted by her afternoon at the Prynnes'.

"No, she is just a friend of mine. What news have you brought me?"

Half an hour later, the man was on his way, anxious to catch the next morning's packet to England if the Rothschilds' yacht was not waiting. He took Felix's latest report to Nathan Rothschild, with a few final words scrawled without waking Anita. Carrying in the tea tray a few minutes later, Fanny found them in the now familiar pose.

"Heavens, are you still holding her? Lay her down on the sofa."

"I don't want to disturb her. No doubt she'll wake any moment, since I see you have brought bixits."

"I thought your courier might be in need of refreshment. He's left already? I'm sorry I was so long."

"He was in a hurry." He accepted a cup

79

of tea and balanced it on the arm of his chair as Anita stirred. "You were dealing with Madame Vilvoorde, I take it."

"Madame is threatening to raise the rent because of all the wear and tear on her house." She laughed. "Believe it or not, she has kept a record since we arrived of every single time any of us or our visitors has gone up or down stairs or opened and closed the front door!"

"Is that what she's been up to? I was beginning to think she must be spying for Boney."

"Nothing half so exciting." She sobered. "I hope I have talked her around. We cannot afford a higher rent."

"I shouldn't worry. Unless I'm mistaken, she will soon have other matters to occupy her attention. Amschel Rothschild sends word that the Russians are nearing Frankfurt. Napoleon must be aware of it, or will be shortly, and he's surely not fool enough to wait until they reach the French border before he attacks the Allies."

Fanny felt the blood drain from her cheeks. How could he be so sensitive and considerate towards Anita and yet speak so casually of the coming war with its attendant horrors? "You think there will be a battle soon?" she faltered.

"No, no, I am a wretch to frighten you so!"

His dismay made her struggle to master her feelings, ashamed of her loss of self-control. She shook her head and managed a smile. "Not frighten; you took me by surprise. Of course I know that we shall have to fight Boney sooner or later, and a lifetime with the army has taught me not to let the uncertain future torment me. You took me by surprise," she repeated, "when I was thinking about Madame Vilvoorde."

Frank, entering at that moment, overheard her and demanded, "What's the old harridan up to now?"

"What's a harridan, Tío?" asked Anita, inconveniently waking at the sound of his voice.

"Never mind, pet. Have a biscuit," said Fanny hurriedly. "She wanted to raise the rent, Frank, because we have too many visitors." She proceeded to describe her interview with Madame in the mixture of Flemish, French, and English used by the landlady. Frank and Felix were soon helpless with laughter, while Anita, nibbling her biscuit, watched them indulgently.

Felix set out for Wellington's dinner party in good spirits. Trevor had spent the day brushing and polishing and ironing and starching; he was prepared to swear that no one would guess his lordship's black evening coat was the only one he possessed, his dancing shoes resoled a dozen times.

The dinner party was a masculine occasion, the guests being foreign diplomats, divisional commanders, and, of course, the Duke's personal staff.

The Prince of Orange had ridden over from Braine-le-Comte, bringing a copy of the French newspaper *Moniteur* with a glowing account of Napoleon's magnificent "Champ de Mai" assemblage on June 1st. The vast demonstration of support for the Emperor shocked Wellington, who had hoped his power was crumbling, into a momentary silence. Felix broke it with his news of the approach of the Russian army. The Duke at once recovered his countenance, and a babble of diplomatic French arose as his guests discussed the consequences of the latest information.

After dinner, there was no sign of the gathering breaking up to go on to Lord Stuart's ball. Port and brandy circulated, cigars were lit, and Felix checked the time every five minutes. Lady Sophia had promised him two dances; she would never forgive him if he missed them.

Several gentlemen had left their seats at

the long table to exchange views with others seated at a distance. Lord Fitzroy caught Felix with his eye on the clock and came to speak to him.

"The Goddess waiting?" he asked knowingly.

"The trouble is, she won't wait. There are plenty of fellows ready to lead her out if I'm not there."

"The Duke won't notice if you leave, or won't mind if he does. I'll explain if necessary — it will amuse him and he could do with a good laugh. Thank you, by the way, for producing the Russians at precisely the right moment. I've never seen him so cut down."

"Have you had any word from King William on the Hanover business?"

"Nothing yet, and we don't expect anything good. Thank God for Rothschild! The Russians wouldn't be at Frankfurt if he hadn't arranged that subsidy, too. Off you go, now, before Lady Sophia gives your waltz to that Belgian count."

When Felix arrived at the Ambassador's residence, a cotillion was in progress and Lady Sophia was dancing it with St Gérard. Discovering that a waltz was next on the program, he was glad he had left the dinner party early, especially since it turned out to be the waltz she had written him down for. He was even more glad when, considerably later, Wellington and his guests at last entered the ballroom as he was going down the set of a country dance with her.

To leave a young lady dangling when she had been so kind as to promise two dances would have been unforgivable. His rivals would have leaped to take advantage of such shockingly ungentlemanly conduct.

CHAPTER 5

Early on Tuesday morning, an orderly delivered to Madame Vilvoorde's a sealed paper inscribed with Felix's name. When it came, he was at breakfast with Fanny and Anita, a pleasantly domestic routine Fanny had come to delight in. As he pried open the seal, a card fell out.

"Another ball?" Fanny asked. "I hope they will admit you with egg on the corner of your invitation."

He picked it out of his buttered eggs, wiped it on his napkin, and read it. "Just an informal party at the Duke's tomorrow evening. I wonder why . . ." He turned to the enclosing sheet and laughed. "This is from Fitzroy. He assures me that the Comte de St Gérard has not been invited."

"Your rival? Then Lady Sophia has, I collect."

"Yes. I doubt many of her other suitors will be there either, though they will be invited to his formal ball later in the month."

"You must make the most of the opportunity," she said dryly. She kept hoping that he'd grow disillusioned with Lady Sophia, but he continued in hot pursuit, and continued to confide in Fanny his progress or lack thereof.

Now frowning at Lord Fitzroy's note, he did not respond to her words. "That's odd. He says Wellington has definite word from Colonel Grant — his head of Intelligence — that Napoleon is at Laon, and on his way to Lille."

"Where is Laon?"

"About eighty miles north of Paris, more than half way to the Belgian border. I cannot believe it! Moving troops takes time. Jakob Rothschild would have informed me if Boney had left Paris."

"Might not his courier have come to grief?"

"Possibly, though I had rather trust a Rothschild courier than British Intelligence. Do you know, our Government will not allow Grant to send patrols into French territory because we are not officially at war?"

"So I have heard, but I didn't believe it. In Portugal and Spain, the information the guerrilla patrols gathered was invaluable."

"It's true. Who can guess where Grant

gets his information? From Boney's agents, I wager. I'm sure he is mistaken. Don't repeat this to anyone, if you please. Fitzroy told me in confidence."

His trust in her discretion gratified her. She knew he never discussed such matters with Lady Sophia, and for some reason that gave her comfort. "Shall you tell Old Hookey you think Colonel Grant is wrong?" she asked.

Felix ran his fingers through his hair. "All I can do is tell him I have heard nothing to confirm the news."

"Then do that. Stop worrying and eat your breakfast."

"Yes'm." He applied himself to his plateful of eggs and muffins.

"You didn't eat all yours, Tía," Anita pointed out. "I finished mine. Tía, can we feed the swans today?"

"Yes, we'll go this morning if you promise not to give the pigeons all the bread." She dipped a corner of her napkin in the finger-bowl set there for the purpose and removed a quantity of jam from sticky little face and fingers.

"I'll go with you," Felix said, consulting his watch, "if you can wait until I've been to Headquarters. I shan't be long."

Fanny guessed he was calculating that

Lady Sophia would not be in the park before noon. When her cynical glance brought a tinge of colour to his cheeks, she was sure she was right, but all she said was, "We shall not be ready to go for at least an hour."

"We won't go wivout you," Anita promised, and to Fanny's amusement his expression became downright penitent. He retreated in disorder.

When Felix reached Headquarters, neither the Duke nor Fitzroy was there. As he had nothing definite to report, he didn't leave a message but returned after accompanying Fanny and Anita to the park. By then Fitzroy had sent word that he would spend the morning at home as his young wife was unwell. Wellington, Cathcart thought, was calling on the Richmonds.

Felix made his way to the Rue de la Blanchisserie and ran his quarry to earth. As he was shown into the Richmonds' drawing room, Lady Georgiana was telling Wellington about the planned picnic to Lille or Tournai.

"You'd better not go, Georgy," said the Duke authoritatively. "Say nothing about it, but let the project drop."

"Must we?" mourned Lady Jane. "We have been looking forward to it so, and William is nearly well enough."

"I'll take you to the Guards' cricket match at Enghien instead," suggested the Commander-in-Chief of the Allied Armies.

Felix could only admire his sang-froid, if he really believed Boney was at Laon. He recalled the remark he had overheard at the Review. "Balls, horse races, le cricket" all added up to convincing wavering Belgians of Wellington's confidence in victory, persuading them it was not in their interest to go over to Boney.

He said as much to the Duke when they left the house together.

"Yes, of course, we must not let them doubt us." His whooping laugh rang out: "Besides, I promised the duchess to keep Richmond's mind at ease. But, 'fore God, Roworth, I'll be surprised if that cricket match takes place."

"It's scheduled for the 12th, is it not? You expect war before then, sir?"

"No doubt Fitzroy has told you that Boney is at Laon."

"I have not heard from Jakob Rothschild that he has left Paris," said Felix doubtfully.

"My dear fellow, I trust absolutely the information you receive from the Rothschilds, but a lack of information is another matter. Though my Intelligence is damnable, I must act as if it is accurate."

"I suppose so, sir."

"Never fear, I'll not do anything irrevocable. The French Army is a well-oiled machine, that breaks down with a little grit in the gears. I treat a campaign like a harness — if it breaks I tie a knot and go on. By the way, you may tell Rothschild that King William has reneged on the Hanover subsidy. It's up to our Government now, Lord help us."

Felix was changing for the Duke's informal party on Wednesday when he heard a rapping at the front door below. A moment later Fanny called up the stairs, "Lord Roworth, someone is here to see you."

"Damn!" he swore, annoyed. Lady Sophia had accepted his escort for the evening and invited him to dine first. Nothing must spoil the occasion. "Damn!" he repeated with more force as he realized he had ruined his neckcloth. He only owned three of the lengths of snowy-white starched muslin, which left little room for error.

"His lordship will be down presently," Trevor called tactfully.

When Felix entered the parlour, Fanny was regaling the visitor with a glass of wine. He looked as if he could do with it. His dark hair was matted with sweat, his face drawn and smudged with road dust. He started to rise as Felix came in, but she pushed him down with one hand on his shoulder and without protest he wearily subsided.

Felix's annoyance faded as he recognized one of Jakob Rothschild's couriers, from Paris. *"Quelles nouvelles?"* he demanded. "You have ridden hard, *mon vieux.*"

"It was necessary, milord. Barely did I slip through." He hesitated, glancing at Fanny.

"You can speak freely in front of Miss Ingram."

"*Alors* — the Emperor has closed the border, milord. Not a carriage may cross, not a horseman, not a hay cart, not a peasant on foot. No fishing boat may leave the Channel ports."

"And Napoleon," Felix asked urgently, "where is he?"

The man shrugged. "He was in Paris when I left. Now, who knows?"

"I shall tell Wellington at once. You, *mon ami,* must be prepared to leave for England with a report for Mr Nathan."

"Not tonight!" Fanny protested.

He smiled at her. "Not tonight. May I leave him in your care? I must go, I'm late."

"For Wellington — or for Lady Sophia?" she murmured almost inaudibly.

He strode through streets aglow with evening light to the Daventrys' hôtel. Lady Sophia greeted him graciously, her flawless beauty set off by an elegant gown of wild rose crêpe lisse caught up with rosettes of Mechlin lace over a darker rose petticoat. The only other guests were Sir William de Lancey, with his perpetual worried frown, his young bride Lady Magdalen, and the Marquis and Marquise d'Assche. No competition there for the Goddess's favours.

If only he were not so impatient to give Wellington his news! Still, an hour or two's delay hardly mattered.

The talk at dinner was of the races at Grammont, of the respective merits of riversides and woods as locations for a picnic, of the Brussels Opera's latest production. The prospect of war seemed to belong to another world, and even the Quartermaster-General's creased forehead gradually smoothed. Not without effort, Felix pushed the closed frontier to the back of his mind and basked in the attention of Lady Sophia, seated next to him.

Soon after dinner they all went on to the Duke's party, Felix in the Daventrys' carriage.

"Our picnic is to be on Friday," Lady Sophia told him as he took his place beside her, opposite her parents, "in the Forest of Soignes. We decided we are less likely to be plagued by flies there, and by undesirable persons, than on the banks of a river."

"If this hot weather continues, you will be glad of the shade," said Felix, wondering whether she remembered she had invited him.

"We hope you will be able to join us," the marchioness put in.

"I shall be sadly cast down if you cannot go," said Lady Sophia dispassionately.

He chose to hear her words rather than her tone. "I would not miss it for the world," he assured her.

Arriving at the Duke's, Felix requested a private word with him.

"Urgent?" Wellington asked, changing instantly from jovial host to keen-eyed commander.

"This evening, sir."

"After the concert, then. I hope La Catalani's visit is long enough past that you won't despise the local diva, Lady Sophia. At least her fee is reasonable and she don't refuse to sing more than two songs."

"Madame Catalani's temperamental character is to be deplored, Duke. I am sure we shall enjoy your concert."

"There will be dancing afterwards. Lovely

young ladies cannot have too much of dancing." He kissed her hand with the gallantry that had won him the nickname of the Beau.

Lady Sophia's genteel composure was no whit disturbed by the attentions of the great man. As they made their way to the music room, she said with considerable satisfaction, "You have Wellington's ear, my lord."

"I flatter myself I have been of use to him more than once," said Felix, delighted with her approval.

Nonetheless, unaccustomed to taking second place, she pouted when, instead of leading her into the first dance, he went off with Fitzroy for his private interview with the Duke. Lord George Lennox came to the rescue. Even the Goddess must be pleased to be partnered by one whose proficiency in the quadrille was justly celebrated. Felix was glad Lord George was not one of her admirers.

"Good choice?" drawled Fitzroy with a grin, leading the way to a small antechamber.

"So you set that up! I might have guessed. Excellent choice."

Wellington joined them a moment later. "What news, Roworth? London? Paris? Frankfurt? Vienna?"

"Paris, sir. A courier just made it through

before they closed the frontier. No one is allowed to cross. Even the fishing boats are confined to harbour."

"Hmm, as when he escaped from Elba. That certainly presages a move." The piercing gaze drilled into him. "Where is he, man, do you know that?"

"He was still in Paris when the courier left."

"Good." The Duke relaxed. "Excellent. Laon was too close for comfort, but it will take him some time to march from Paris. Anything else to report? Then off with you both, there are any number of young ladies waiting for partners."

The quadrille ended at last, and Felix led Lady Sophia into the country dance that followed. Despite the absence of her other beaux, she refused to stand up with him more than twice — to dance three times with the same gentleman would be shockingly fast, he had to agree. However, since it was a informal affair, she agreed to take supper with him later, and in the meantime to sit out a set with him.

With her on his arm, he was seeking a secluded corner when he caught sight of Wellington seated on a sofa with the Duchess of Richmond and Lady Daventry. His laugh rang out as he loudly complained that no one would care for his ball after the proposed magnificence of the duchess's.

Once again Felix had to admire the Duke's sang-froid. With the borders closed, the emperor bound to make a move soon, he was discussing his ball in a fortnight's time as if he believed it would take place. Did he really trust the Rothschilds' reports, as he claimed, or would he once again wait for confirmation from Colonel Grant?

"I wonder what Boney is up to?" Unintentionally, Felix spoke his thought aloud.

"Pray do not speak of the wretched man, my lord!" Lady Sophia gracefully seated herself on a striped satin loveseat part-screened by potted palms. "Surely we can find more interesting topics of conversation."

So he poured compliments into her shell-like ear, so much more attractive and, he hoped, attentive than the Duke's. It took some skill to avoid the narrow line that separated the acceptable from personal remarks she would consider vulgar. Nonetheless, all the while he was wondering what Fanny would think of Wellington's casual reaction to his news. Tomorrow morning, after sending off the courier revived by her efforts, he would speculate with her about what the Emperor was concealing behind his impenetrable barrier.

The Goddess eventually tired of hearing her own praises sung and they talked of the Duchess of Richmond's ball.

"Mama says the duchess is preparing a great surprise," Lady Sophia told him, "but she will not reveal it."

"Lady Daventry is on intimate terms with her grace, is she not?" asked Felix, a brilliant idea suddenly dawning on him.

"They have known each other for ever. That is why I count Lady Georgiana among my friends, for in truth I find her a trifle too spirited for my taste."

"The duchess would accept as a guest anyone your mama brought with her, would she not?"

"Certainly," she said, puzzled, "but you have received an invitation, I am sure."

"Yes, I'm not thinking of myself. Lady Sophia, let me beg a favour of you. Ask your mother to take Miss Ingram with you to the Richmonds' ball."

"Miss Ingram!"

"She is a young lady who resides at my lodging house, the sister of an officer . . ."

"Lord Roworth, how dare you mention that loose woman in my presence!" Her voice vibrated with fury. "To ask me to associate with your . . . your chère amie goes far beyond the bounds of what is permissible even in a foreign country!"

Felix was aghast at her misconception, and angry. "In plain English," he said tightly, "Miss Ingram is my dear friend. She is not and never has been my mistress."

Lady Sophia flushed. "Since you say so, of course I must believe you. However, everyone knows she has an illegitimate child."

"Anita's birth is irrelevant, since Miss Ingram is not her mother. She is the daughter of a Spanish lady and a British soldier."

"You are excessively credulous, my lord."

"If she were Miss Ingram's child, how much easier Miss Ingram's life would be if she called herself a widow! No one would challenge such a claim, for many of her friends died in the Peninsula and those who survived are very protective of their own."

"Supposing her to be telling you the truth, she would do better to put the girl in an orphanage. She will never find a husband with a love-child on her hands."

Felix had to admire her change of heart once she knew the facts: now she was expressing concern for Fanny's well-being. She was not to blame, gently raised as she was, for being unable to comprehend the impossibility — the horror! — of the notion of Anita in an orphanage.

"Miss Ingram has chosen a difficult life," he admitted. "All the more reason to give her a little gaiety for once."

"I respect your kindness in wishing to give her the pleasure of a fashionable ball," Lady Sophia said stiffly, "but alas, it will not do. I am willing to accept that Miss Ingram is respectable. However, I cannot possibly ask my mother, let alone the Duchess of Richmond, to lend countenance to such a nobody." Her air of finality was softened by a sweet smile as she added, "Come, my lord, I believe they are striking up our waltz."

As he led her onto the floor, Felix realized he had been too precipitate. That she should progress in a few minutes from believing Fanny his mistress to issuing an invitation was not to be expected. She had been brought up to consider a respectable nobody to be beneath her notice.

Suddenly recalling the Ingrams' noble connexions, he realized why they never mentioned them. An unsupported claim must inevitably be disbelieved, making them appear the worst sort of social climbers. It was better forgotten.

All the same, even without that inducement, he'd try Lady Sophia again at the picnic. After all, he wasn't asking her to accept Fanny as an intimate friend, only to take her to a ball where, among hundreds of guests, her presence would doubtless go unnoticed.

He imagined how Fanny's face would light up if he told her he was trying to snabble an invitation to the Richmonds' ball for her. No, best not breathe a word. He was too uncertain of the outcome.

Lady Sophia was particularly charming for the rest of the evening, and his spirits soared. He almost forgot Boney, lurking in his lair.

CHAPTER 6

"Some of our fellows are giving a picnic tomorrow," Fanny told Felix when he returned to the parlour next morning after sending off the courier. "Frank was here last night and he suggested that I invite you. I don't suppose you'd care to go with us?"

"I'm going," said Anita happily. "And Billy and Jane and Peter."

"Major Prynne's children," Fanny explained. "I expect it will be a noisy, rowdy affair, not at all what you are accustomed to."

Felix grinned. "That's what you think."

"Indeed!" She raised her eyebrows questioningly.

"Well, harking back to schooldays and . . . hm . . . some of the less refined amusements of my years on the town — no, don't ask for details! I'd like to go to your picnic, but I'm already engaged tomorrow."

He looked almost as disappointed as she

101

felt. "I wish I had been able to ask you sooner, but the date was only settled last night. Our batteries are scattered all over the countryside so it was difficult to consult everyone."

"Where are you going?"

"To the river bank near Ninove. Some of ours are quartered there. I daresay I shall spend my time keeping Anita out of the river."

"So that is why I was invited!" he quizzed her.

"Not at all! I can always find someone to watch her if I want to."

"I been't going to fall in," Anita announced. "The river will make my new dress dirty."

"I'm not going to fall in," Fanny corrected absently.

"I hope not," said Felix, laughing, "but if you do there will be plenty of stout fellows eager to pull you out."

She smiled. "What a horrid, teasing humour you are in this morning. You enjoyed the party last night?"

"Lady Sophia was all that is amiable, and none of my rivals was present. She was impressed by the Duke's willingness to grant me a private interview in the middle of his soirée."

She should have known that if he had enjoyed himself it was because the Goddess had been kind for once. To forestall the expected paean of praise, she asked, "And what was the result of that interview?"

He told her of his concern that Wellington was ignoring the implications of the closed border.

"Old Hookey doesn't like anyone to know his plans," she pointed out, "and you have said yourself that he is much concerned to persuade the Belgians of his confidence. Panic among his guests last night would have achieved the precise opposite. I daresay your pride was piqued because he did not at once act on your report, but only consider how many factors he must take into account."

"True. You are thoroughly commonsensical, Miss Ingram."

Any praise was better than none, she thought with a silent sigh. She stood up. "Common sense tells me that if I don't go to market, we shall not dine tonight, and I have promised to bake a spice cake for the picnic."

"I'll take care of Anita while you are out."

"Why don't we all . . ." Seeing his dismay, she shook her head and mocked, "No, the heir to the Earl of Westwood carrying a basket of groceries is an image altogether too mortifying to contemplate."

Flushing, he snapped, "I don't expect you to understand . . ."

"I beg your pardon," she said, contrite. He had every reason to be vexed. No wonder he preferred Lady Sophia's indifference to her sharp tongue. "I have no right to cavil when you are so generous with your time looking after Anita. Thank you for your offer. I shall be as quick as I can."

"One does not always appreciate hearing a home truth." He smiled wryly. "Come, Anita, shall we play at soldiers or horses?"

"Horses," she decided.

"So much for my dignity!" he groaned, and Fanny, still upset, was forced to smile.

He had so many good, endearing qualities, it was none of her business to point out his faults. Indeed, those who moved in his world — Lady Sophia, for instance — would see nothing objectionable in his high notion of himself, counting it, rather, a virtue. She had spoken out of hurt, she realized, hurt that he considered her daily duties so much beneath him. His easy friendship was making her forget the gulf between them. Beware, she told herself. Beware!

The next day dawned perfect for picnics,

whether on the banks of the Dendre or in the shady aisles of the beech woods. A shower during the night had settled the dust and cooled the air, and a breeze was chasing the last clouds from the sky.

The artillery officers had hired a farm wagon to take women and children to Ninove. Felix had not yet left when it arrived to pick up Fanny and Anita. Anita clapped her hands at the fat horses, their harnesses bedecked with tassels, fringes, and gleaming brass. The Flemish driver, in his embroidered blue smock, red cap, striped stockings, and wooden sabots, grinned gaptoothed at her excitement.

Felix saw them seated on bales of straw and waved goodbye, then went to fetch his hired hack. For once he had obtained a decent-looking mount, a showy chestnut, though he'd not have counted on the beast's pace over any distance.

He rode to the Rue de Belle Vue, where he was disappointed but unsurprised to find that the outing was as much the Comte de St Gérard's party as the Daventrys'. Indeed, Lord Daventry had made himself scarce.

The marchioness, Lady Sophia, an unknown, plump brunette, and the count's hatchet-faced, overdressed, spinster sister had already taken their places in St Gérard's barouche. The Misses Ord, youthfully pretty girls often considered indistinguishable, were each driven in a gig by equally youthful and indistinguishable young officers.

Tempted though he was to go straight to the Goddess, Felix refused to push in among the colorful crowd about her. St Gérard, mounted on a superb bay, was holding his own at her side against Viscount Garforth, Major Bissell, Lord Albert Faversham and his fellow Guardsman, and a dashing Hussar. Gold braid and silver laces glittered in the sunshine.

Felix attacked from the flank. He drew up his chestnut on the other side of the barouche and greeted Mademoiselle de Saint Gérard. She introduced him to the plump damsel, who giggled and blushed. Lady Daventry, seated next to Mademoiselle, turned to welcome him.

"Sophie, here is Lord Roworth," she said, and common politeness obliged her daughter to divert her attention from his massed rivals to exchange a few words with him.

Whether more than common politeness animated her, he could not guess. Perhaps he had imagined that last night she had made a particular effort to please him after her refusal to act in Fanny's behalf. Still, he was gratified with the success of his tactics in outmaneuvering the military, however briefly.

The cavalcade set off, leaving the city by the Namur gate then trotting through the suburbs. The ladies furled their lace-trimmed parasols as the road entered the shade of the forest of Soignes. On either side, the smooth grey trunks of beeches rose like pillars to a roof of green. Here and there shafts of sunlight broke through to the floor of rich russet leafmould. A pair of squirrels scampered across the road and sped chattering up the nearest tree.

They turned off the road onto a winding track and soon approached a delightfully dappled glade.

Felix was too busy planning his campaign to take much notice of the scenery. He dropped back to where a closed carriage brought up the rear with servants and hampers of food. The Daventrys' butler was perfectly willing to reveal the contents of the hampers and which delicacies Lady Sophia was especially fond of.

While a bevy of beaux rushed about making the Goddess — and, as an afterthought, the other ladies — comfortable with rugs and cushions, Felix was filling three plates. As the rest of the gentlemen clustered about the hampers, Felix handed well-chosen luncheons to Lady Daventry and Mademoiselle, and joined Lady Sophia on her cushions.

"Have I guessed correctly what you will like?" he asked, as she spread a snowy linen napkin over her peach sarsnet carriage dress. He passed her a selection of salmon in aspic, chicken vol-au-vents, and a salad of artichokes.

"Perfect," she murmured, taking the silver fork he offered. "But you have nothing."

"As long as I can feast my eyes on your beauty, what need have I of aught else?"

"You are fantastical, sir. Pray take a vol-au-vent. I cannot eat so much."

So Felix ate from the Goddess's plate while the rest of her suitors scrambled for sustenance. And as he bit into the pastry, delicately flavoured with truffles, he wondered what coarse fare Fanny was subsisting on. Cold chicken eaten with the fingers, farmhouse ham, hard-boiled eggs, crusty loaves torn apart and slathered with yellow butter, perhaps a treat of oranges for the children. And the fragrance of her spicy cake had filled the house this morning.

Suddenly he was hungry.

However, after his extravagant compliment he couldn't very well desert Lady Sophia in search of food, especially as his rivals would at once usurp his place.

"About Miss Ingram . . ." The words escaped him against his will. He had meant to lead up carefully to a second request. "Now that you know her to be respectable, will you not reconsider?" he said to her stony profile.

She turned a blank stare on him and said in glacial tones, "I wonder at your persistence, my lord. Such persons cannot expect to mingle with Society."

The count came up just then and sat down on her other side. Felix was presented with an excellent view of pale gold ringlets beneath the upturned rear brim of a Leghorn hat adorned with three curling, peach-coloured ostrich plumes. Gloomily he contemplated pulling them out, one by one, to recapture her attention — but it would hardly be the sort of attention he wanted.

What a muttonheaded fool he was! He knew very well she set herself on high form, as was only right and proper in the daughter of a marquis. He recalled his momentary anger yesterday when Fanny had teased him for being too high and mighty to go to market with her. She was from another world, and the two worlds rarely mingled happily. If he had obtained an invitation for her, what, for instance, would she have worn?

With a last, useless, pleading glance at the back of Lady Sophia's head, he stood up and went over to the picnic hampers. Sir Henry Bissell narrowly beat out Lord Garforth to take his place.

Felix filled a plate and went to join Lady Daventry and the count's sister. The plump brunette was simpering under the attention of Ensign Faversham, a well-brought-up young man who restrained himself from all but an occasional jealous glance at the Goddess. Felix made polite conversation and picked at his food. He had lost his appetite.

At last the company broke up into small groups to wander through the woods. Attempting to join the gentlemen around Lady Sophia, Felix was treated to another frigid glare. He dropped back, retrieved his horse, and set off riding aimlessly between the trees.

He came out of the forest close to a village. In a huddle of brick and stone cottages, opposite a curious domed church, stood a small tavern. Hitching the chestnut to a post, he went in and ordered a glass of beer.

"What is this place?" he asked the tapster.

"Waterloo, m'sieur. A village of no importance."

"How far is it to Ninove?"

The man shrugged his shoulders. "By road it is best to go into Brussels. Perhaps thirty miles. As the crow flies, twenty or less."

Felix considered the unknown quality of his horse, the chance of losing his way, the possibility of missing the picnic site by the Dendre, the probability of the Ingrams leaving before he arrived. He, too, shrugged his shoulders. He had nothing better to do. He'd prove to Fanny that he wasn't too toplofty to enjoy the company of her friends.

The tapster described landmarks along the way — a winding lane to Hal, church steeples, a hill top spinney — shaking his head at the curious behavior of the English. Felix found his way with ease. Crossing a canal and river at Hal, he skirted fields of red and white clover, purple-blue flax, wheat and rye already shoulder-high in the fertile soil. Splashes of blood-red poppies brightened the hedgerows.

However, as he had half expected, the showy chestnut went lame. Fortunately, he had reached the banks of the Dendre by that time. He dismounted, checked the hoof for stones, found none, and walked on along the riverside path leading the limping beast.

The Horse Artillery picnic announced itself from a distance. Plodding round a bend of the river, Felix heard male voices upraised in song, the singers hidden from him by a row of willows. Next came the squeals of children, then a female voice called to Billy to stop pulling his sister's hair. A girl with blond pigtails dashed around the nearest tree, skidded to a halt, and regarded him thoughtfully.

"I've seen you before. Aren't you Anita's Uncle Felix?"

He smiled. "Yes."

"You're a lord, aren't you? I'm Jane Prynne. Horrid name, isn't it!" She wrinkled a freckled nose. "Do you want to see Aunt Fanny?"

Felix felt a slow, inexplicable flush rising in his cheeks. "Or Captain Ingram," he said indifferently. "My horse has gone lame."

"I expect you can go back to Brussels with us in the wagon." She turned and ran back along the muddy path, calling, "Uncle Frank, Uncle Frank, guess who's here!"

Following, Felix came to a water meadow tinted palest pink by lady's smock, with a few late marsh-marigolds adding touches of brilliant yellow. A pair of dedicated anglers sat on the bank with their backs to the gathering. On the grass nearby sprawled the male chorus, tankards in their hands, their dark blue uniform jackets unbuttoned. He recognized the dark, stocky Captain Lloyd, but Frank was not among them. Beyond, young Jane Prynne, pigtails flying, raced towards a group of women sitting in the shade at the edge of a copse of oak and alder.

Fanny wasn't with the women, as far as Felix could see, but one of them held a sleeping Anita on her lap, and Frank stood close by talking to two other officers. Felix recognized one as Major Prynne. The other was an older man, with a colonel's insignia.

Jane Prynne tugged on her father's sleeve, then bobbed a curtsy to the colonel, said something, and pointed at Felix. Frank came to meet him.

"My lord, what an unexpected pleasure. Fanny thought you were going in the opposite direction. You know Major Prynne, do you not? Let me present . . ." He looked from Felix to the colonel and back and laughed. "Dashed if I know aught of precedence. Lord Roworth, Colonel Sir Augustus Frazer."

They shook hands. "I just dropped by to see how my lads are doing," said the colonel, "and to admire the pretty girls." He chucked Jane under the chin and she giggled.

"My horse is gone lame." Felix gestured disgustedly at the chestnut, standing behind him with drooping head. "I hope your lads will take pity on me, colonel, and somehow convey me back to Brussels." He made no attempt to explain what he was doing in the environs of Ninove when he had set out for a picnic in the Forest of Soignes.

"We'll get you home, never fear," said Major Prynne.

"In the wagon with the women and children," Frank added, grinning.

"It's fun," Jane assured him.

Felix looked back at the main group of officers, who seemed to be having a difference of opinion as to which tune to strike up next. "I daresay one or two of your fellows will be more fit to travel by cart than on horseback," he said.

The men laughed. "Let them have their spree," said Colonel Frazer indulgently. "There'll be time enough for sobriety when we go after Boney. I must be on my way. A pleasure to make your acquaintance, my lord." He returned Frank's and the major's salutes and went off towards the road, where a mounted trooper held the reins of his horse.

Captain Cavalié Mercer joined them, a fishing pole over his shoulder, his face mournful. "Not a bite," he said. "Fresh fish would have made a nice change from my landlady's everlasting *carbonnade*. Where's your sister, Frank?"

"She spotted anemones growing in the wood and went to look. You know how she is about flowers."

"The devil! I was afraid of that. I saw Barnstaple heading — or rather stumbling — towards the trees a few minutes ago. You know how he is with a few pints in him."

"Don't worry, Cav. Fanny can deal with Barnstaple, drunk or sober. Oh, very well, if you will look at me like that, I'll go and find them."

"I'll come with you," said Felix grimly. "We can split up and search quicker."

"I assure you it's unnecessary, Roworth," Frank's insouciant voice followed him as he plunged into the copse, "but if you insist . . ."

A narrow, winding path, one of a maze of rabbit tracks, led to his right between slender alders, gnarled oaks, and a tangle of stumps and underbrush. A woodpecker's rat-a-tat-tat rang through the green stillness. Scattered clumps of fragile, purple-veined wood anemones suggested he was on the right track, then he saw the imprint of a small foot in a patch of soft earth. He hurried on. Where was she? Was she even now struggling in the brutal embrace of a drunken soldier?

He quickened his pace, his heart thundering with dread and fury. Ahead a shaft of sunlight struck down where a tree had fallen, and there was a flash of pink . . . He frowned; surely Fanny had been wearing blue, like Anita.

Flaunting across the fallen trunk, an exuberance of dog-roses raised their pink petals and golden centers to the sun, scenting the moist air. Loving flowers as she did, the sight must have drawn her like a bee to honey. And there she was, just beyond, a small, supple figure writhing in the arms of the tall, fair lieutenant.

In two long strides, Felix reached the tree trunk and leapt atop it, his fists clenched, silent rage screaming in his head. As he sprang down, Fanny made some quick move he couldn't follow. Barnstaple toppled backwards into the briars, doubled up, gasping in pain and clutching his groin.

"I'm sorry, James," said Fanny sadly. "I wish you will learn to take no for an answer."

By that time, Felix's sympathies were divided. "Are you all right?" he asked her, but his gaze was on the unhappy, squirming lieutenant.

"Fe . . . Lord Roworth! What are you doing here?" Hurriedly she smoothed her tousled curls. "Yes, I am perfectly all right. The silly boy has torn my lace a little but it will mend."

"You are not going to swoon?"

"Swoon! I haven't the least idea how to go about it. Since you are here, pray give James what aid you can. He is a trifle green in the face. Perhaps he will swoon."

Felix thought the unfortunate young man a great deal more likely to shoot the cat, the ultimate humiliation before the woman he loved. "Frank's looking for you," he said. "You'd better go and call him off."

"You won't abandon him? No, I know you will not. I daresay he will feel the better for my absence."

"I daresay he might," he told her retreating back. Any properly brought up young lady would have fainted dead away, but he had to admit her reaction was a good deal more practical. What an extraordinary creature she was, mingling courage and compassion! He knelt beside her victim.

Some time passed before Lieutenant Barnstaple was able to rise groggily to his feet, and then he sank to a seat on a stump, head in hands. Casting up his accounts had sobered him somewhat and he was very hangdog.

"You probably think I'm a loose fish," he muttered, "but I love her! I want to marry her, even if she won't give up the child."

"I take it you have offered and she has refused you?"

"A dozen times. Half the fellows have asked her to marry them . . ."

"You mean half the officers in your regiment want to marry Miss Ingram?" Felix asked, incredulous. He had never given the matter much consideration. If asked he would have supposed that a female with neither dowry nor useful connections, nor the kind of beauty to make a man forget the lack, was unlikely to suffer from an excess of suitors.

Of course, in character Fanny was no ordinary female. He frowned. She was too good to marry one of these rough-and-ready artillerymen.

"Most of 'em gave up when she took on the baby. I mean, a by-blow, even if her father was one of ours. But I don't care," the lieutenant went on with stubborn determination. "I'll keep on trying."

"Not when you are pot-valiant!" His fury re-awoke. Fanny had proved able to take care of herself, but she should not need to. This was one of the hazards of following the drum that she had not mentioned.

"N-no, my lord . . . It's just that when I'm top-heavy I just can't seem to . . . Oh lord, here comes the captain."

A jaunty whistle preceded Frank into the little clearing. "So there you are. I was going to leave you to take your medicine but Cav persuaded me to rush to the rescue." He scrutinized the lieutenant. "By the look of things, Lord Roworth didn't arrive quite in time." Turning to Felix, he asked, "I must have just missed Fanny when I went back to the others. Was she upset?"

"Cool as a cucumber," he said, with more than a hint of irony. "Truth to tell, I was under the impression it was her rescue I was rushing to. I felt it unnecessary to punish the lieutenant further."

"She hates having to use that little trick I taught her. What a confounded bacon-brained nodcock you are, Barnstaple! Come on, old chap, let's get you back to the river. It looks like rain and everyone's packing up to leave."

As he gingerly stood up, the lieutenant moaned. "I can't ride back to Brussels!"

Dispassionately, Frank surveyed the hunched figure. "It would serve you bloody well right, but I suppose it's too much to ask."

"You can go in the wagon with the ladies,"

said Felix smugly. "I engage to return your horse safely to Brussels."

Frank set off down the narrow path and Barnstaple stumbled after him. Felix paused, something niggling at the back of his mind. He glanced around the clearing, no longer bright with sunlight. Ah, that was it.

He bent to pick up Fanny's straw hat. A military boot had demolished the crown, completing the extinction of the drooping plume. Never more than passable headgear, it was now the sorriest of sights. He tossed it into the bushes. Perhaps some day a bird would nest in it.

As he turned, a briar caught at his sleeve. On a sudden impulse he picked one of the roses, carefully broke off the thorns, and stuck it in his buttonhole to take to Fanny.

By the time he reached the riverbank, the petals had fallen off. A pointless gesture anyway, he thought moodily, dropping the remains on the path.

In the south-west, over France, towering storm clouds loomed black.

CHAPTER 7

Lady Sophia was "not at home." That the phrase deserved quotation marks Felix knew, because he saw Garforth's superb Thoroughbred being walked by a groom up the Rue de Belle Vue. She was still miffed, whether by his solicitation on Fanny's behalf or by his departure from the picnic. With the rest of her suitors constantly dancing attendance, she was unused to being deserted.

Disconsolate, his pride hurt by her denial, he strolled to Headquarters and dropped in to chat with the officers on duty. The latest rumour, according to Gordon, was that Boney had reached Maubeuge, on the frontier.

"Grant can't confirm it and the Beau don't believe it," the plump colonel added, "but De Lancey's talking of sending Lady Magdalen to Antwerp. I suppose you haven't heard anything definite?"

"Not since Wednesday, when the border was closed."

"Pity. I half expect your couriers to take wing and fly over the border. By the way, some of us are having a little dinner at the Hôtel d'Angleterre this evening. Join us, if you're not otherwise engaged."

"A little dinner?" drawled Lord Fitzroy, entering the room at that moment. "Come now, when did you ever eat a *little* dinner, Gordon?"

"I expect he meant there'll be devilish little dinner for the rest of the company once he's been served," Felix suggested. "Still, feast or famine, I'm delighted to accept." The musicale he'd been invited to held no charms if Lady Sophia was going to give him the cold shoulder. He'd send his regrets.

"I'll tell you what," said Fitzroy, "Emily's been complaining that she hasn't seen you this age. Why don't you call in around four o'clock and she'll feed you up in preparation for an evening of starvation."

"Confound it, you fellows, can't a chap put on a spot of weight in peace?" complained Colonel Gordon.

"A spot of peace is what I'm waiting for," Fitzroy punned. "I've letters to write. See you later, Roworth."

Felix took his leave and headed homeward at a leisurely pace to add a word about Maubeuge to his latest report. The rumour was too vague for urgency, just as well since he had no courier on hand at present. Certainly it did not call for him to speed to England.

Crossing the Grand' Place, his eye was caught by a stall in the market opposite the magnificent medieval pile of the Hôtel de Ville. The counter was heaped with straw hats of every conceivable size and shape, while bundles of feathers, ribbons, bows, and silk flowers dangled from the awning. A trio of giggling Flemish girls clustered about a fourth who was directing the stall-holder in the placement on one of the hats of a huge rose in an unlikely shade of purple.

Felix watched as, satisfied, she tried it on, admired herself in a square of mirror nailed to an upright, and paid the woman. The girls moved away and he took their place.

A few minutes later he walked on with a hat in his hand, praying he wouldn't meet any acquaintances. The straw, though not of the finest quality, was closely woven. Instead of extravagant plumes he had had the woman adorn it with a circlet of daisies and a big white bow. Lady Sophia would have looked upon it with incredulous contempt.

He hoped Fanny would like it, with her love of flowers, and he knew she would accept it in the spirit in which it was given. It would suit her fresh prettiness very well.

"Oh Roworth, how delightful!" Setting it atop her curls she rushed to the looking glass. First he had turned up at the picnic, and now a new hat, as though to prove to her that he was not the toplofty creature she had accused him of being. He made it very difficult to remember the difference in their stations. Pink-cheeked, she turned and beamed at him.

He smiled back. "Charming."

"How very kind of you. But you shouldn't have. It was entirely poor James's fault I lost my hat."

"Undoubtedly, but I found it. And judging by where I found it, it was my clumsy foot that extinguished its last hope."

She laughed. "Last hope is right. I could not have gone on wearing the wretched thing much longer." All the same, she had seen James step on it. Felix was giving her an excuse to accept his gift as reparation, but ought she to accept? Suddenly shy, she said, "I was saving for a new one. Will you not let me pay you for this?"

"Madam, do you think to impugn my honour as a gentleman?"

"Heavens, no, I should not dare. Thank you, my lord. Thank you very much."

"Shall we take Anita to the park to show it off?" He spoke with an air of defiance, and Fanny realized that Lady Sophia might well be taking the air at this hour. Apparently he'd decided not to let her whims rule his actions. "You haven't already fed the swans today, have you?" he asked.

"No, and I'd love to go, but Anita is napping. She was downright crotchety this morning, still exhausted from the picnic and from the excitement of having children to play with. Later perhaps?"

He shook his head, regretful, but also slightly relieved. "I'm engaged for afternoon tea."

"At the Daventrys'?"

"No, the Somersets'. Lady Sophia is offended with me."

"I'm so sorry," said Fanny, more tactful than truthful, "but as you said before, she will doubtless relent. What is she vexed about now? For several days now you have only been to the park with us too early for her ladyship to be about," she pointed out, concealing her hurt behind a teasing manner.

Felix appeared to be hunting with some desperation for an answer when the door knocker sounded. Fanny went to the front door and found a boy with a huge bouquet of crimson roses. Her nose buried in the blooms she returned to the parlour.

She extracted a card from the fragrant flowers. "From James Barnstaple, with his humble apologies. How sweet of him, when I was so unkind."

"You are too forgiving!" said Felix roughly. "He got what he deserved."

"I came to no harm," she pointed out, surprised at his tone.

"No, I daresay you have often had to employ such methods. Barnstaple told me you have been courted by half the officers in the regiment."

She flushed as crimson as the roses. "He had no business telling you any such thing."

"But it is true? Why did you marry none of them?"

And that was none of his business, yet her answer burst from her with such vehemence that her voice shook. "I shall never marry a soldier!" War had robbed her of too many people she loved, father, mother, friends, and a certain stalwart young officer . . .

But one must not live in the past. Once more she buried her face in the flowers, this time not to enjoy the fragrance but to hide her emotion. "Are they not beautiful? I must find a vase for them."

She escaped to the kitchen, still wearing the hat. Felix had the lowering feeling that she had forgotten all about his gift.

Some time later, he was about to leave for the Somersets' lodging when again there came a knocking at the front door. Fanny was above stairs, so he answered it himself, ignoring Madame Vilvoorde's scowling surveillance.

It was a courier from Nathan Rothschild in London. He brought advance news of another shipment of gold, arranged by Mr Herries who was back in England. Of more immediate interest was a report that the previous morning Napoleon had still not left Paris.

Mr Rothschild's letter advised him to keep the courier at hand in case of need, so he sent the man to a hotel. Since he didn't know the Duke's whereabouts and was about to see the Military Secretary, he went straight to the Somersets' with his news.

Lady Fitzroy, her bloom showing her fully recovered from her confinement, presided over the tea-tray, watched with fond pride by her husband. Lady Georgiana and Lord George Lennox were there, too, and Colonel Sir Alexander Gordon, and one or two others.

After making his bows, asking after the baby, and accepting a cup of tea in fragile Limoges porcelain, Felix drew Fitzroy aside into a window embrasure.

"Boney was still in Paris yesterday morning," he said.

"How the devil do you know that already? Did your courier find a leak in the dam?"

"Not exactly. As Gordon suggested, my courier sprouted wings and flew over the wall. My employers only use those particular couriers in emergencies as they are less reliable, though faster, than the usual. And they don't want it generally known that they use them at all." He grinned at Fitzroy's puzzlement. "Pigeon post, Paris to Dieppe, Dieppe to London."

Fitzroy laughed. "May I tell Gordon?" He called the colonel over.

Gordon arrived with a plateful of cucumber sandwiches and queen cakes. "I'm filling up so you needn't fear starving at dinner," he said. "What's new?"

"Roworth's courier took your advice and flew across the border."

"Huh?"

"Pigeon post," said Felix.

He and Fitzroy grinned as, after a startled moment, Gordon guffawed.

"What is the joke?" cried Lady Georgiana.

"Do tell us, pray."

"It is never wise to ask what gentlemen are laughing about," Lady Fitzroy chided gently.

With a barely perceptible shake of the head at the colonel, Fitzroy said, "Sorry, Georgy, Emily's right. I can tell you, though, that the Monster is still in Paris." He turned back to Felix. "I'll make sure the Duke hears tonight. He still thinks it likely we'll be waiting for the Russian and Austrian armies to arrive and then marching into France. Now come and have some sandwiches before Gordon snabbles the lot."

When Felix returned to Madame Vilvoorde's to change for dinner, Frank was in the parlour reading a newspaper while Fanny put Anita to bed. Trusting the captain's discretion as he trusted Fanny's, he waited until she came down, then told them the courier's news, and how it had reached England.

"I have never understood how pigeons can be counted on to deliver messages," Fanny admitted. "They always seem such silly birds."

"Perhaps that's why they can do it," Felix proposed. "They only have a single idea in their heads, which is the location of home. Nothing can distract them."

"Nothing but a hawk or a sportsman with a shotgun," grunted Frank. "To be sure they are fast, and Old Hookey may be glad to know Boney was in Paris yesterday, but I'd like to know where he is now."

"Don't be such a crab-apple," said Fanny.

"I just wish we had some of the 12-pounders the Duke keeps trying to get us. Or these new 24-pounder carronades, though I daresay they would go to the Field Artillery, being too heavy for us. They are supposed to be good with Colonel Shrapnell's case shot."

"Do you find Shrapnell's shells effective?" Felix asked.

"The French don't like 'em," he said, grinning, restored to good humour.

"And Whinyates' rockets?"

Frank pulled a face. "We are not so enamoured of Whinyates' rockets. Mind you, they'd frighten the horses to death if they went anywhere near 'em."

Felix laughed. Fanny was glad they were on such friendly terms, though she wished they would talk about something other than weapons.

Though by no means a regular church-goer, Felix attended morning service at the English church the next day. He was already feeling virtuous, having been most abstemious at the Hôtel d'Angleterre the previous night. Lieutenant Barnstaple's drunken example had reinforced the lesson of an embarrassing episode in the south of France, when overindulgence had led to his embracing Miriam — unexpectedly, if not precisely against her will. He still was not sure just how to interpret her response at the time.

Admittedly, after the dinner last night he had called on his mistress, but only to find her gone. Katrina Lisle had left a letter for him, explaining that in view of flying rumours she had sought refuge with relatives near Bruges. Under the circumstances, he wasn't sure whether his continence counted as a virtue.

Virtue, however, was not his chief purpose in going to church. He knew that Lady Sophia had far too great a sense of propriety to turn her back if he addressed her in the church yard afterwards.

In a modest walking dress of Pomona green silk, and a thoroughly immodest bonnet with no less than five green and white ostrich feathers, the Goddess was a delectable sight. Major Sir Henry Bissell shared a pew with the Daventrys, his smug air suggesting that he considered he had stolen a march on the count, who was, of course, a Catholic. The dark Rifle green of his uniform admirably set off Lady Sophia's lighter green gown. He was not at all pleased when Felix approached them after the service.

"Good day, Lady Sophia."

"Good day, my lord." She was reserved but not, he thought, more so than usual.

They exchanged commonplaces on the weather and then, knowing that she would spend the afternoon at home reading sermons, he requested, "May I have the pleasure of riding with you in the park tomorrow?"

She looked unwontedly uncertain. "Thank you, sir. I have been invited to the Guards' cricket match at Enghien . . ."

"Lord Roworth." Her mother, who had been chatting to a friend, turned towards them. "I cannot allow Sophie to go so far as Enghien squired only by those delightful — but so very young! — Guardsmen, even though the Duke was quite positive last night that Bonaparte is still in Paris. As it happens, Daventry and I are otherwise engaged tomorrow."

"I am on duty," said Bissell, scowling, then added with a hint of malice, "and even for Lady Sophia's sake, St Gérard will have nothing whatsoever to do with that English madness called cricket."

Taking Lady Daventry's hint, pleased with her confidence in him, Felix said promptly, "I shall be honoured to escort Lady Sophia, if you will entrust her to me, ma'am."

"Most kind," said the marchioness, bestowing a smile of approval. "You will be quite safe with Lord Roworth, Sophie."

"Yes, Mama," she murmured.

In the event, the outing proved singularly tedious. Though Felix had enjoyed playing cricket in what he was rapidly coming to think of as his distant youth, as an uninvolved spectator he found it boring. Besides, he received only a third share of Lady Sophia's scrupulously divided attention, since Lord Albert and his fellow-ensign accompanied them. Their puppylike infatuation with the Goddess he found only briefly amusing. Nor did he enjoy the good-natured but dismissive way they treated him as a venerable elder, and a civilian at that.

"As if I were ninety, not nine-and-twenty!" he exploded to Fanny when he reached home. She giggled. "And as if a pair of colours were the only important thing in the world."

At that she looked sad. "Those Hyde Park soldiers will learn soon enough what war is about, poor boys."

"What's Hyde Park?" Anita asked. "Is there swans there, like in our park?"

So Felix took her on his lap and told her about the swans and ducks on the Serpentine, and of the fashionable parade every fine afternoon during the London Season, where ladies showed off their best hats.

"Tía Fanny weared her best hat today, when we did feed the swans. Tío Cav said it is dev'ish smart."

"Anita, you must not repeat that word," said Fanny, and then she caught Felix's eye and they both burst out laughing, for no particular reason that he could afterwards discern.

He was glad he had bought her the devilish smart hat, even if that was not quite how he'd have described it. Was Mercer in love with her, to throw compliments about like that? She deserved better than that profane captain. He recalled with relief that she had sworn never to marry a soldier.

Late the following afternoon, another of her admirers arrived at Madame Vilvoorde's. Moses Solomon had galloped ahead of a slow-moving coachload of gold from London to bring electrifying news.

Following Fanny into the parlour, he announced importantly, "Napoleon left Paris yesterday, my lord, in the early hours of the morning. His headquarters are said to be at Beaumont, though Mr Rothschild had no definite word on that." He gave Felix two letters, one addressed to the Duke of Wellington.

Felix had just come in after riding in the park with Lady Sophia — and the count and Lord Garforth. He seized his hat and gloves from the table. "This cannot wait. I'm off to the Duke's."

He strode out, knowing he could rely upon Fanny to take care of the weary courier. Moses failed to hide his delight at being left in her hands.

As he hurried towards the Rue Royale, Felix read his letter from Nathan Rothschild. After repeating the news of Bonaparte's movements, his employer went on to stress the utmost importance of keeping him informed of developments in Belgium. Felix had two couriers at his disposal. Once they had been despatched back to England, in the event of further urgent news he must come himself.

Rothschild went on to discuss business matters, closing with an assurance of his complete confidence in Felix. The wisdom of his decision to employ Viscount Roworth had been proved again and again.

Felix was gratified to have earned the gruff

banker's rare praise. Fanny would be pleased and proud of him. Folding the three close-written sheets, he slipped them into the inside pocket of his coat and entered the Duke's Headquarters with a spring in his step.

"Good news, my lord?" asked young George Cathcart, looking up from a hand of cards.

"Not exactly, though you might call it positive."

"Boney's made his move," stated Lord Arthur Hill with placid certainty, dropping his cards as Felix nodded, and heaving his bulk out of the chair. "Fitzroy's with the Beau now, but for this I'll risk losing my head."

"If you're lucky he'll put you on bread and water and you'll find your waistline," observed another officer. "It's true, Roworth? What have you heard?"

None but the Duke's personal staff was present, so Felix told them what little he knew.

"Beaumont?" said Canning, consulting a map pinned to the wall. "The devil! That's where the road to Mons splits from the road to Charleroi. He could be aiming to outflank our right, or to divide us from the Prussians, or even to march directly on Brussels."

The Duke said the same when Felix reported to him. "Things are moving at last, and I don't doubt we shall have a fight of it, but I cannot make a move until I have definite word from Grant at Mons or from the Prussians at Charleroi. Fitzroy, send a couple of the fellows to inform them of this latest. My thanks, Roworth. I shall see you at the Richmonds' ball, I expect?"

"Yes, sir, if you think . . . ?"

"Her grace would never forgive me if I broke my promise that she could hold her ball without fear of interruption."

By the following evening, when Lady Conynghame held a soirée, everyone had heard talk of serious French troop movements on the border. Felix had been in and out of Headquarters all day, but he refused to confirm the rumours until Wellington came in and calmly corroborated the most recent report: the French had crossed the frontier.

Felix was flattered when Lady Daventry consulted him as to the advisability of removing herself and her daughter from Brussels immediately.

"Just to Antwerp," she said anxiously, "until we see what happens."

"No one else is leaving, Mama. Can we not stay for the Duchess's ball? There will be time enough to go to Antwerp afterwards," she said, dispassionate as always.

"I daresay you are right, my love," said her mother weakly, throwing a helpless glance at Felix.

It was true that very few of those privileged to be invited to the Richmond ball were talking of departure. "I suggest you prepare to leave at short notice," he advised her in a low voice. "Then you will be ready for any eventuality without disappointing Lady Sophia unnecessarily."

And without disappointing himself, since he was to take the Goddess in to dinner at the Richmonds' before the ball — and none of his rivals had been invited to dine. He was sorry Fanny was not to have a chance to enjoy it, but surely the French would not be so cruel as to attack before the long-awaited ball.

CHAPTER 8

In the morning, Felix joined Fanny, Anita, and Moses for a hearty, companionable breakfast. He was sure Fanny must be oppressed by the news of Boney's approach but for the child's sake she concealed it admirably behind a cheerful, serene countenance.

Afterwards, he again repaired to Headquarters. Rumours abounded, but there was no firm news and he was told that Fitzroy was walking in the park with the Duke.

He joined them there, finding the Duke of Richmond with them. Wellington had heard nothing from either Charleroi or Mons, but he meant to dine at three so as to be ready to deal with whatever might arise.

Felix declined an invitation to dine with them, but he went back with them to Headquarters. He was just leaving when the Prince of Orange dashed in. Already in his dress uniform for the ball, Slender Billy announced that with his own ears he had heard gunfire from the direction of the Prussian positions around Charleroi.

Unwilling to leave the center of affairs, Felix lingered, accepting a glass of wine. The diners were still at table when a Prussian officer, covered in dirt and sweat, brought a long-delayed despatch. It was dated nine o'clock that morning, and reported that soon after daybreak the French had attacked in force.

"Fitzroy, send for De Lancey. Everyone — the whole army — is to report to divisional headquarters and to be ready to march at a moment's notice."

Having sent off a messenger, Fitzroy returned to the table, looking worried. Felix wondered if he too had expected the Duke to deploy his troops, not merely to gather and arm them. "No doubt we shall be able to manage those fellows," said the Military Secretary diffidently.

"There is little doubt of that," Wellington snapped, "provided I do not make a false movement. Charleroi might be a feint. I must wait for word from Mons."

The situation was unchanged when Felix had to go home to change his dress for dinner and the ball. News awaited him at Madame Vilvoorde's.

Fanny and Frank were in the parlour, Fanny pale but composed and dry-eyed. "Frank's battery is to be deployed at Quatre Bras," she said. "He has just come home to . . . to. . . ." She bit her lip.

Her brother put his arm around her shoulders. "To say goodbye," he finished her sentence bluntly.

"Quatre Bras? Where is that?" Felix hoped explanations might steady her. At least Anita was already abed.

"It's just a farm at a crossroads on the road to Charleroi. Prince Bernhard's Dutch-Belgians had a bit of a set-to there with a few skirmishers late this afternoon. Drove them off, but he thought he saw Marshal Ney reconnoitering later."

"Ney himself!"

"So I heard. Ney can't have seen much, though, because of the tall rye, or he would have attacked. The prince's brigade has no more than four thousand men and eight guns. Since Slender Billy isn't at Braine-le-Comte to be consulted, thank heaven, his aides are sending reinforcements. Well, duty calls, I must be off."

Felix shook his hand heartily. "Goodbye, then. I'll keep an eye on your womenfolk until you've sent Boney running with his tail between his legs."

Frank grinned, and kissed Fanny, who hugged him convulsively and then stood back, taut as a bowstring, letting him go. He strode out without a backward glance, a resolute figure in his dark blue jacket and riding breeches.

"Goodbye," Fanny whispered as the door closed behind her brother.

Somehow his departure brought home to Felix the reality of the approaching battle, in a way all the talk at Headquarters had not. No longer was it just a matter of reports and maneuvers. Men were going out to fight.

He desperately wanted to comfort Fanny, to hold her and stroke her curls and tell her everything was going to be all right. But any words of reassurance would strike false, and probably precipitate the tears she was so nobly holding back.

"I must send a courier to London," he said abruptly.

"Mr Solomon?"

Moses Solomon was staying in the house, and might be of use to her. "No, I'll send the other fellow. He ought to leave tonight."

"Here's your pen and ink and paper." She was obviously glad of something practical to do. "Shall I send Trevor with a message?"

"If you please. Tell him to hurry back."

The courier was despatched. Already late for dinner, Felix went upstairs to change, feeling as if he were abandoning Fanny. She had sat nearby with some sewing while he was writing to Rothschild, but he noticed from the corner of his eye that she did not set a single stitch. He was glad young Solomon was there to dine with her.

When he reached the Richmonds', the company was already at table. He made his apologies to the duchess, who assured him that since everyone was at sixes and sevens, she had ordered several dishes kept hot for late arrivals.

"We thought you had deserted us too," Lady Georgiana greeted him.

Looking around the table as he took his place beside Lady Sophia, he saw that his was not the only empty chair. Lord March was present, but his brother George was not. An excess of the female sex prevailed. Small wonder, then, that the Goddess smiled on him despite his tardiness. It was a pity that the general talk of war distracted him from the enjoyment of her undivided attention.

The duchess led her dinner guests to the ballroom in time for them to appreciate its glories before the dancing began. The rose-trellis wallpaper was almost hidden by draperies swathed to give the appearance of a pavilion. Looking around, Felix wondered whether Fanny would be awed, or shocked, or would burst into laughter at the sight of such wildly extravagant decorations.

Crimson, gold, and black hangings; pillars wreathed with ribbons, leaves, and flowers; banks of roses and lilies, their heavy scent vying with the odour of hot wax from glittering chandeliers — the tiniest crease marred Lady Sophia's smooth forehead. Amid the sumptuous splendour her spangled lemon-yellow gauze paled to insignificance.

As the ball guests began to arrive, Felix was no better satisfied with his sober black. Despite the call to arms, well-born officers in full dress uniform swarmed into the ballroom. Lord Garforth appeared, dripping with silver lace, and Lord Albert in his scarlet and gold. Felix felt an unexpected sympathy with the Comte de St Gérard, a drab fellow-civilian among the military magnificence.

He could not help feeling useless, though he had played an essential part in the preparations for war.

Lord Garforth led Lady Sophia out for the first set. Felix watched, not unwilling to stand still by one of the open French doors, for he feared his neckcloth was wilting. The heat was stifling. With luck, the night would grow cooler by the time he waltzed with her. Going in search of champagne, he met a friend, and stopped to discuss the latest disturbing rumour. He hoped Fanny was not hearing any of the alarming stories flying about Brussels.

When he returned to the ballroom, the floor had been cleared and a skirling of bagpipes announced the appearance of the duchess's much discussed surprise. A detachment of Highlanders marched in and, kilts swinging, performed strathspeys and sword dances for the amusement of her guests.

Shouts of "Bravo!" rewarded their efforts, and they were bombarded with roses by appreciative young ladies. As they departed, the orchestra returned to strike up a waltz. Felix hurriedly sought out Lady Sophia.

"Did you enjoy the Scotch dancers?" he asked as they circled the room.

"An original diversion, but I cannot think it was proper for Lady Georgiana and those others to throw flowers. Why, the men were mere privates. It is always unwise to encourage the lower orders."

"There was no harm in it," Felix disagreed. Sometimes her sense of propriety and of her high rank went too far. "Tomorrow, after all, the French may be throwing shells and bullets at them."

"Pray do not talk of war," she said, with a touch of petulance. "It is all anyone can think of, I vow, and it can hardly be considered an agreeable subject of conversation."

A disagreeable subject, to be sure, but unavoidable. When Felix returned Lady Sophia to the marchioness's side, she was at once swept away by the count, but Lady Daventry detained him to quiz him about the outbreak of hostilities. All over the ballroom, while young ladies and their uniformed suitors danced with a desperate gaiety, their elders gathered in groups to wonder why Wellington had not yet put in an appearance. Already here and there an officer bid farewell to a fainting sweetheart, a pallid mother or wife or sister, and slipped out into the night.

After his second dance with Lady Sophia, Felix was tempted to dash home just to check that Fanny was holding up. He went so far as to head for the door, reaching it just as Wellington at last arrived with several of his staff in tow.

Georgiana Lennox darted off the floor, dragging her partner behind her. "Oh, Duke," she cried, "do pray tell me: Are the rumours true? Is it war?"

"Yes, they are true. We are off tomorrow."

The news whipped around the ballroom like a whirlwind, leaving consternation as it passed. Felix found himself next to Lord Fitzroy.

"What the devil are you fellows doing here?" he asked. "Don't tell me the Beau didn't dare risk the duchess's displeasure!"

"What better place to find all the ranking officers? We heard from Mons at last — not a sign of the French — so we're deploying eastward."

"Towards Quatre Bras?"

"Yes. You know it?"

"The artillery captain at my lodgings said there was a scuffle there this afternoon."

Fitzroy stared. "I've heard nothing of it."

"I didn't rush to tell you because it's little more than yet another rumour. Ingram was not actually present. And if it is true, since our fellows were involved, I was certain you'd have been informed."

The Duke's Military Secretary glanced indecisively over his shoulder at his commander, now seated nearby on a sofa chatting with Lady Dalrymple-Hamilton. Every now and then he would break off and call a passing officer to him to give directions. Felix saw the Prince of Orange, who had been dancing with his usual exuberance, and the Duke of Brunswick conferring with Wellington for some minutes.

"You're right," Fitzroy said, "it's just another rumour so far, and if it's true we are aimed in the right direction."

Felix was glad he'd be able to tell Fanny that the entire British army was on its way to reinforce her brother's position. He had half a mind to leave right away, but there was always the hope of further news.

The Duke rose to his feet as Lady Charlotte Greville came up to speak to him. At that moment one of Slender Billy's aides, in riding dress, brought in a despatch. The prince gave it to the Duke unopened and, excusing himself, Wellington read it. His expression of forced gaiety turned grim.

He called back the prince's aide. Felix heard him order, "Four horses instantly to the Prince of Orange's carriage!" Turning back to the prince and Brunswick, he told the former to return at once to Braine-le-Comte. Brunswick left with him.

"Braine-le-Comte is not far from Quatre Bras," said Fitzroy softly. "I'd best go to him."

The Duke's staff converged on him in a brief flurry of activity. Half the ball guests pretended not to see, while the rest watched anxiously. Wellington emerged calm and smiling and proceeded towards the supper room with Lady Georgiana Lennox on his arm.

Sir Alexander Gordon, on his way out, paused beside Felix. "Charleroi's taken," he muttered. "Blücher has fallen back on Ligny." He shook Felix's hand and hurried on.

"Roworth!" Lord Garforth strode up to him. "I'm off. I was supposed to take Lady Sophia in to supper but I can't stay. Be a good fellow and take my place."

"Of course."

As the Dragoon blue and silver vanished into the night, Felix bitterly recalled the rousing speech from Henry V that had once sparked his desire to be a soldier:

And gentlemen in England now a-bed
Shall think themselves accurs'd they were not here
And hold their manhoods cheap whiles any speaks
That fought with us . . .

He was not in England; he was not a-bed; but he might as well be for all the good his manhood was doing for his country.

He found little consolation in being able to take Lady Sophia in to supper. He could

149

not help worrying about Fanny. Still, another hour or so would not make any difference.

He went to find the deserted Goddess, explained Lord Garforth's departure, and escorted her to the supper room. No sooner were they seated than Slender Billy came in, looking serious for once. He spoke at length in a whisper to the Duke. Everyone watched.

"Very well," said Wellington loudly at last, "I have no fresh orders to give. I advise your Royal Highness to go back to your quarters and to bed."

For some twenty minutes, he continued his conversation with Georgy Lennox and his flirtation with the lady on his other side. Then he turned to the Duke of Richmond, sitting opposite him with the Marquise d'Assche.

"I think it's time for me to go to bed likewise," he said, his voice once more resounding through the subdued chatter of the remaining guests.

People began to disperse, drifting back to the ballroom, where the orchestra was tuning up again, or calling for their wraps and their carriages. The count came to claim Lady Sophia. Felix made his way to the entrance hall. He wanted to go home, just to see how Fanny was getting on, but then he decided good manners demanded that he take his leave of Lady Sophia in due form.

Fitzroy came up to him and nodded towards Wellington, who was standing nearby, speaking to the Duke of Richmond. "I must just have a word with him before I go home to . . . to say goodbye to Emily. Felix, will you drop in on her when you can? I wish I had sent her to Antwerp, but she is the Beau's niece, after all, and would not go."

Felix clasped his hand. Goodbyes everywhere. Fanny was not alone in her distress, though that made it no easier to bear.

In a momentary hush, he heard Wellington say in a low voice to Richmond, "Have you a good map in the house?"

Richmond nodded and led the way toward the back of the house. Wellington caught sight of Fitzroy and beckoned him to follow.

Felix lingered, hoping for the latest news to take to Fanny. He was still in the hall when they came out of Richmond's study a few minutes later. Fitzroy hurriedly informed him that Slender Billy had only just received a despatch from his headquarters confirming what Frank Ingram had said of

Prince Bernhard's engagement that afternoon.

"The Duke said Napoleon has humbugged him, gained twenty-four hours march."

"I wish I had told him as soon as I heard it!"

"He wouldn't — couldn't — have acted on an unsubstantiated report, leaving the right undefended. We'll engage the French at Quatre Bras but he don't expect to stop them there. Have you ever heard of a village called Waterloo? He said weeks ago he'd fight just to the south of it if he had his choice, and it looks as if he will get it."

The orchestra in the ballroom fell silent at that moment, and they heard a bugle in the distance. Fitzroy clapped Felix on the shoulder and left without another word.

Waterloo — the village where he had stopped after that ghastly picnic. It no longer mattered that Fanny had not been invited to the ball. She'd not have dreamt of dancing the night away when her twin brother was on his way to face the enemy.

Time and past time he went home. He returned to the ballroom to take leave of Lady Sophia.

Few people remained amid the extravagant decorations, but the orchestra was beginning another waltz. Half a dozen couples took to the floor. Lady Sophia was seated beside her mother, a hint of a pout taking shape on her lovely lips. It changed to a smile as Felix approached.

"Roworth, you are just in time for the last waltz."

"We have already danced twice," he reminded her, eager to get away. Only the horrid prospect of being a wallflower could have prompted her suggestion.

"Sophie, dear, I really think it is time we were going. Are you leaving Brussels, Lord Roworth?"

"I?" he asked, startled, though it was a reasonable question. "No, not for the present." Not when the urgent news Rothschild awaited was the outcome of the approaching battle. "But I trust you are?"

"Yes, tomorrow, or rather, today," said Lady Sophia. "It may be an age before there is another ball." The pout returned full force.

For a gentleman there was no choice. Felix stood up for the third time with Lady Sophia. In the prevailing chaos, it was most unlikely that anyone would notice.

Afterwards he went to look for the Duchess of Richmond to pay his respects. She was nowhere to be found, but he came across Lady Georgiana, white and distracted.

"Mama is saying goodbye to March," she said. "I helped him pack. I haven't seen George all evening. Lord Roworth, what is going to happen?"

Felix had no answer for her. Gently he pressed her shaking hands. "Wellington will pull us through, if anyone can," he said.

She tried to smile. "Yes, that is what Papa says. He was so angry not to be allowed to join the Staff. Goodnight, sir. At least I know I shall see you again."

Filled with admiration for her bravery, Felix set out through the torch-lit streets. The air rang with the clamour of trumpets, bugles, fifes, and drums, and the tramp of marching men. Soldiers stuffed their knapsacks with provisions thrust upon them by the townsfolk they had been billeted on — the British were popular because they paid in gold, Rothschild gold. A boy ran beside a Rifleman, carrying his weapon, while his older sister blew kisses and wiped her eyes on her apron. A little girl rode on the shoulder of a wiry Highlander, her mother clutching the Scotsman's arm.

War demanded quite as much courage from women as from men, Felix realized, and theirs might be the more difficult part.

Waiting was always much harder to bear than action. He lengthened his stride. Fanny might be sleeping peacefully but he doubted it.

She was walking up and down the parlour with a sniffling Anita in her arms. Looking exhausted, she gave Felix a tired smile. Her dimples were not in evidence.

"The noise woke her and frightened her."

"Where is Solomon?"

"He was all agog to see what is going on, so I sent him out. Hush, love, hush. You've heard the drums before."

"Let me take care of Anita while you rest."

"Thank you, but I shan't sleep."

"Then would you like to go out to walk about a little?"

Anita perked up at once. "Let's go to the park and feed the swans."

"They will be sleeping, darling. All the same, Roworth, that is a good notion, if you are not anxious to seek your bed."

"I shouldn't sleep either." He took Anita from her and she went to fetch a shawl and the child's cloak.

Anita on his shoulders, they wandered through the streets. The Grand' Place and the Place Royale swarmed with troops. They came across Captain Mercer, rounding up his men, horses, and guns.

"I'm to proceed to Enghien," he said, " 'with utmost diligence.' Such is my diligence that I was giving orders while I put on my stockings, though one order was for breakfast, I admit."

"Oh, Cav!" Fanny managed to laugh.

"I heard Frank was bound direct to Quatre Bras. Don't fret, my dear, we'll whip Boney till he wishes he'd never been born." Impulsively he hugged her and she clung to him for a moment. Felix reminded himself that the man was one of those she considered her extended family.

He coughed. The captain saluted him, patted Anita's cheek, and returned to directing his men.

They went on to the park, where the Highlanders were assembling in the chilly light of dawn. Struck with the contrast, Felix told Fanny how, a few hours since, some of those men had been dancing in an extravagantly decorated ballroom for the amusement of the Richmonds' guests.

"They were very popular," he said.

"Was the ball a success?"

"Hardly, in the circumstances. I was fortunate in that many of Lady Sophia's beaux were absent and she was especially kind to me." Though he had not intended the statement to be ironic, that was how it

156

sounded and that was how Fanny took it.

"Was she, indeed!" she snorted.

The sun inched above the horizon, sparkling the dewy grass. The bagpipers struck up "Hieland Laddie," and the Scots brigades marched out in formation, a brave sight in their tartans and black-plumed bonnets.

Anita cheered, but before the column had passed she was wilting with fatigue, barely able to hold on. Felix took her in his arms and they went directly back to Madame Vilvoorde's, where he laid the sleeping child on the sofa. It was too late to think of going to bed. Fanny went to the kitchen and made tea.

Felix was pacing the floor when she carried the tray into the parlour and set it on the table. "I wish I were a soldier!" he burst out. "I feel utterly useless when I see them all marching off to glory."

"You wish you were a soldier!" Fanny rounded on him furiously. "What do you know of soldiering? All you see is parades and pretty uniforms. Those poor boys in their fancy clothes are marching not to glory but to mud, and blood, and death, and dismemberment!"

A storm of tears engulfed her. After a moment of shock at her outburst, Felix strode across the room to hold her shaking body close, to murmur useless words of comfort, his heart aching with sympathy.

As she grew calmer, he was ashamed to realize that another part of him was aching in response to the feel of her slim, yielding form in his arms. Her small, soft breasts pressed against his chest. The downy nape of her neck felt fragile beneath his tenderly stroking fingers. He had only to bend his head to bury his face in her rosemary-scented curls or to touch the silken smoothness of her temple with his lips.

The hot wave of desire took him by surprise, for he had never regarded her with an amorous eye.

She was his friend. He respected her too highly to take advantage of her momentary weakness, even to allow himself to dwell on the unexpected temptation she presented. Nor did he forget the unhappy Lieutenant Barnstaple's fate. He gave her his handkerchief and turned away to pour the tea.

Mopping her eyes, Fanny shivered. For a brief time, all too brief, she had felt safe and cared for in the strong circle of his arms. How wonderful it would be to be loved by this man, and what a fool Lady Sophia must be to treat him with indifference!

But he was her friend, not her lover. The comfort of his embrace was not for her and she must be strong, not give way to over-wrought sensibilities. Life with the army demanded self-control. There was no room for weaklings.

CHAPTER 9

Madame Vilvoorde rapped on the parlour door. She was departing for the country and she wanted a fortnight's rent in advance.

Felix was almost glad of the demand, for worrying about it distracted Fanny from her chagrin over having given way to the vapours, as she referred to her tempest of anger and grief. Red-eyed, she was still in no state to argue with their landlady, but Felix succeeded in persuading the woman to accept a single week's rent. She went off scowling.

Moses Solomon, having seen Wellington ride off at the head of his staff, returned shortly before Anita woke up hungry. Happily, stout Henriette was less alarmed, or less mobile, than her mistress and provided a good breakfast.

After eating and changing, Fanny took Anita round to Mrs Prynne's to help prepare bandages and dressings. Felix admired the way she had recovered her spirits, outwardly at least, despite the prospect of this gruesome task. He sent Moses to bed, lest he should have need of him, and sat down to write a report.

When he finished, he went out. The streets seemed empty after the ordered chaos of the night. In the Grand' Place, provision wagons were being loaded, their Flemish drivers preparing to follow and feed the army. Their fellows, drivers of the tilt-carts drawn up nearby in neat rows, slumbered in the shade of the awnings designed to shelter the wounded. They would not be sent for until battle was joined, until there were injured men to be brought back to the city.

Fanny was right, as usual. What did he know of soldiering? From a distance it was easy to see the glory and forget the suffering of which the tilt-carts were an ominous reminder.

Felix walked to the Richmonds', where he found the duchess attempting to dissuade her husband and Lord William, still bandaged, from riding after Wellington to offer their services. He laughingly refused to take sides. He suspected they would be in the Duke's way, which made it easier to resist the temptation to join them. His duty was to Rothschild, he reminded himself sternly, to gather information and see that it reached his employer as soon as possible.

He went on to Lord Fitzroy's lodging and left his card, with a scrawl on the back begging Emily to let him know if he could be of assistance. Then he made for the Daventrys' hôtel.

As he expected, the knocker had already been taken off the door. Lady Sophia was gone.

In the middle of the afternoon a distant dull rumbling made itself heard. People came out of their houses to join those in the streets, to glance up at the clear sky and then rush to the south end of the city. Felix joined the crowd on the ramparts, gazing towards Quatre Bras. Nothing was to be seen but a slow procession of supply wagons crawling towards the sound of the guns.

Felix went home to change into riding clothes. Though the thunder of the cannonade was audible indoors, it was possible to ignore it. In the parlour, Fanny was playing cards with young Solomon while Anita took a nap.

"I'm going to ride towards Quatre Bras, to see if I can discover what is going on," Felix told them. Fanny's look of painful anxiety made him add quickly, "Don't worry about me, I shan't go anywhere near the battlefield. And I'll be home for dinner."

At that she smiled. "Good. Madame's absence has inspired Henriette to attempt a 'rosbif à l'anglaise.' Since she obtained the receipt from a neighbour who has a Yorkshireman billeted on her, I daresay there will be Yorkshire pudding as well."

"I shouldn't miss it for the world," he promised.

He found it surprisingly difficult to hire a decent mount. The Daventrys and Madame Vilvoorde were not the only ones to have decided that morning that discretion was the better part of valour. Both carriage and riding horses were in short supply. He had to pay an outrageous price, in advance, putting it down to Mr Rothschild's account.

He rode as far as Waterloo, but most traffic was heading in the same direction and he learned nothing of the battle. Recalling his promise to Fanny, he turned back. He'd come out again later, for the long summer evening would be light for hours yet.

At dinner, Henriette's Yorkshire pudding caused a subdued merriment, for she had altered the proportions of the ingredients to turn it into a soufflé. The roast beef was excellent, however, and Felix set out again well fortified. He was beginning to feel the effects of missing a night's sleep, and Fanny declared her intention of retiring at once.

He had kept the hired horse so he quickly left the town behind. About half way to Waterloo, he met a string of emptied provision wagons returning to Brussels. They carried wounded soldiers.

Lightly or badly hurt, they were all neatly bandaged. The earliest casualties had the best of care, before the surgeons were too overwhelmed to do more than save what lives they could. Among the Dutch-Belgian lads, some moaning for water, some sitting in stolid silence, Felix saw the funereal black uniforms of a few Brunswickers, little more than boys themselves. Here and there Highland plaids and the green jackets of Riflemen stood out.

One of the Scots called out to him, "Ye'll no hae a wee dram aboot ye, sir?"

Apologizing for not having had the forethought to bring a pocket flask with him, Felix asked for news. The man, whose splinted leg seemed not to abate his cheerfulness a jot, knew nothing but his own small part in the fighting. Nor did any of his companions who were capable of speaking.

Felix rode on, unable to force his eyes

from the wounded. This was the side of war Fanny knew, had lived with all her life. No wonder she flared up at talk of glory.

And then the evening sun's golden rays picked out a familiar dark blue coat with scarlet facings. Dark stains surrounded a dozen rents in the fabric. No one wore it; it had been draped across a still figure so enveloped in bandages that only the face was visible.

The face, white as the bandages, was Fanny's brother's.

Without a second thought, Felix abandoned his quest for news, turned his horse's head back towards Brussels and urged the beast to a gallop.

Bursting into the parlour, he startled Moses Solomon to his feet.

"Where's Miss Ingram?"

"S-sleeping, my lord."

"Don't go out. She may need you." He took the stairs two at a time but tapped gently at Fanny's chamber door, not wishing to rouse Anita. No response. He knocked a little louder and called softly, "Miss Ingram!"

A moment later she opened the door, hair tousled, feet bare beneath a cambric nightgown, scarcely half awake. "Roworth! What is it?" In sleepy brown eyes the beginnings of alarm dawned. "Frank?"

"Wounded. I don't know how badly." He reached out as the blood drained from her face.

She gripped his hand tight for a moment. "I'll get dressed at once."

"The cart won't arrive for another hour or so. They've put up hospital tents by the gates, but I thought you'd want him here."

"Yes, oh yes! How could I leave him to strangers?"

"I'll bring him to you directly."

Lady Fitzroy would lend the curricle, but it was the wrong vehicle to transport an unconscious man. The Richmonds' had several carriages. Leaving Fanny to her preparations, he rode to the Rue de la Blanchisserie.

He was ushered into the drawing room where the family was gathered. Georgiana jumped up and came to greet him, took one look at his face, and faltered, "Not March? George?"

"No, a friend of mine. Duke, may I borrow a carriage? Just to carry him home from the city gate."

"The barouche," said the duchess calmly. "Sit down, Roworth, while it is brought round. Have you news? The guns ceased a few minutes ago."

166

He had not noticed the end of the bombardment. "I know nothing," he said, "but that the Highlanders, the Rifles, and the Duke of Brunswick reinforced the Dutch-Belgians early."

"Lots of others came up later," said Lord William eagerly, "one after another to the rescue. The Guards, for one. The cavalry had not arrived, though, when we left."

"They had a long way to go," his father pointed out, almost as enthusiastic. "We held off the Frenchies, Roworth."

"We had to leave just as Wellington counter attacked." William pulled a face at his mother, who had no doubt insisted upon an early return. "I heard the Duke of Brunswick was hit rallying his men. Some of them ran away, with the Dutch-Belgians."

Lady Jane brought Felix a glass of wine. He sipped it, impatiently listening to their talk, until the butler came in to say the carriage was at the door. Gulping down the rest of the wine, he thanked them and hurried off.

The Richmonds' coachman drove him through the dark, tensely quiet streets to the gate. As they reached it, he heard a commotion beyond the ramparts and a moment later a disordered troop of uniformed horsemen galloped through, shouting in French

167

and Flemish.

"All is lost! The French are here!"

They raced on, hooves ringing on the pavement, cries echoing from the walls. Behind them rattled a stampeding rabble of carts, mingled with stragglers from the troop, panic on every face.

Felix jumped down and dodged through the chaotic mass that filled the roadway. The wagons bearing the wounded were just outside the ramparts, blocked from entering by the crush of vehicles.

Fanny counted on him. With grim determination, Felix seized a bridle here, a whip there, calmed horses, struck drivers, and cleared the way.

An orderly from the hospital tent helped him carry Frank to the barouche. The captain groaned once but didn't open his eyes. His cheeks were sunken, his forehead wet with sweat, and he constantly licked his lips with a dry tongue. Felix had brought a bottle of water. As soon as he was settled in the carriage, supporting the wounded man, he raised his head and held the flask to his mouth.

Frank swallowed, greedily but painfully. The barouche set off through streets now alive with townsfolk and English visitors wailing that the French were coming.

Felix wondered if the moment had come to send Moses to London with a report of defeat — but he had seen only Belgians fleeing. He recalled Fanny's description of them as farm lads, fresh from the plough. And Fitzroy had said Wellington expected to be driven back from Quatre Bras to make a stand at Waterloo. No, he'd wait till morning at least to send young Solomon.

When he carried Frank into the house, he was glad to find that Mrs Prynne, the major's robust, energetic wife, had come to help. He had no time for more than a brief exchange of words with Fanny — heartfelt thanks on her part, a disclaimer on his — before he went out again to fetch a doctor.

He brought back a Belgian surgeon, sent him up to Frank's chamber, and sat down on the sofa in the parlour to await news of the captain's condition. The next thing he knew was an agonizing crick in his neck, daylight peering around the window-blinds, and Mrs Prynne standing over him.

"I've taken the liberty, my lord," she announced, "of ordering your man to fill you a bath, and the servant to make breakfast. Fanny's given me her word that she'll eat a bite and then go to bed. I've to be off to my family. I'll take Anita with me, and it seems to me between you and your man and the cook-girl and that other young fella-me-lad you ought to be able to take care of Frank."

"Certainly, ma'am," he responded with as much dignity as he could muster given his position, his unshaven chin, and his gummed-together eyelids. He forced himself to sit upright. "How is he?"

"He looks as if he'd been peppered by a shotgun at close range. Upwards of a score of flesh wounds, some of 'em nasty, broken ribs, black and blue bruises you wouldn't see on a prize-fighter. He's lost a lot of blood, but it's infection that's most to be feared. Any sign of a fever and you send for a doctor right away."

"I will indeed, ma'am. I can't thank you enough for your help."

"Fanny helped me when Prynne near lost his arm to a French sabre," she said gruffly, and marched out.

Much restored by the bath, Felix met Fanny at the breakfast table while Moses sat with Frank. She drooped in her seat, pallid and hollow-eyed, scarcely able to lift the fork to her lips. He cut up her food as he would for Anita, and stirred plenty of sugar into her tea, coaxing her to drink the syrupy brew from the thick china cup before he supported her up the stairs.

When he opened her chamber door, she

clung to his arm. "You won't leave him alone?"

"Not for a moment."

Though he had every intention of keeping his word, he had other responsibilities so he crossed to Frank's chamber to ask Moses to stay with the captain. The young Jew was only too delighted to do Fanny any service within his power. Felix was shocked by Frank's appearance. Grey-faced, his vitality gone, he seemed to have shrunk as he lay motionless beneath the incongruously gay patchwork quilt.

Calling on Lady Fitzroy, Felix found her reading a letter from her husband, written the previous evening after the battle. She was delighted to see him.

"Fitzroy has not a scratch. Would you like to read this?" she offered, then blushed and reclaimed the letter. "No, I will tell you what he says. 'The Prussians and we have repulsed the French.' But oh, Roworth, he and my uncle were nearly captured when trying to rally the Belgians, and the Duke of Brunswick is dead. Such a charming, solemn young man!"

"I'm sorry to hear it. Wellington was nearly captured, you say?"

"He and Fitzroy had to ride for their lives. Only think, Uncle Arthur had to jump a bank and ditch lined with Highlanders all with their bayonets at the ready. 'Ninety-second, lie down!' he shouted, and just cleared them. Fitzroy says that on a worse horse he might not have escaped."

"Nor if he were a worse horseman. In general, the news is good, then."

"Yes, except that Colonel Gordon was sent out towards Ligny to reconnoiter and found no sign of the Prussians, only French scouts. He was to go again at first light. But Uncle Arthur has every confidence in Marshal Blücher."

"And we all have every confidence in your uncle Arthur. Are you and the baby quite comfortable, ma'am? Is there anything I can do for you?"

Assured that there was not, he took his leave.

By noon, rumours of the Prussians' rout at Ligny had been confirmed. They had fallen back eighteen miles, to Wavre, and Wellington was said to be in full retreat towards Brussels. Everywhere people were fleeing the town, on foot if they could not beg, borrow, or steal horses or squeeze onto overfilled canal boats.

Consulting a map, Felix noted that Wavre was only ten miles from Waterloo. He sent Moses to get a couple of hours sleep, while he sat beside Frank and wrote to Rothschild that the Duke was engaged in a strategic withdrawal.

Just as he finished, the captain roused. A startled look flashed in his brown eyes as he saw who was at his side, and he said in a voice that was scarce more than a whisper, "My lord, you should not . . ."

"It's as good a place as any to finish my report," Felix told him. "Are you hungry? Thirsty?"

"Thirsty." He paused, seeming to search deep within his torn, battered body. "And hungry, I think."

On the dresser, Felix found a carafe of murky water. He sniffed at it and poured a glass. "Barley water, I'd say. It takes me back to nursery days." But at Westwood barley water had always been flavoured with lemon. Probably lemons were beyond Fanny's purse — he'd buy some next time he went out.

He helped Frank to drink, a painful process that reminded him of the dislocated shoulder he had suffered in the Pyrenees. Then he sent Trevor down to the kitchen to see what Henriette had to offer.

Frank watched him sign and seal his report. "What happened?" Breathing obviously hurt him but he was determined to speak. "I was hit . . . early in the game. Slender Billy had eight thousand men . . . and sixteen guns . . . and he reckoned Ney had twenty thousand . . . against us."

"Your eight thousand, your sixteen guns, kept Ney busy until reinforcements arrived." Felix told him all he knew, and was glad to have his judgment confirmed. The captain was sure Old Hookey was only moving back to keep his communications with Blücher open.

"What happened to you?" Felix asked, curiosity outweighing compassion. "Mrs Prynne said it looked like a shotgun blast, but I can't believe you tangled with a gamekeeper."

"Hoist with . . . my own petard." He managed a wry smile. "French shot . . . hit one of Colonel Shrapnell's shells . . . as we were loading it. Bloody lucky . . . only shell's charge . . . low velocity."

"So the case shot peppered you."

Frank closed his eyes, his mouth tightening. "Killed two . . . of my gunners. Fanny knew them. Don't tell . . ."

"I won't."

Trevor came back with bread and cheese for Felix and a beef broth specially prepared for the patient. Felix set the valet to feeding Frank, spoonful by spoonful, but soon decided his man's all too evident pique was no sauce to the appetite. He took over the task himself, despite Frank's weak protest.

Meanwhile, he sent Trevor to wake Moses Solomon. Though he was as reluctant to lose his willing help as the young man was to leave, both of them had a first duty to Mr Rothschild.

He regretted the loss still more when, soon after Moses departed, Jane Prynne brought Anita home.

"Mam says she's sorry but there's lots of wounded coming in and she's needed," the girl reported with a touch of ghoulish relish.

Fortunately, Anita was worn out and at once fell asleep on Felix's lap in the armchair Moses had wrestled up the stairs to Frank's chamber last night. Felix soon followed suit.

He woke with a sense of déjà vu — a crick in his neck and Fanny standing over him, smiling, though this time no sun peered in at the narrow window. Instead it admitted the steady, relentless drumming of a downpour.

"You slept through the most tremendous thunder and lightning," she said. "There is always a deluge before Old Hookey's biggest victories."

Sleepily returning her smile, he thought how much he'd rather have her standing over him than Mrs Prynne who, however obliging, was no beauty. Refreshed by sleep, pretty Fanny in her practical brown cambric-muslin sprigged with green was an altogether pleasanter prospect to wake to.

He saw little of her in the twenty-four hours that followed. Frank developed a fever, a sure sign of infection, and even with Trevor's huffy aid they were both stretched to the limit. Felix had to practically kidnap a grossly overworked doctor, who could do little but give advice on what he appeared to consider a hopeless case and a waste of his time. Anita had to be kept from the sickroom. And Felix had to continue gathering information for his employer.

The thunderstorm had covered the Allies' retreat, he heard, bogging down the Emperor's troops in mud. According to Lord Fitzroy's latest letter to Emily, "Wellington proceeded leisurely towards Waterloo," stopping along the way to laugh over the scandal column of the London *Sun.*

So Felix and Frank had been right: a strategic withdrawal, not defeat.

Not until half past eleven on Sunday morning was the sound of guns heard again. At half the distance of Quatre Bras from

Brussels, their reverberating bellow was shockingly loud in the city.

All through the afternoon, a stream, a river, a torrent of wounded men poured into Brussels, each bringing a tiny scrap of the story. The Duke of Richmond had popped up from behind a hedge to start a charge of the Household troops with a cry of "Go along, my boys! Now's your time!" General Picton was dead, as was De Lancey, the perpetually worried Quartermaster-General. Fleeing Dutch-Belgians had fired on Wellington. Two French eagles had been taken. Prussian scouts had been seen but there was no sign of Blücher's troops. Old Hookey was everywhere, the mere sight of his great chestnut, Copenhagen, putting heart into his men.

The wounded flooded the streets and courtyards and welcoming homes of Brussels. Slender Billy, Colonel Gordon, and Lord Fitzroy Somerset were hit. Ney had broken through Wellington's center, and still the Prussians did not come.

In the drab chamber at Madame Vilvoorde's, another battle was fought. Turn and turn about, Felix and Fanny bathed Frank's burning body, forced him to drink, held him as he moaned and tossed on the narrow bed.

Fanny had just returned from putting Anita to bed when suddenly the constant booming of the guns ceased. She and Felix stared at each other. Still an hour and more of daylight left — then Frank cried out in delirium and she forgot everything but her twin brother's struggle for life.

Felix went out, hoping for news of Fitzroy and Gordon as well as the battle, but no one knew what had become of them. The Prussians had turned around and marched away. Napoleon had thrown in the Imperial Guard, undefeated in a dozen years. Dusk and darkness came and he heard nothing more. Why had the guns stopped?

He returned home. Fanny was fast asleep in the armchair in Frank's room, a small, fragile figure with dark rings about her eyes. Dread clutched Felix's heart as he turned to look at the bed. The captain lay unmoving, his face whiter than the sweat-soaked, threadbare pillowcase. No, not unmoving! The patchwork quilt barely rose and fell with his breathing. The fever had broken.

Slumped on the straight chair by the bed, Felix joined them in sleep.

A heavy-handed thumping on the front door below roused him. As he stumbled to the head of the stairs, lamp in hand, the door opened. A black-faced, tattered, blood-stained man staggered in, crossed the hall, and sank onto the bottom step.

"Who is it?"

The figure hauled itself to its feet, came to attention, and saluted. "Beg pardon, m'lord. Didn't know you was there an' I'm a mite tired. Corporal Hoskins reporting, m'lord."

"Sit down, man! What are you doing here?"

"Cap'n Mercer got leave for me from the colonel to come and see after my cap'n. How is he, m'lord?"

"Better, I think, but in need of your help. What has happened?"

"Boney's half way to Paris by now. We beat off the Guards, though I won't say it were easy, an' blow me if the rest o' the Frogs didn't start shouting out *La Garde recule,* an' take off after 'em. So Boney rallies 'em, see, but then up comes Ol' Marshal Forwards just in the nick o' time."

"Blücher?"

"That's it, Marshal Bloosher, an' didn't he put the cat among the pigeons! We could hear them Frenchies yelling out 'Noo som tree,' which is to say 'We been betrayed,' an' 'Sove key per,' that's 'Save your own skin.' An' there was Ol' Hookey standing up in the stirrups on the ridge, an' a sunbeam hit him, like, an' he waves his hat at the French lines, three times he did, an' this great cheer goes up. So us gunners stops firing and off they goes — our cavalry that is, m'lord. We just stands there and watches 'em, and the Frogs turned tail an' 'opped it."

"They just ran away?"

"Well, it weren't quite that easy, m'lord. Them Guards o' theirs is nothing to sneeze at, but we cut 'em to pieces." He grinned, teeth white in his black face. "I heard the Duke asked their general to surrender an' what he said was *'Merde!'* That means . . ."

"I know what it means," said Felix hastily. Fanny had come to join him at the head of the stairs.

"So do I," she said. "Hoskins, we have won? You are quite sure?"

He beamed up at her. "Like I said, Miss Fanny, Boney's half way to Paris by now, if Ol' Forwards ain't caught him yet."

Felix looked at Fanny. Her eyes were huge, dark, and fathomless in the flickering lamplight. "I have no one to send to London," he said. "I must go."

She turned and hurried back to Frank's chamber.

She had no right to feel deserted, yet somehow the tears would come. These last

180

dreadful days, his very presence — quite apart from his help — had been a tower of strength, a crucial buttress without which she might have foundered.

"Fanny?" Frank's voice was scarcely a whisper. Concern mingled with the ever-present pain in his eyes.

She took his hand and essayed a smile. She was not very good at smiling these days. "I shall be all right in a moment. Lord Roworth is leaving."

"Duty."

Yes, he had his duty to Mr Rothschild, as she had hers to Frank and Anita. She was a soldier's daughter. She understood duty.

But when he waved goodbye, when he cantered down the street, tall and straight in the saddle, she knew she had struggled against her heart in vain. She loved him.

CHAPTER 10

Felix stood at the stern rail of the Rothschilds' ketch, watching the port of Ostend fade into the haze. His mind returned yet again to the shabby parlour in Brussels where he had bade Fanny farewell. Had he done everything for her comfort that he possibly could?

In the dawn that followed hard upon Corporal Hoskins' heels he had ordered Trevor, after preparing a bath for the gunner, to pack his saddlebags. The valet would follow at a slower pace with the rest of their belongings. Felix felt the less guilt at withdrawing his man's services because they had always been grudging, and because of Frank's batman's arrival.

As for himself, he was torn in two. He yearned to be able to stay to support Fanny but his duty was owed to Rothschild just as much as any soldier's to his superior officer. There was no one he could send to London with news of the victory.

He had offered her money, intending to borrow twenty guineas from his employer. He'd pay it back somehow. She refused it, even under the guise of a loan. Then Hoskins mentioned that, on Captain Mercer's orders, he had brought Frank's horse with him. Jumping at the chance to acquire a decent mount while helping Fanny, Felix bought the gelding. Admittedly, a trooper was not precisely the horse he would have chosen for a fast seventy-mile ride, yet he had seldom been so pleased with a purchase.

All the same, he doubted whether he'd have had the heart to leave had not Frank fought off the fever. He was out of immediate danger, though his ultimate victory over death was by no means assured. He opened his eyes when Felix went to take leave of him, but the effort to speak was beyond him. Every bone in his face seemed about to cut through the skin.

No wonder, then, that Fanny's eyes were once more red-rimmed when she brought Anita down to the parlour to say goodbye. To spare her embarrassment, Felix had concentrated on the child. When he picked her up, she flung her arms about his neck and gave him a smacking kiss.

"Bye-bye, Tío Felix. I wish you didn't be

going away," she said dolefully.

"So do I, pet, but duty calls." In her short life, besides her father, how many honorary uncles had "gone away"?

"That's what Tío Frank awways says. I don't like Duty."

Hugging her, he looked over her head and said, "Miss Ingram, I have left the direction of my London lodgings on the table. I beg you will write to me to let me know how you go on."

"If you wish, my lord," she had said with unwonted formality, not meeting his eyes.

Felix turned away from the ship's taffrail with a sigh. If all went well with the Ingrams he might hear from them. If matters went badly, she would turn to her military family for succour. She had too much pride to ask help of an outsider like the Viscount Roworth, now that their accidental intimacy was at an end.

He was going to miss her, her cheerfulness, her courage, her practical kindness, even her teasing.

Though the sea was calm, the ketch's motion was beginning to make him decidedly uncomfortable, for he was a poor sailor. He went below to his cabin. On the bunk lay the copy of the Dutch *Gazette* he had bought in Ostend. He had picked up enough

German in Vienna to understand the Dutch headlines and parts of the article. Corporal Hoskins' report was confirmed: the Battle of Waterloo was an Allied victory.

Nathan Rothschild would be pleased to learn that his family's investment in the French monarchy was safe.

Slinging the hammock he always used, since it abated somewhat the horrors of seasickness, Felix retired to sleep away the Channel crossing. By the time they sailed into Dover, he was well rested. At the Ship Inn he ate a quick meal while one of the horses the Rothschilds stabled there was saddled for him, and then he set out on the last segment of his journey.

As he rode across London Bridge into the City, another dawn brightened the skies. To his left the dome of St Paul's floated serene in a golden mist. After the alarms of the last few days in Brussels, the great metropolis seemed a haven of peace, though Felix knew that in an hour or two it would wake to bustling life. He had lived for years in London, and as much as Westwood it was his home — parts of it, at least. The City was devoted to business and commerce; Mayfair and St James's were the haunts of the ton. As soon as his business with Rothschild was done, he'd hurry to St James's

Square to see if the Daventrys were back in England.

The Daventrys! Shocked, he realized he hadn't spared a thought for Lady Sophia in days. His work, the battle, the Ingrams had absorbed all his attention. Nor had he time now to dwell admiringly on the Goddess's image. Cannon Street — St Swithin's Lane — he turned into New Court.

His horse's hooves rang loud in the stillness and all around the courtyard windows stared down blankly.

After his race from Brussels, Felix was in no mood to wait until the bank opened. Utmost urgency Nathan Rothschild had stressed; utmost urgency he should have. Dismounting, he tied the tired beast to a rail and strode up to the front door of the Rothschild residence.

A sleepy maidservant with a broom answered his imperative knocking.

"I am Lord Roworth. I must see Mr Rothschild at once on urgent business."

She gaped at him and fled, so he walked in. Weary after the ride from Dover, he dropped hat, gloves, and whip on a half-moon table and sat down. With a sigh he leaned back, eyes closed, wondering when he'd sleep in a proper bed again.

Before he had time to grow impatient, a

butler appeared, still buttoning his waistcoat. "My lord, my apologies for that stupid girl. Mr Rothschild's man has gone to inform him of your arrival. If your lordship will be so good as to step this way . . . Might I enquire if your lordship has breakfasted?"

He was ravenous. Was Fanny eating properly now that he was not there to coax her?

Felix was digging into a plateful of cold beef and fried eggs when Nathan Rothschild, in a plain cotton caftan and nightcap, joined him in the dining room. A stocky, balding man of about forty, he grunted a greeting as he sat down and helped himself to eggs and toast. The butler poured coffee and discreetly vanished.

"Well, my lord?"

"Victory, sir." Accustomed to his employer's terseness, he responded in kind. "On Sunday, at Waterloo. I have a newspaper." He reached for his inner pocket but Rothschild stopped him with a wave.

"Your word is good enough." The banker still spoke with the accent of the Frankfurt ghetto, despite nearly two decades in England. "The government must be informed. We'll go to Herries."

"Not at this hour, sir!"

"No." The faintly amused expression that generally confined itself to his full lips reached the dark, piercing eyes. "Public officials do not understand the importance of speed, as you and I do."

He applied himself to his breakfast. Felix followed suit, very much aware that behind the placid amusement a remarkably shrewd mind was planning a strategy as complex and as flexible as Wellington's.

A little after eight, Mr Herries, the Commissary-General, received them in his dressing gown. He was reading a report in the Times of the Prussians' defeat at Ligny and Wellington's retreat from Quatre Bras. "Shocking news, gentlemen," he said gravely, shaking their hands. "Since you are here, Lord Roworth, I assume the French have taken Brussels."

"On the contrary, sir." Felix gave him the Dutch Gazette. "The French are doubtless back in Paris by now, those who are not our prisoners."

"Good God! So the Duke has done it again! You are quite sure?"

"I had an eyewitness account of the final stage of the battle, a gunner who watched our cavalry join the Prussians in putting the enemy to flight."

"I must tell Liverpool. Mr Rothschild, Lord Roworth, will you be so good as to go with me to Downing Street?"

His eyes gleaming, the banker grunted his assent.

Before he went to dress, Mr Herries sent a messenger to Lord Liverpool to advise him that he would arrive shortly with momentous news from Belgium. Despite the still early hour when they reached 10 Downing Street, Lords Castlereagh and Bathurst awaited them with the Prime Minister.

At Mr Herries' request, Felix repeated his news. Lord Liverpool took the Gazette, glanced at it uncomprehendingly, and tossed it aside.

"The Dutch are unreliable, alas."

"Who, precisely, is your eyewitness, my lord?" asked Castlereagh, the Foreign Secretary.

"A Horse Artilleryman, sir. The guns were silenced, I collect, to avoid firing upon our cavalry as they charged the French lines, so Corporal Hoskins was able to watch all that transpired."

"A mere corporal! Such fellows cannot be expected to understand the course of war. I had thought you spoke with an officer. I fear you have been misled by wishful thinking, Lord Roworth."

"All we have heard leads us to believe that matters go ill with General Wellington," the

War Minister agreed.

Though Lord Liverpool thanked them courteously for their communication, he was quite as incredulous as his colleagues. Felix would have argued, but weariness made him doubt his own judgment. For all the good his hurried journey had done, he thought bitterly, he might as well have stayed in Brussels to help Fanny.

Mr Rothschild stood silent. Mr Herries looked crestfallen.

The banker's coachman drove them back to Mr Herries' residence, where the Commissary-General apologized for taking them on a fool's errand.

"Not at all," said Mr Rothschild with unusual geniality. "It had to be done. Good day to you, sir."

He directed the coachman to Albemarle Street, where Felix kept rooms. As they set off again, he turned to Felix. "We have done our duty in informing the government. Do you feel obliged, my lord, to spread the word?"

"Sir, if the government which depends upon your services will not believe me as your agent," said Felix angrily, "why should anyone believe me? The information is yours, since I obtained it in your employ."

"Very good, very good. You shall have a

percentage of my profit from your diligence. I must go to the 'Change. You will be the better for catching up on your sleep, I daresay. Come and see me tomorrow morning."

Felix's landlady welcomed him back to London and fussed over him. How much easier Fanny would be finding life if Madame Vilvoorde had been the same kind of woman! Yet despite her ministrations he missed Trevor, who was a superior valet as well as a starchy, self-important grumbler. Nonetheless, after a bath to remove his travel dirt, he fell into bed and slept the clock round.

In his dreams, he saw Nathan Rothschild in his customary pose at the Royal Exchange. Leaning against the first pillar on the right by the Cornhill entrance, hands in pockets, the banker stood motionless, stony-faced, while cannon thundered about him. Gaudy-uniformed officers rode up to him, received their orders and a purse of gold, and galloped away. One of them was Lord Fitzroy, but his features merged into Frank Ingram's suffering face. Then Felix noticed that Rothschild had imperceptibly turned into the Duke of Wellington, 'Change into the Duchess of Richmond's ballroom. Slender Billy waltzed by with Fanny in his arms.

Waking, Felix was vaguely surprised not to have a crick in his neck. He lay luxuriating in the comfort of his bed, until he remembered with annoyance that Trevor was absent. He struck a light and checked the time.

Without his valet's assistance, he'd not be fit to present himself at his club much before midnight. There he would find friends and a neat supper — but he was by far too hungry to wait. (Was Fanny eating properly?) He flung on a dressing gown and went to rob his landlady's larder. And somehow, after cold mutton pie, plum cake, and a long draught of ale, it was all too easy to tumble back into bed and make up for a bit more lost sleep.

In the morning he set out for the City with an indistinct memory of his employer offering him some reward for bringing the news of victory, even though it had not been believed. Perhaps he'd get enough blunt to order a new coat from Weston before he called on Lady Sophia. A spring in his step, he walked towards New Court.

He quickly learned, from newspaper hawkers and from snippets of conversation overheard, that Waterloo was on everyone's lips. Late last night, while he slept, Colonel Percy had reached London with Wellington's despatches and two French eagles.

Wishful thinking, hah! he thought. So much for ignorant corporals and credulous bankers!

He voiced the thought when he was ushered into Mr Rothschild's private office. "I wager they will take your word for anything at all after this, sir," he added.

"No matter. They gave me time enough to do my business." His gaze not wavering from the ledger before him, he slid a sheet of paper across the desk. "Here is your bonus."

Felix took the bank draft, read the figure on it, and blinked twice. "Sir, you have put down too many noughts."

His employer looked up. "My lord, are you accusing me, a Rothschild, of mistaking my figures?" he asked with cynical amusement.

"No, sir. Yes, sir. But, sir . . ."

"The figure is correct. Your speed and your discretion allowed me to make a great deal of money on 'Change yesterday, of which I promised you a percentage. I pay well for work well done."

"I'm not about to argue with that!" He stared in awe at the draft. "How can I thank . . ."

"Enough," snapped Rothschild impatiently. "Don't tell anyone or all my agents will be at my door. You have been abroad for me for a year or more, have you not? Take a month off. Go and see your family. Nothing is of more importance than the family. Good day to you, my lord."

He returned to his ledger. Felix put nineteen thousand pounds in his pocket and walked out, treading on air.

Nineteen thousand! And all because the Government had chosen to disbelieve him. In the midst of his euphoria, he wondered how much Mr Rothschild had gained from his early intelligence of victory.

Of course, the Rothschilds did not deal in shillings and pence. The last gold shipment Fanny's faithful admirer Moses Solomon had brought to Brussels had raised the total sent to the army to over a quarter of a million pounds, Felix knew. That did not include the foreign subsidies. His reward might well be a small percentage of yesterday's profit.

Felix touched the draft in his pocket. Perhaps he had earned it after all.

Now he was well to pass, surely Fanny would not refuse his financial assistance. He'd send her some money before he went down to Westwood.

What would his father say when he presented the draft? Rothschild was right, nothing was more important than the family. Felix had once heard the banker's little son ask how many nations there were in the world, only to be told, "There are only two you need bother about. There is the family, and there are the others."

The windfall would pay off a good part of the mortgage that strangled Westwood. Then the estate might provide enough income to pay for a Season in London for Felix's sisters, even marriage portions. He tried to picture his father's astonished delight, Connie's transports, but another thought intruded: The reward made it possible to leave his employment and offer for Lady Sophia.

With money in his pocket he was a more than acceptable suitor. Nor would he be taking anything from his family, for her dowry was large enough to restore the family fortunes and they'd greet the daughter of the Marquess of Daventry with open arms. She might turn him down, as she had many another unexceptionable match, but the chance to make the Goddess his wife was at last within his grasp.

He was pondering whether to try his luck with Lady Sophia before dashing down to Westwood when he reached the courtyard.

Crossing it towards him came Moses Solomon.

"My lord," cried the young courier, "how was M-miss Ingram when you left Brussels? Is her brother recovering? Has she anyone to help her n-now you are gone?"

Felix told him of the captain's fever and Hoskins' arrival. With a troubled frown, Moses went into the bank, and Felix continued slowly out into St Swithin's Lane.

Hoskins was a soldier. How long would he have leave to stay with the Ingrams? Suppose, even now, Fanny was struggling to care for Anita and Frank, alone and short of funds in the chaos of a city overwhelmed with wounded men. Her haggard face rose before him, so drastically changed in so short a time from her usual stoic cheerfulness. He recalled Anita's drooping mouth and farewell kiss, Frank's deathly pallor.

Almost against his will he turned back into New Court.

Moses was already in Mr Rothschild's office. He looked up startled as Felix strode in. The banker merely raised his eyebrows.

"Sir, I'm going back to Brussels, on personal business. May I use the ketch?"

The dark eyes seemed to search his soul, then Rothschild nodded. "Certainly. You may carry my letter to Wellington. It is not urgent; you need not leave until tomorrow morning. Your month's leave begins when you return."

With the greatest reluctance and a glance of burning reproach, Moses handed over the letter.

"I'll convey your regards to the Ingrams," Felix told him, grinning, but not without sympathy.

Since the rest of the day was at his disposal, he thought of calling on Lady Sophia, not to propose immediately but to prepare the ground. Then he might spend the evening at Brooks's, where he'd meet friends and everyone would be celebrating the news from Waterloo.

A pleasing prospect, yet one that somehow failed attract him. Driven by his own sense of urgency, he called for one of the bank's horses and rode back to his lodgings to repack his saddlebags.

How could he possibly enjoy himself while Fanny was suffering?

CHAPTER 11

Scarce two hours later, Felix turned off the Dover road, cantered through country lanes, and rode up to Nettledene. Leaving his horse at the stables, he strolled to the walled garden where the groom had said he would find the mistress of the house.

He pushed open the door in the wall of Kentish ragstone, overgrown with creeping jinnie and orange lichen. The air was full of the heady fragrance of sun-warmed herbs: thyme, lavender, mint, rosemary, a dozen he could not name. Rosemary — the scent of Fanny's hair when he had taken her in his arms to comfort her.

Among the beds of herbs, her back to him, moved a tall, graceful woman dressed in lavender-green, a straw hat hiding all but a single lock of dark red hair. He paused to admire the scene. After four years and two children, Miriam must be thirty, yet her splendid figure was as tempting as ever.

Isaac was a lucky devil.

A little boy, about Anita's age, with hair the bright copper colour of a new penny, ran up to her and tugged urgently on her sleeve.

"Mama!" He pointed and she turned, shading her eyes. The sun had touched her pale porcelain complexion with colour.

"Felix! Amos, you remember Uncle Felix. What a wonderful surprise! I hope you can spare us more than an hour or two this time."

"I fear not," he said regretfully. "I am come to ask a favour."

"What can we do for you? Isaac is in the library. At least come into the house to see him and take some refreshment before you dash off." She picked up a watering-can, took Amos's hand in hers, and came to meet him. "Mr Rothschild keeps you busy. You have been in Brussels ever since we last saw you?"

"Yes. Hello, Amos. How is your little sister?"

"She's on'y a baby," he said with scorn. "She's too liccle to play catch prop'ly. She tried to eat my horse."

"A wooden horse," Miriam said hastily, "a present on his third birthday. Leah is crawling already, driving poor Hannah to distraction with her poking and prying. Tell me, did you leave Brussels before the battle? The morning papers announced a victory, but they had no details as yet."

"I brought the news to Mr Rothschild," Felix said as they left the garden and turned towards the long, low manor house. "Liverpool, Castlereagh, and Bathurst refused to believe it until Wellington's despatch arrived. As a result, Rothschild made a fortune on 'Change. He gave me a share, Miriam, a most generous share." Accustomed to confiding in Miriam and Isaac, he told her, "I can afford now to think of asking for Lady Sophia's hand."

"Lady Sophia Gerrold? Whom you met in Vienna? You called her a Goddess, I recall, but I did not realize you were hoping to marry her."

"She was in Brussels, too."

"You said she is very beautiful."

"She is, but more important, she is everything even my parents could look for in a future countess, the daughter of a marquis, well-bred, dignified, elegant . . ."

"Spare me the rhapsodies," she said, laughing. "I am prepared to believe that Lady Sophia is a pattern-card of perfection in every conceivable way."

Not in every way, he conceded silently.

But she was young, she would learn. He himself had been five and twenty when Miriam had taught him to appreciate people for themselves, not their station in life. Unfortunately, his parents had different notions.

They had thoroughly disapproved his going to work for Nathan Rothschild. It was up to him to please them with his marriage.

"Have you come for advice on proposing?" Miriam asked.

Felix snorted. "From Isaac? When he had recourse to a matchmaker? Not likely."

They went into the house. As always, Felix felt instantly at home. Miriam's wealthy father had provided luxury, but her mother's taste for formal elegance had been defeated by her own desire for comfort, a result of impecunious years of travel on the Continent with her uncle. More important, the atmosphere of the house seemed permeated with the generous warmth of her personality. Felix was reassured that he had made the right decision. Fanny would be welcomed here.

However, he waited to broach the purpose of his visit until Amos had gone up to the nursery and Isaac had joined them for a cold collation. Tall and dark, his host's slender build belied a resilient strength that had twice saved Felix's life. It was difficult to believe he had once hated Isaac Cohen with a bitter passion.

"Felix has just returned from Brussels," Miriam told her husband, "and he is already off again. We should never see him if we did not live near the Dover road."

"Where are you bound for now?" Isaac asked, carving a chicken into neat slices.

"Back to Brussels, but on my own account. Friends of mine need my help, a brother and sister who shared my lodgings. Frank was badly wounded on the first day of fighting. The trouble is, there's no point going back just to help Miss Ingram take care of him. A servant could do that as well. And if I offered her money to hire a servant, she is too proud to accept it."

"If your friend is fit to travel," said Miriam at once, "you must bring him here."

"May I?" He had known he could rely upon their generosity! "That is what I hoped, I confess. My lodgings in London are barely adequate for myself and my servant, and I cannot take them to Westwood."

"Of course not. Somerset is much too far for an injured man to travel."

Felix nodded agreement, though distance had been a minor consideration. He had tried, and failed, to imagine explaining to his parents the arrival of an unknown artillery captain in dire need of medical attention, his shabby sister, and their illegitimate ward. Fanny and Frank would most definitely not receive the warm reception at Westwood he expected for Lady Sophia.

"Just as you supposed, my love," Isaac said teasingly, "we owe his visit to our position near the Dover road. No doubt your medical skills also have something to do with the matter. Felix, you had best explain your friend's injuries to Miriam so that she can mix up the appropriate witch's brew."

"I shall. But before you confirm the invitation, I ought to tell you . . ." He hesitated, unsure how to proceed. "It's not just Frank and Miss Ingram, there is Anita, too. She is the daughter of a friend of theirs who died at Ciudad Rodrigo, and I must warn you that she is a . . . a love-child."

"Yes, it's best to know," said Miriam, "so that one can be sure not to say anything that might hurt or offend."

"You don't mind?" Felix's relief was mingled with curiosity. "Does Jewish law not discriminate against illegitimacy?"

"Jewish law! You will have to ask Isaac. Common humanity ought not to lay the faults of the parents upon the innocent child."

Felix turned to Isaac, who grinned, his rather serious, intense face transformed. "As long as the child is old enough to throw a ball and not to chew on wooden horses, she will be warmly welcomed in the nursery. If she is an infant in arms, Amos for one will not be pleased."

"Isaac, how can you speak so! Of course Anita is welcome, Felix, whatever her age, and she cannot be a baby since her father was killed in Spain."

"She is three and a half. I daresay I had best visit the nursery before I leave and try to turn Hannah up sweet."

"You always could twist Hannah around your little finger," Isaac said. "I don't know if it's your handsome face or your devastating charm."

"Both," said his wife promptly, adding, to quash Felix's smugness, "and your title doesn't hurt a bit. In any case, Hannah would be sadly disappointed if you didn't drop in to say hello. Are you sure you cannot stay the night?"

"Thank you, but no. Brussels is in turmoil, overwhelmed by the numbers of wounded. Fanny is pluck to the backbone but I cannot bear to think of her struggling alone."

His sense of urgency reanimated, he turned his full attention to his luncheon, ignoring the enigmatic glance that passed between Miriam and Isaac.

When Felix let himself into Madame Vilvoorde's house, he was taken aback to hear Fanny's laughter floating down from above. His spirits rose at the sound yet, tired and hungry after the ride from Ostend, he could not repress a certain pique. She seemed to be getting on very well without him.

He trudged up the stairs. Half way up, he recognized the masculine voice issuing from Frank's chamber: Captain Mercer. His resentment swelled.

From the doorway where he paused, unnoticed, he saw Frank lying back against a heap of pillows, a faint smile on his pain-sculptured face. Fanny sat slumped in the armchair. Even in the dusk, Felix noted the smudges under her eyes; she propped her head on one hand as if it were too heavy for her slender, delicate neck.

". . . and there were Boney's lancers," Mercer was saying. "We opened fire and a moment later that black cloud burst like a magazine blowing up. You couldn't hear the guns for the thunder. Lord Uxbridge — he was commanding the rear guard — yelled at us to fire a last round then gallop for our lives. The lancers would have caught us if not for the deluge. After that it was just skirmishing. One of Whinyates' rockets blew up a French gun, Frank, but another of the bloody things turned arsy-versy and chased me up the road."

That brought the faint smile back to Frank's lips. Fanny, laughing again, turned slightly and caught sight of Felix.

"Lord Roworth!" The incredulous joy that lit her face was ample compensation for his journey, even including a choppy Channel crossing. She started up from the chair and came to him, both hands held out.

As he took them in his, an odd tremor shook him. Pity, of course, aroused by the thin, pale face in which her brown eyes seemed huge. "I brought a letter for the Duke," he explained, reluctant to admit that he had returned for her sake — and Anita's, and Frank's.

"Evening, my lord," said Mercer, sketching a salute. "Well, I'll be on my way, Miss Fanny. The next episode will keep for another day. We'll have you on your feet again in no time, Frank."

"I'll see you out, Cav," Fanny said, pulling her hands from Felix's clasp.

"No, you stay here, I'll see the captain out," Felix offered promptly. He stepped back onto the landing.

Mercer followed, and Fanny came after him. Now she gave him her hand, and he took it in both his. "Thank you, Cav. Your visits take his mind off the pain," she said in an unsteady voice.

"He'll be all right, my dear. It's a matter of time."

"I know there are many others with worse injuries, it's just that . . ." Biting her lip, she retreated into her brother's chamber.

"When someone you love is hurt, no one else counts," Mercer completed her sentence. "It was a bloody business, my lord."

"I heard Lord Fitzroy Somerset and Sir Alexander Gordon were hit," Felix said, leading the way down the stairs. His friends had never been far from his mind. "Do you happen to know how badly?"

The captain answered with a soldier's bluntness. "Colonel Gordon lost his leg and died in Wellington's own bed. Lord Uxbridge lost a leg, too, at the last minute when the French were in retreat, but he'll survive. He told the Marquise d'Assche he'd soon be dancing with her with a wooden leg. Colonel Canning's dead."

"And Fitzroy?"

"His right arm. It's said that he called out to the surgeon, 'Hallo, don't carry away that arm till I've taken off my ring.'"

"The ring Emily gave him." There were others he ought to enquire after, but tonight he couldn't face it. He opened the front door. "Thank you, captain."

"Shall you be here long?"

"Until Ingram is well enough to travel. Then I shall take the three of them back to England."

It was nearly dark outside and he could not see Mercer's face, but the surprise and suspicion in his voice were unmistakable. "To England! Why the devil . . . ?"

"He'll receive better medical care there."

"No doubt. But you're not related, my lord; you're not even connected with the regiment . . . Oh, so that's it."

Felix guessed that the captain believed his motive to be a civilian's guilt at having escaped the carnage of war. Let him. It was as good an explanation as any for the unaccountable, quixotic impulse that had brought him back to Brussels.

He went back into the house. Fanny was coming down the stairs, every step a visible effort. She smiled at him.

"Frank is sleeping. Roworth, it is so good to have you back. Have you eaten?"

"Not since Ostend, and not much then. I was humiliatingly seasick."

"But you are recovered? I shall see what

Henriette can provide."

"You'll do nothing of the sort. I'll throw myself on Henriette's tender mercies, while you go and sit down. We must talk."

"Yes, my lord." Miraculously her irrepressible, irresistible dimples had survived her ordeal.

A few minutes later he entered the parlour carrying a tray. On it a pot of tea stood beside a plate of steaming stew in which, he noticed, turnips, carrots, and onions were more in evidence than meat. Fanny was curled up unselfconsciously in a chair by the empty fireplace. He poured her a cup of tea, then sat down opposite her with the tray on his lap.

Even Henriette's talents had not succeeded in rendering the vegetable stew better than edible. As he picked at it, she could not tear her gaze from him, still scarcely able to believe he had really returned.

"Tell me, how is Anita?" he asked.

"Well, but a trifle crotchety. The poor child has had a sad time of it for she does not understand that I cannot give her my full attention. Hoskins has been splendid with her."

"I'm glad you've had his help. I saw him just now in the kitchen."

"He must return to his unit soon, alas. I

believe Henriette will miss him as much as we shall, or more!" She sipped her tea, avoiding his eyes. He must not guess how desperately she longed for him to stay. "Shall you be here long?"

"That depends on Frank. Is he fit to travel?"

"To travel?" Bewildered, she stared at him. "I don't know. It is difficult to find a doctor who has not more urgent cases to deal with. But in any case . . ."

"There are doctors aplenty in England. I want you to come back with me."

Her mouth quivered. If only she could accept! "Oh Roworth, it is excessively kind of you to offer us your escort, but we have nowhere to go in England."

"I have found you somewhere." There was a note of triumph in his voice. Setting aside the tray, he leaned forward and said earnestly, "I have spoken of your plight to friends of mine, and they will be more than happy to take you in."

"We cannot possibly accept the hospitality of people we have never even met!"

"Not in general, perhaps, but the Cohens would never turn away anyone in need."

"Miriam Cohen?" she cried, agitated. Miriam Cohen, whom he had loved and still admired? "I will not beg her charity."

210

"Do you mislike Jews? You have too much sense to be as stupidly prejudiced as I once was."

"How can you ask? Have I not welcomed Mr Solomon and others of your couriers? But how can the Cohens be your friends when . . . when . . ."

"When Miriam turned me down in favour of Isaac? If you meet them perhaps you'll understand. Won't you reconsider, for Frank's sake? Miriam learned a great deal of medicine from her doctor uncle. She still treats her dependents and the local people, and she is certain she'll be able to help your brother."

"Will she?" Her resolve weakened.

"She saved me the use of my shoulder. Besides, she has a son near Anita's age who is in despair because his baby sister is too young to play catch with him."

Fanny gave him a tentative smile. "And toy soldiers?"

"What little boy worth his salt doesn't want to play with toy soldiers?"

She sighed. "None, unfortunately. Did you tell them about Anita's . . . birth?"

"I did. It is of no account. Will you come?"

"You did not persuade Mr and Mrs Cohen to invite us against their better judgment?"

"Miriam offered before I had even asked."

"Then how can I let a scruple stand in the way of Frank's recovery? Yes, we will come."

"Frank won't object?"

"Frank is in no case to object. Now, my lord, finish your dinner, pray, or Mrs Cohen and I shall have two of you to nurse."

He grinned, happy to hear the ironic note returned to her voice. Nearly cold, the stew was even less appetizing. Pushing the remains around his plate, he silently vowed to send Hoskins out first thing in the morning with a fistful of the ready to restock the larder.

He hadn't told Fanny yet about his huge bonus from his employer. She'd be happy for him that he was able at last to help his family.

As he opened his mouth to tell her, he realized she was fast asleep, her cheek pillowed on her hand. A stiff neck was inevitable if she stayed there all night, he thought with a twinge of fellow-feeling.

The scarcely touched dinner delivered to an offended Henriette in the kitchen, Felix went upstairs to open the door to Fanny's chamber. A night-lamp revealed Anita's dark, tousled locks and cherubic face on one pillow. Smiling, he held the lamp high and studied her long black eyelashes and delicate features. A good thing Amos was too young to have his heart broken.

He turned back the counterpane on the other bed, then went back downstairs. Fanny stirred as he picked her up but did not wake. His heart swelled with gladness that he had returned as, featherlight in his arms, she nestled her head trustingly against his shoulder.

CHAPTER 12

Wielding his title, Felix had no trouble finding an army surgeon willing to examine Frank. He arranged to meet him later at Madame Vilvoorde's and went on to deliver Nathan Rothschild's letter to the Duke of Wellington.

The atmosphere at Headquarters was more like mourning than celebration. Felix ventured to congratulate the Duke on his victory.

"By God, it is difficult to rejoice in a victory that has cost me so many friends!" Wellington exclaimed. "It was a dreadful business, and a close-run thing. I hope to God that I have fought my last battle." He scanned the letter. "Tell Mr Rothschild, if you please, that I shall do myself the honour of calling upon him when I return to London. He is as responsible as I for our success. You'll see Fitzroy and Emily before you leave?"

214

"Yes, sir, if he is well enough to receive visitors."

Unexpectedly, the Duke's whooping laugh rang out. "He's already learning to write with his left hand. I expect to have him back as my secretary in short order."

Felix went directly to the Somersets' lodgings. They welcomed him, and he was glad to see how well Fitzroy was adjusting to the loss of his arm, but it was a somber visit. Gordon's memory hung between them, and Canning's, and other mutual friends.

To raise his spirits, on the way home he stopped at the Marché aux Fleurs and bought lilies-of-the-valley for Fanny. As an afterthought he added a posy of pansies for Anita. Then, crossing the Grand' Place, he bought hothouse grapes for Frank and some strawberries, and a basket to carry them in. Compared to the events of the past week, the ignominy of the heir to the Earl of Westwood carrying a basket through the streets paled to insignificance.

Fanny was sewing at the table in the parlour, with difficulty for Anita had pulled up a chair right to her side as if she couldn't bear to be more than a few inches away. She tended to cling since Fanny had had to spend so much time with Frank. However, when Felix entered she jumped down and ran to him.

He handed her a posy of flowers, then set down a basket on a small table by the door. Fanny raised her eyebrows. Lord Roworth gone a-marketing? She had not expected him to take her words to heart.

Crossing the room, he bowed deeply, and with a flourish presented a nosegay. "Madam, I beg your acceptance of this small token of my regard."

"My lord, you are too kind," she responded, matching his implausible formality, forcing the words past the catch in her throat. Flowers for her? Feeling silly tears rising, she lowered her eyes as she raised the bouquet to breathe in the sweet fragrance of the delicate blooms.

"Tía, look, my flowers has faces. Look!" Anita insisted, tugging on Fanny's arm, forcing her to regain her equanimity.

"Have faces. Pansies — how clever of you, Roworth. The very thing for a little girl. Anita, love, did you thank Tío Felix?"

"Not yet. Will you hold my pansies, Tía?" The flowers safe, she spread her pink muslin skirts and carefully curtsied. "Thank you, Tío Felix. Do you want a kiss?"

"Yes, please." As he picked her up, over her head he cast a teasing gaze at Fanny.

Blushing, she prayed that he had not the

slightest notion how happy she'd be to follow the child's example. She hurried into speech. "When she is a little older, I shall have to teach her not to pay with kisses when a gentleman offers flowers."

"A pity." He heaved a heavy sigh and watched with shameless amusement as her cheeks grew still hotter. "I daresay at least she must learn to be discriminating about whom she kisses. Thank you, Anita. I've brought some strawberries, too. May I have another kiss?"

She giggled and complied. Fanny went over to the table where he had put the basket.

"Grapes, at this season!" she gasped.

"I hoped they might tempt Frank's appetite."

"They will, I'm sure, but they must have cost a fortune."

"Only a small fortune. You needn't worry that I'll land in the River Tick; I can stand the nonsense," he announced grandly, setting Anita down and striking a pose. "I'm rich."

"Rich! Not a week since, your valet was ready to quit because you had naught but rags to your name. Have you been gambling?"

His face darkened. Fanny was momentarily afraid her query had crossed the bounds of impertinence and she was about to receive a set-down. But that would be unjust, since he had frequently confided to her the irksome details of his purse-pinched condition!

That thought must have crossed his mind, for he said mildly, "I haven't played for more than chicken-stakes in years." Nathan Rothschild had rewarded him most generously, he explained, for the early news of the victory that had enabled the banker to make a fortune.

"And the Prime Minister, the Foreign Secretary, and the War Minister all refused to believe you?" she said, as incredulous as those gentlemen. "What fools!"

"But their folly was to my advantage," he pointed out, grinning.

"So you will not need to pinch pennies any more to keep up your position in Society," she said with forced cheerfulness. At least while his pockets were to let they had had something in common. She returned to the table and bent over her sewing. "I hope, for Trevor's sake, you mean to buy a new coat."

He laughed. "That was my first thought. He will appreciate removing to decent lodgings, too, and not having to travel on the stage."

Of course, he would not stay at Madame Vilvoorde's now he could afford better. With an effort, Fanny dismissed a lurking sense of desolation and reminded herself that he had offered his escort and a refuge with his friends in England. There were practical matters to be settled.

"I wanted to ask you about that. Frank cannot travel on the stage, even if a doctor says he is fit to be moved. I was too tired last night to think of it, but this morning I realized that we cannot afford the journey to England. Only, if you can afford it, we could pay you back gradually, over a period . . ."

"Gammon! There is not the least need . . ."

"Even if I agreed, which I shall not," she said obstinately, "Frank would never consent to hang on your sleeve." She'd accept Miriam Cohen's charity for Frank's sake, but to accept Felix's was unthinkable.

Felix drew himself up with a haughty stiffness belied by a quizzical glint in his blue eyes. "Then permit me, ma'am, to pay the reckoning for your services to Mr Rothschild's agent and couriers over the past several months. Housekeeping, hospitality . . ."

"You odious, odious man!" She wrinkled her nose at him. "You know perfectly well that I did not do that for money."

"If you will permit me to finish a sentence," he said, grinning at her indignation, "I wish to point out that what is sauce for the goose is sauce for the gander. Mr Rothschild will absorb some of the cost of the journey, since I have to make it anyway and we shall use his yacht. For the rest, I shall consider myself grossly insulted if further mention is made of the word 'money.' I may even call you out."

Fanny had to laugh, and Anita came running to her. Strawberry stains about her mouth betrayed the way she had taken advantage of her elders' preoccupation.

"What's funny, Tía?"

"Your face, lovie."

Felix swept up the child and held her up to the tarnished looking-glass. "See?"

"Strawbies is good," she explained earnestly. "I didn't eat some of Tío Frank's grapes."

"Didn't eat any," Fanny corrected, "— at least, I hope that is what you mean!"

"Can I give them to Tío Frank?"

"If you promise to be very good and quiet. It's time I checked on him anyway. Or do you wish to present your gift with your most

220

elegant bow, Roworth?"

"No, go ahead." The last thing he wanted at present was to find himself next at odds with the invalid over accepting his aid. He was well satisfied to have put Fanny in a position where she'd find it difficult to refuse anything further he chose to do for her. "I'll wait here for the surgeon. He should turn up at any moment."

"You persuaded a doctor to come? Oh Roworth, thank you. Why did you not say so sooner?"

"Because, ma'am, you have scarce let me get a word in edgewise since I came home!" Nor had he yet told her that he was now in a position to offer for Lady Sophia. That news could wait.

The young doctor arrived a few minutes later. Felix took him up to Frank's chamber and brought Anita down to the parlour. He kept her amused for what seemed like an age with a story about a little girl who ate too many strawberries and turned bright red all over.

At last he heard footsteps on the stairs and went out to thank the man. "Do you think Captain Ingram can safely travel?" he asked.

"Yes, my lord, as long as he makes no attempt to exert himself. He must be carried, helped to sit up and lie down. Any effort of the limbs is likely to break open wounds which are just beginning to heal. You see . . ."

"You need not explain, doctor. I know you are needed elsewhere. Miss Ingram will tell me the rest."

The doctor looked at him in tired surprise. "But all I told Miss Ingram was that her brother can be moved, with care. I would not wish to alarm a lady with the unpleasant details of his condition."

Felix was affronted on Fanny's behalf. She was no milk-and-water miss to have the truth kept from her. On the other hand, he himself had a squeamish lack of desire to delve into the intricacies of healing wounds. However, someone had to know, and the doctor's weariness was evident.

"You had best come and sit down." He led the way into the parlour and waved him to a chair. Anita appeared to be tucking her soldiers into a bed composed of Fanny's sewing. Crooning a lullaby, she ignored the men. "Go on," Felix said.

"You see, my lord, the scar tissue over a wound is inflexible, so that stretching is liable to crack it. When the wound is near a joint, healing is often delayed by excessive motion. The captain has many wounds —

indeed, he could scarcely have survived had he not been standing at an angle to the explosion. I deeply regret having to tell you that, even with straightforward healing, an accumulation of scarring will probably limit your cousin's freedom of . . ."

"My cousin? Captain Ingram is no relative of mine."

"I beg your pardon, my lord." His shoulders slumped. "I assumed, since you were seeking care . . ."

"No matter. I beg your pardon, for interrupting." He hadn't wanted to hear, but the worst must be faced. "If I understand you aright, whatever we do, Ingram is going to be crippled."

"I would not put it so harshly. As I was about to say, his freedom of movement will be limited to some extent. The resultant lack of use, unfortunately, may atrophy the muscles."

Felix's mind flew back to a tiny chamber under the rafters of a cottage in the Pyrenees. Miriam had forced him to exercise his agonizing shoulder to stop it stiffening, to stop a permanent loss of function. She had succeeded — he was as strong as ever and rarely felt the least twinge. "We must get Frank to England at once," he said.

The doctor appeared to think he was

slightly mad, but he gratefully pocketed a small supplement to his army pay and took his leave.

On second thoughts, Felix decided there was no need to disclose Frank's gloomy prognosis to Fanny. He could not bear the thought of her horror, when Miriam might be able to prevent the terrible outcome.

He went to rescue Fanny's sewing from Anita's depredations. It was a plain white chemise, unadorned with lace or ribbons except for a tiny satin bow. The hint of a sternly suppressed longing for finery touched him, and the intimate garment reminded him all too clearly of the feel of Fanny's slender body in his arms. That bow would nestle between her breasts . . .

Hastily he folded the chemise, set it aside, and started picking up the pins scattered on the table. Their quantity suggested that he had arrived rather too late to save the sewing, but Anita happily helped him stick them in the pincushion. In fact, her neat little fingers managed it much better than he did. He was sucking a pricked thumb when Fanny came in.

"Will you go up to Frank?" she entreated. "He is fretting about something, he will not tell me what, and he asked to see you."

Felix could think of any number of matters that might be worrying the captain, from the doctor's report to the cost of travel. He had no wish to discuss any of them with a sick man. Reluctantly he went upstairs.

Frank was lying with his eyes closed. Felix paused in the doorway to study him. The resolution that had characterized his face was missing. Defenceless, vulnerable in his weakness, he appeared much younger than his twenty-five years, his likeness to his sister more pronounced.

Not that anyone could accuse Fanny of a lack of resolution!

"Ingram?" Felix said softly.

The captain's brown eyes, so like Fanny's, were alert and watchful. "My lord. Fanny tells me you want to take us to England. Why?"

Felix told himself the man's bluntness was due to the pain caused by speaking, not to discourtesy. "Because I believe I can procure you better medical attention there," he said with deliberate patience.

"There are many others in worse case than I."

"But I'm not acquainted with them as I am with you."

Frank hesitated, then blurted out, "Lord Roworth, what are your intentions towards my sister?"

So that was what troubled him. Felix hadn't even considered the possibility that might be a source of worry. Guilt flashed through him. Only a moment ago he had been thinking of Fanny in a way that would have justified her brother in taking a horse-whip to him, had he acted on his thoughts.

But she was not the sort of female one might set up as one's mistress, any more than she was a conceivable bride for the heir to an earldom. He did his best to reassure Frank.

"My dear fellow, I have none, neither honorable nor, I assure you, dishonorable. I have the greatest admiration for Miss Ingram and I am concerned for her welfare, and for Anita's, but as for tenderer feelings . . ." He felt the oddest sense of betrayal when he said that. He hurried on. "You are aware, I daresay, that I have been attempting to fix my interest with Lady Sophia Gerrold."

"So I have heard." The captain's lips quirked.

Of course he knew. Half Brussels knew. All the same, Felix would hardly have spoken of so personal a matter if it had not been necessary to remove Frank's doubts. "At last I can declare myself to Lady Sophia

226

with some hope of success. Fanny must have told you that it's high tide with me?"

"She did, and that's another thing. High tide or low, I cannot allow you to pay our way to England."

His protest was expected. Felix put on an air of arrogant disdain and said, "You mean you cannot subdue your pride for the sake of your sister and the child. What do you suppose will become of them if you insist on repaying with scanty funds a debt I don't even recognize? Or do you prefer to linger here in a decline while Miss Ingram struggles to support you?"

With that unsporting leveller, Felix departed.

He had a certain sympathy for Frank's pride, though, so when he went in search of a comfortable, well-sprung carriage he decided to borrow one if he could. Without the expense of hiring a vehicle, he hoped, the Ingrams' sense of obligation would be that much less.

The Richmonds had helped before. He went to the Rue de la Blanchisserie and found Lady Georgiana and her sisters rolling bandages under the supervision of the duchess. Lord March was there, too, and Slender Billy, his shoulder heavily bandaged, his spirits no whit depressed. The prince insisted on repeating for Felix's benefit the story of how March had carried him off the battlefield. Felix suspected that it grew more dramatic with each retelling.

When Felix mentioned his errand to the duchess, Slender Billy eagerly interrupted. "Captain Ingram of the Horse Artillery? His battery was the first to reinforce us at Quatre Bras, remember, March?"

"How could I forget, sir, when he instantly doubled the number of our guns."

"Lord Roworth, you shall have my carriage to take you to Ostend. No, I insist! Keep it as long as you like, the longer the better. Can you imagine a better reason not to visit my royal parents?" He burst into laughter, and even the duchess smiled though she tried to frown on the prince's combination of filial impiety and *lèse majesté.*

Drawing Lord March aside, Felix said dryly, "I've no desire to cause dissension in a royal family."

The young man shrugged. "No fear of that. If King William insists, we can always find a way to get to the court. Believe me, I have worse to contend with than the lending of a carriage, and Ingram really did turn up in the nick of time. When do you want it?"

"Tomorrow morning, if possible." He did not want to give the proud twins time to come up with further objections.

"Give me your direction and I'll see to it. I'm sorry to hear Captain Ingram was badly hurt. Convey my best wishes, will you?"

Felix stayed a little longer for politeness' sake, then hurried home, impatient to impart his news. To his disappointment, Hoskins told him that Fanny, taking Anita with her, had gone to inform Major Prynne of their intention to return to England.

"She don't expect no trouble," he added.

"Trouble?"

"The cap'n's still in the army an' under orders, m'lord, same as what I am."

Another complication he hadn't considered. Still, a word with the major, or Colonel Frazer, or even Wellington, would solve any problem. The advantages of being heir to a peer were legion.

He went up to see Frank, who was gazing bleakly at the ceiling. Felix's conscience pricked him for having hit a man when he was down. "I've just been to the Richmonds'," he said. "Lord March sends his best wishes for your recovery. He and Slender Billy were telling me how you rushed your guns to the rescue at Quatre Bras."

"Orders."

"Orders or no, the prince remembers you with gratitude. He insists on lending us his carriage to drive to Ostend."

Frank turned his head and stared. "The Prince of Orange's carriage?" he asked incredulously. "You're gammoning me. You must be."

"Not I. Wellington may never have a good word for the artillery, but others are more appreciative. So will you please stop worrying your head about what you owe me, you nodcock, and . . ."

". . . And start worrying about what I owe the heir to the throne of the Netherlands?" The note of laughter in his voice came as a vast relief to Felix. "I don't pretend to guess how you did it, Roworth, but I'd give a mint to see Fanny's expression when you tell her."

"You can tell her yourself. I think I hear her now." He went to the top of the stairs and called, "Miss Ingram, will you come up here for a moment?"

She stopped in the act of taking off her daisy-garlanded hat and turned an anxious face up to him. "Is Frank worse?"

"No, no! I am a wretch to alarm you. No, I have something to tell you."

Anita scrambling ahead of her, she came

230

slowly to join him, every step a small but distinct effort. He picked up Anita and went into Frank's chamber.

"What is it?" Fanny asked, following.

Felix gestured to her brother, who announced, "Roworth has talked no less than Slender Billy into lending us his travelling carriage."

Her eyes widened and her mouth dropped open in the most satisfactory manner, but Felix demurred, "It was none of my doing. He offered it entirely of his own accord."

"The *Prince of Orange* offered us his carriage? With the royal coat of arms on the door panels? And footmen in royal livery?"

"I didn't like to demand the footmen. It don't do to look a gift horse in the mouth, you know."

Fanny laughed, her tiredness momentarily banished. Her brother unwisely followed suit, and gasped with pain.

"We shall take the journey very slowly," Felix promised. He'd take the reins himself if the prince's coachman possessed the neck-or-nothing proclivities of his master.

Doubtless at March's command, the coachman drove at a pace so staid that they were a full two days on the road to Ostend. Despite the lack of footmen, at every stop they were received and treated like royalty.

Nonetheless Frank was exhausted by the time he was carried on board the Rothschilds' ketch. Fanny went below with him while Felix stayed on deck with Anita, eyeing the water uneasily and praying that it would be calm enough for him to devote his attention to the child.

She watched, fascinated, as a carriage almost as splendid as the prince's was winched aboard the packet at the next berth. A crowd waited to embark, among them a number of soldiers with bandaged heads or arms in slings, and a few prone on hurdles. Others besides Felix had rushed to Brussels to bring their wounded back to England.

As the first of them started up the gangway, a vaguely familiar figure caught Felix's attention. A small man in a battered hat stood with his back to the ship, scanning the faces of the people boarding, even stooping to examine those borne on stretchers. Felix frowned. Where on earth had he seen him before?

The ketch's crew began to cast off and he had to keep Anita from lending a hand. When he glanced back at the packet, all but a few passengers had embarked. The little man was talking to a sailor, who shook his head and pointed at the ketch.

As the breeze caught the ketch's sail, the man ran along the quay towards them, too late. The gap between ship and quay widened. Hands on hips, he stared after them with an expression of wrathful frustration.

Felix recognized the frieze coat, catskin waistcoat, and disreputable hat. It was the man who had been asking questions about the Ingrams in Brussels. What the devil did the fellow want? If he made any attempt to persecute Fanny, he soon find out that she had an able defender!

CHAPTER 13

The Cohens' footmen bore Frank into the house on a hurdle. He lay very still, semiconscious, his breathing painful. Fanny was horribly afraid she had been wrong to subject her brother to the fatigue of the journey, though they had travelled in the greatest possible comfort.

She was tired enough herself. Drooping, she plodded beside Felix. Anita, in his arms, had been half woken from a nap by their arrival at Nettledene.

As they stepped through the front door into the entrance hall, Fanny saw a tall, red-haired woman bending over Frank. She held his limp wrist for a moment, then nodded to the footmen. They started up the stairs with their burden and Fanny moved forward to follow, but Mrs Cohen came to greet them.

"Miss Ingram, I am happy to welcome you to Nettledene." Her gaze swiftly took in the crumpled travelling gown, pale face, and shadowed eyes. "The journey must have tired you half to death. Felix shall take you into the drawing room and Samuels shall bring you tea in a trice. I beg your pardon for deserting you, but of course I must see to your brother's comfort first. Cheer up, my dear, we shall pull him through. And you will feel much better for a cup of tea." With a swirl of blue cambric skirts, she hurried after the footmen.

Overwhelmed, Fanny said uncertainly, "I ought to go to Frank."

"Miriam will do all that is necessary. Come and sit down."

He turned away from the stairs. By an open door stood a small man in black with a rosy, benevolent face and a fringe of white fluff around a shiny pate topped with a Jewish skullcap. Fanny was wondering in surprise if this could possibly be Isaac Cohen, husband of the gracious, beautiful Miriam, when Felix addressed him.

"Good day, Samuels. I hope I see you well?"

Samuels beamed. "Very well, thank you, my lord, and all the better for seeing your lordship."

He must be a servant, Fanny decided; probably a butler.

"And Mrs Samuels?" Felix enquired.

"Flourishing like a cedar in Lebanon, my lord. The tea tray will be here in a moment, but perhaps your lordship would care for something a little stronger?"

"I'll take a glass of Madeira." He glanced at Fanny. "And a glass for Miss Ingram would not come amiss," he added.

Anita fixed Samuels with a pleading gaze. "Do you got some bixits, please?"

"I'll see what Mrs Samuels can do, miss," he said gravely. He turned to Fanny and bowed. "Is there anything in particular I can bring for you, madam?"

"For me?" She was flustered at having her wishes consulted. "Oh no. No, thank you, tea will be very welcome."

The butler bowed again and departed. Felix led the way through the open door into a parlour — no, Mrs Cohen had called it the drawing room. Fanny glanced around.

Its walls painted white, the room seemed light and airy despite its low ceiling with age-blackened beams; the brick fireplace, with a simply carved wood mantelpiece, was surmounted by a large landscape painting, handsomely framed; the furniture was not only well-stuffed and cushioned but graceful, upholstered in blue and grey figured damask, gleaming with polished wood; a luxurious carpet covered most of the floor. Fanny had never seen a room so elegant.

"It's very grand, isn't it?" she whispered apprehensively. "I didn't realize your friends had a butler."

Felix looked taken aback. "To tell the truth, I've always regarded Samuels as a sort of elderly cherub," he said, "and I'd describe the room as cosy. No wall hangings, no gilt, not a fashionable inch of spindly faux bamboo, and the picture's by some modern fellow — Beadle or Constable or something of the sort — not an Old Master."

Fanny wasn't sure what an Old Master was. She felt lost, out of her element.

Anita wriggled out of Felix's arms and darted over to inspect a long-case clock with a zodiacal face. Gazing up at it in wide-eyed awe, she announced, "I like this house. Specially if there's bixits."

Fanny smiled. "Don't touch," she warned.

Taking her arm, Felix led her to a group of chairs at the far end of the room, arranged in a semicircle facing French doors that stood open to a stone terrace and the garden beyond. The vista of roses, pink, white, and crimson, distracted her from her uneasiness. She went to the open doors and breathed in the fragrance.

"Mrs Cohen must love roses."

He laughed. "I daresay she enjoys their beauty, but she is equally interested in their medicinal qualities. She uses the petals to scent lotions, and rosehips to make syrups and jellies."

"Oh. She must be very clever." Dismayed again, Fanny sank into one of the chairs as Samuels brought in a hissing silver tea urn. A maid in grey with a frilly, starched white apron and cap came after him with a tray.

Anita abandoned the clock and sped to investigate. Half way across the room she stopped and stared towards the hall door. Fanny saw a small, carrotty head poking around the door.

"What are you doing here, Master Amos?" Samuels scolded.

"I runned away from Hannah."

Amos ventured into the room, his gaze fixed on Anita. They stood regarding each other solemnly. Fanny crossed her fingers — and saw Felix doing likewise. If the children took a dislike to each other, she was in for a difficult time.

"Do you want a bixit?" Anita offered hopefully.

"Is there bixits? Sam'els, is there bixits?" Turning his head, he saw Felix and ran to stand at his knee. "Uncle Felix, can I have a bixit?"

Anita scurried to Fanny and squeezed into the chair beside her. Each provided with a gingerbread man, the children nibbled with a stolid lack of interest in each other belied by occasional furtive peeks.

Samuels raised bushy white eyebrows enquiringly at Felix, who said, "Leave him." The butler bowed in acquiescence and withdrew with the maid.

Leaning against Felix's leg, Amos ate every last crumb and then said in a stage whisper, "Uncle Felix, will she play catch wiv me?"

"Ask her," Felix suggested.

He stumped across to Fanny's chair, eyed Anita warily, and said, "Will you play catch wiv me?"

"I got so'jers. Wood so'jers. Calvary an' infantly an' artirelly."

"We can play so'jers, too."

Anita slipped down from the chair. "Awright."

"Uncle Felix, can I show her to Hannah?"

Fanny answered his questioning look with a tentative nod. Hannah must be his nurse, she supposed. A household with a butler must surely possess a nurse. Perhaps she ought to go and make the woman's acquaintance but the effort of rising from her chair was beyond her.

Felix told the little boy, "Yes, take Anita up to the nursery."

Amos took Anita's hand and tugged her towards the door. Anita suddenly panicked and ran back to Fanny.

"Tía, you won't go 'way?"

"No, love, I shall come and see you in the nursery by and by."

Reassured, Anita gave her a kiss and rejoined Amos. "I got a sister," he told her. "But she's on'y a baby."

"Tío Frank's artirelly," she said grandly as they left the room hand in hand. "My daddy was, too."

Fanny leaned her head against the back of the chair and closed her eyes. Relieved for the moment of responsibility for Frank and Anita, she surrendered to weariness. Felix was blessedly silent and she fell into a half-doze.

A few minutes later she sat up with a start as Mrs Cohen came in.

"How is Frank, ma'am?" she asked anxiously, guilty at having forgotten him for a moment.

"Sleeping, which is quite the best thing for him at present. I daresay a nap would not do you any harm either, Miss Ingram. Let me take you to your chamber."

"Thank you, but I have promised Anita to

go up to the nursery."

"I'll go," Felix volunteered. "If she's not happy I shall bring her to you, but I'd wager by now she's instructing Amos in Wellington's strategy."

She smiled her thanks.

He was tempted to offer to carry her up to her bedchamber, but he had a feeling she wouldn't appreciate the liberty in a strange house. She had never spoken of the time he had put her to bed — fully clothed — in Brussels. Either she was embarrassed, or she had been so tired she never realized she hadn't got there by her own exertions. Naturally, he was too gentlemanly to mention it.

She trudged away with Miriam. Felix repaired to the nursery, where he paid his respects to Hannah and admired a blue and red chalk scribble on a slate.

"It's Tío Frank," Anita explained. "Amos drawed a horse."

She seemed perfectly content to start on a new picture, so he went back to the drawing room and poured himself another glass of Madeira. Miriam soon joined him.

"What an amiable, unassuming young woman Miss Ingram is," she said. "She is very anxious not to give any trouble, but I managed to persuade her to have her dinner taken up on a tray. She is burned to the socket. In fact, I doubt she will wake to eat. I hope the child will let her sleep."

"With luck she'll be satisfied with a good-night kiss from me. She and Amos are well on the way to being bosom friends."

"You always were good with children, Felix. You ought to have some of your own by now."

"Perhaps I shall soon. I'm on my way to propose to Lady Sophia, remember."

"Ah yes, the Goddess. You will be leaving in the morning, then?"

He frowned. "I was going to, but perhaps I ought to stay for a day or two until Miss Ingram is settled. She finds your magnificence a trifle intimidating."

"Magnificence! You are bamming me."

"Not at all. She has had a hard life, Miriam, though she laughs about it. Our dingy lodgings in Brussels were luxury compared to what she endured in Spain. This is magnificence." His gesture encompassed the pleasant room and the butler, who appeared at that moment with fresh tea for his mistress. "Yes, I'll stay a day or two if you will have me."

"Have I not been begging you for years to spend more than an hour or two with us?"

she retorted. "Thank you, Samuels. Tea, Felix?"

"Thank you, I'm quite happy with the wine. An excellent vintage."

"It ought to be, you chose it for Isaac. He will not be home until late, by the way. He had to go up to town. We shall dine tête-à-tête."

"Would that it were true! I suppose you mean with none but Samuels and a footman or two in attendance, alas."

"Really, Felix, you are an incorrigible flirt. Now tell me, please, what you know of the captain's injuries. Miss Ingram was too tired for me to interrogate her."

He repeated what the doctor had told him.

"Does Miss Ingram know?"

"I was incensed with the doctor for thinking her too weak to hear the worst — but in the end I couldn't bring myself to tell her that her brother was going to be a cripple."

"Of course we shall not let him be crippled," she said briskly. "I have oils and unguents to keep the scar tissue supple, and the proper exercises will restore vigour to his limbs, but first we shall build up his strength with good food. Beef tea and calves' foot jelly for a start. I must go and consult Mrs Samuels."

Deserted again, Felix strolled out into the

garden. A gardener was weeding one of the rose beds. His dilapidated hat reminded Felix of the inquisitive man who kept turning up on the Ingrams' trail, and he wondered whether he ought to warn Miriam. He couldn't conceive of any way the fellow could possibly trace them to Nettledene.

Nonetheless, he mentioned the matter at dinner.

"What does he want?" Miriam asked.

"I've not the least idea. He may be a debt collector, for all I know."

"I cannot have my patient harassed over an old debt, but I rather doubt he will find them. I have already told the servants not to gossip in the village about the Ingrams' presence, to avoid a lot of fuss over a hero of Waterloo. No one can talk of anything but the victory, as if bloodshed were something to be proud of."

"Fanny has as low an opinion of military glory as you could wish."

"She is a woman of sense. I had rather hear about the Duchess of Richmond's ball. Were you there? Tell me all about it."

Felix obliged, avoiding the subject of war. He described the splendid decor, the noble guests, the Highland dancers, and Lady Sophia's taking supper with him and granting him a third dance. Miriam displayed a disappointing lack of interest in the Goddess's kindness.

She would be more interested when she was acquainted with his bride-to-be, he told himself, banishing a slight unease at the prospect of introducing his friends to Lady Sophia.

When Felix woke the next morning it was raining. A steady drip-drip-drip-plunk from the tree outside his curtained window suggested a solid drizzle set in for the whole day. His bed was warm and comfortable and after his recent exertions he had every excuse to enjoy a lazy morning. He turned over, closed his eyes, and pulled the covers up to his chin. Drip-drip-drip-plunk. In a while he'd ring for a newspaper and a cup of coffee. A pity Trevor was not here, but Isaac's man would do for him. Later he'd send for Trevor, since he had decided to stay a few days for Fanny's sake.

Poor little Fanny, bewildered by the grandeur of the Cohens' simple country life — he groaned and sat up. She had retired early last night, and she was accustomed to early rising. Was she even now wondering at what hour it would be proper to leave her chamber? She had eaten no dinner last night. She must be famished but he doubted she'd dare ring for breakfast in bed, even if the

245

possibility crossed her mind.

He tugged on the bell-pull. By the time Isaac's valet came in a few minutes later he had donned stockings, drawers and pantaloons under his nightshirt.

"Hot water, my lord?"

"If you please. Do you happen to know whether Miss Ingram is down yet?"

"I understand, my lord, that miss has already visited the captain and the nursery and is at present taking breakfast with the master and mistress."

"The devil she is!" Felix muttered under his breath. He should have guessed that Fanny was not one to let herself be intimidated by a novel situation, especially where the welfare of Frank and Anita was concerned. After the tent camps, open-air bivouacs, and Spanish goatherds' huts she had described to him, she had the sense to enjoy the comforts of an English country manor house. She'd never have survived had she not been both courageous and adaptable.

He cast a longing glance at his bed. A proper nodcock he'd look if he countermanded the order for hot water and tried to go back to sleep.

Washed, shaved, and dressed, he went down to the breakfast room. The Cohens and Fanny were still at table, chatting over tea and coffee. Already Fanny's face had lost its tautness, though still thin and pale.

Under the influence of Miriam's warmth and concern and Isaac's grave kindliness, Fanny was beginning to feel quite at home at Nettledene. She no longer needed Felix as an intermediary between herself and her generous host and hostess, but she was glad of his presence. Miriam had told her he meant to stay several days, an unexpected pleasure due, no doubt, to his finding a rare opportunity to spend some time with his friends. She smiled at him.

"How are Frank and Anita today?" he asked, as he helped himself from the sideboard.

"Frank is very tired, but Mrs Cohen has just been explaining to me what she means to do for him and I know now he will recover." Fanny found it impossible to doubt Miriam's calm certainty of her own abilities.

"Miss Ingram will help me this morning in the stillroom," said Miriam, "making up the potions we shall need. As for Anita, she and Amos are no longer being scrupulously polite to each other, so they are well on the way to being friends."

Isaac grinned. "I interrupted a squabble

over who was infantry and who was cavalry, but they agreed wonderfully well that Leah was Boney."

"I fear Anita always wants to play at soldiers," said Fanny with a sigh.

"She'll soon stop now she isn't surrounded by soldiers," Felix consoled her, sitting down next to her. He no longer showed any sign of envying military glory, she noticed. A glimpse of reality had cured that fantasy.

"By the way, Miss Ingram," said Miriam, "I have been wondering why it is she calls you *tía* rather than aunt."

"Her mother was Spanish." The explanation sounded sadly inadequate, so Fanny added defensively, "Somehow, 'aunt' had a ring to it that seemed to me horridly staid and . . . aging."

They all laughed. Felix came to her rescue and changed the subject. "Isaac, how did your meeting go yesterday?"

"Very interesting. Ricardo, the economist, talked to us, and then he and Rothschild led a debate on political economy."

"Spare me the details!"

"Are you a banker, too, Mr Cohen?" Fanny asked.

"Nothing so practical, Miss Ingram. I and others of like mind are working to obtain the vote for Jews, Catholics, and Dissenters."

"And women," said Miriam firmly.

"And women, my love. But for women it will take a century, for the rest of us fifteen or twenty years."

"Why is that, sir?" Fanny was curious, though the ideals of democracy and the excitement of elections had had no part in her vagabond life.

"Listen. Felix, how old is your father?"

"Nearing sixty," Felix answered, puzzled.

"I don't wish Lord Westwood any harm, but in the natural course of things you are likely to take his place in the House of Lords in the next decade or two. Will you vote to extend the franchise to Jews, Catholics, and Dissenters?"

"Certainly, as you know very well."

"And to women?"

"Good Gad, no!" he said incautiously.

"Shame!" cried Miriam, and she and Fanny glared at him.

He hastened to make amends. "If all females had the courage, intelligence, and practical common sense of those present, it would be a different matter."

"Fair words butter no parsnips," Miriam snapped. "If women received the same education as men . . ." She was obviously off on one of her favourite subjects. Fanny listened in fascination. Such ideas had never come her way before.

After breakfast, she went with Miriam to the stillroom and learned to mix salves and lotions. Felix, meanwhile, went with Isaac to the library. He learned a great deal that he didn't want — but doubtless ought — to know about the probable effect of Napoleon's defeat on the British economy. He tried to concentrate. If Lady Sophia accepted his hand, he'd settle at Westwood and learn to manage the estate. The price of corn would become a matter of more than abstract concern.

Nonetheless, he was far from vexed when Fanny interrupted Isaac's disquisition. "Lord Roworth, if you please, when you can spare a moment will you come with me to see Frank?"

"At once, Miss Ingram." Avoiding the mocking gaze of his host, who was quite aware of his reluctant attention, he leapt to his feet with gallant alacrity. "Isaac, you can explain the wages of farm labourers later. Is anything wrong?" he asked Fanny as he closed the door behind them.

"Frank is being pigheaded. Just like a man! Can you credit it, he questions Mrs Cohen's competence only because she is a female and he wants a male doctor to approve her remedies. I cannot insult her by sending for another physician!"

"Lord, no, I shouldn't dare. Never fear, I have personal experience of her methods. I'll persuade him."

"I'm sure you will, because he trusts you. As do I." She laid her hand on his arm and looked up at him earnestly. "How could we not when you are the best friend we ever had?"

She had proved her trust by coming with him to England, yet to hear her say it was an unexpected joy. To hide his delight, he said quizzingly, "Even though I am not a member of your regiment?"

Dimples danced. "Even though you are not a member of the regiment."

CHAPTER 14

June slid into July and the sun shone again. Felix walked with Fanny in the gardens and orchards and rode with her through the countryside. He played with the children, discussed weighty matters with Isaac, and constantly reassured Frank that the exercises Miriam was beginning to torture him with were worth the pain.

Colour returned to Fanny's cheeks and the spring to her step. She helped Miriam massage her brother's scars with rose-scented oils that made him complain he smelled like a flower garden, though her fortitude failed at putting him through the exercises. With Anita's needs taken care of by Hannah, she had leisure aplenty to stroll abroad with Felix. She also discovered the pleasure of reading — to carry more than a very few books about in the army's train had been impossible. She was often to be found in the library with Isaac.

Miriam had metamorphosed from a bene-factor into a dear friend. Working together in the stillroom, or sitting with the baby on the terrace, watching the children play, they talked of household and nursery matters. Fanny spoke of travels with her father's and then her brother's artillery unit. Miriam reciprocated with tales of her wanderings about Europe with her doctor uncle, ending with her dash across France with Isaac and Felix.

"How Felix has changed since that day we met at Jakob Rothschild's house in Paris!" she remarked one day, shaking her head with a smile. "To be forced to consort on equal terms with commoners was bad enough, but to add to his horror, we were Jews."

"Oh, he has changed, then," Fanny came hotly to his defense. "Right from the first he was perfectly amiable, never the least bit condescending. He even walked in the park with Anita and me, though I did think the first time would be the last when Lady Sophia . . ." She let her voice trail away. Though she couldn't imagine the haughty Goddess on intimate terms with the Cohens, if Felix married her he would want to make her aquainted with his friends. It was not for Fanny to prejudice Miriam against her.

"You have met Lady Sophia?" asked Miriam, her tone casual.

"Only in the sense of coming face to face with her in the park." Fanny's good intentions crumbled under the assault of jealousy and remembered indignation. "She gave Felix the cut direct! He was sadly cast down, yet he apologized for her. He said that as daughter of a marquis she was entitled to hold herself on high form and in general her manners were perfection."

"He extolled her to me as a pattern-card of perfection, guaranteed to please his parents and to become an admirable countess."

"I daresay she will."

"I don't recall that he ever mentioned her good nature, or her warm heart."

"Nor to me. I don't believe she possesses either! No, that is not fair, Miriam. I never made her acquaintance and ought not to judge her. I only hope she will make him happy."

Yet that was not quite true. Fanny nurtured a tiny, secret hope that Felix had forgotten the Goddess. As the days passed he never spoke of her, made no move to leave Nettledene, appeared perfectly contented with Fanny's company, and the Cohens', and the children's. Fanny found it more and more difficult to keep reminding herself of his determination to take a bride of rank and fortune.

She abandoned herself to the joy of being with him, enhanced by the rapid improvement in Frank's health, and by the Cohens' friendship.

In fact, she was perfectly at home at Nettledene, as Felix noted. He had no excuse for lingering. He woke one morning to the realization that over a fortnight had passed since Rothschild presented him with that incredible bank draft — and his parents still knew nothing of his luck.

"I must go to Westwood," he announced at breakfast. "I haven't been home since before I went to Vienna, ten months ago."

"And I daresay you have not written to your mama since Waterloo to tell her you are unscathed!" said Miriam. "What of Lady Sophia? Shall you go via London to see her?"

Startled, Felix sought to conceal the fact that the object of his attentions had somehow slipped his mind. "The Daventrys are unlikely to be in Town in July," he said. "Their place is in Northamptonshire, in quite the wrong direction. My first duty is to my parents. Besides, it's only proper that I should inform them of my intentions before I offer for Lady Sophia."

"Naturally." Isaac frowned at Miriam, who appeared unaccountably amused. Felix had more than once been baffled by her sense of humour at his expense. At least when Fanny laughed at him he always knew why.

Fanny was not amused now. Her woebegone eyes caused a peculiar pang somewhere beneath his waistcoat.

"Cheer up," he said. "I'll be back long before Frank is fit to report to Horse Guards' Parade, either to tell you I've won Lady Sophia's hand, or to weep on your shoulder because she refused me."

She made a pitiful attempt to smile. "Pray do not disappear to Vienna again in the interim. We cannot keep Frank abed much longer, can we, ma'am?"

"No, he is by no means the docile kind of patient I prefer," said Miriam lightly. "How shall you travel, Felix? Do you want to borrow a carriage?"

"Thank you, no, I shall ride. It's quicker cross country via Salisbury than trying to stick to the post roads. Poor Trevor will have to endure yet another journey by the Mail."

They talked of the route to Somerset. Fanny gradually recovered her countenance, but Felix could not forget her dismay at the news of his departure. Before he went up to say goodbye to Frank and the children, he asked her outright, "Are you uncomfortable here?"

"Oh no. The Cohens are all that is kind; indeed, they have made us feel a part of the family." She could not blame him for the cold, hollow sense of desolation that engulfed her. It was entirely her own fault for allowing that tiny seed of hope to take root. Yet he had seen her unhappiness and it distressed him. She did her best to disguise its cause. "I . . . I am a widgeon to worry a little about what we shall do when Frank is recovered."

"A great widgeon," he said severely. "I imagine the army will have a new posting for Frank, but if you find yourselves in any difficulty, I shall not abandon you. Did you not say that you trust me?"

"We do," she assented, dismayed, wishing she had thought of a reason for her low spirits that would not make him doubt her faith in him. Of course she trusted him. Had he not come to the rescue in Brussels when she was on the verge of despair?

But her trust did not lessen her heartache when he rode off down the drive.

As Felix rode west through the green countryside, Fanny's sad face haunted him. Did she really trust him not to leave her in the lurch? Her agreement had been subdued, not the hearty confirmation he had hoped for.

Perhaps she guessed that he had forgotten Lady Sophia's existence for days on end. Perhaps she thought it was "out of sight, out of mind" with him. He hadn't told her it was a vision of her sufferings that had taken him back to Brussels, only that Rothschild had sent him with a letter for Wellington.

Yet the closer he came to Westwood, the more persuaded he was that he had made the right decision. The knowledge that he had returned for her sake could only have aroused unwarranted expectations, even in so sensible and modest a young lady as Fanny.

Riding across the Somerset plain, he fixed his mind on his parents' delight when he told them about his windfall and his intention of asking for Lady Sophia's hand.

The neatly pollarded willows along the drainage channel hid the house from Felix until he cantered across a flat wooden bridge. On the far side he drew rein and gazed at his birthright.

Marble pillars glowed pinkly in the evening sun. Challenging the precipitous limestone slope of the Mendip Hills that rose behind the mansion, the Palladian façade was Felix's grandfather's ostentatious contribution to Westwood. The family had nearly been bankrupted by his father's determination to modernize the interior of the sprawling Tudor house, after an elaborate and expensive design by Robert Adam.

There was no place here for the Ingrams, Felix thought sadly. If Fanny had at first found Nettledene alarmingly grand, his home would overwhelm her, though lack of funds had reduced the ceremony observed by the household.

For instance, a groom permanently on the watch for visitors was a luxury long since dispensed with. Felix rode around the side of the house to the stables. A stable boy he didn't recognize received his hired horse with scorn, his announcement that he was Lord Roworth with suspicion. It was a long time since he had spent more than a few days at Westwood.

At least the butler knew him, though it would have been beneath his dignity to give even his master's heir a welcome as warm as Samuels'.

"The family are dressing, my lord," he said. "I shall send a footman to wait upon your lordship."

The direst poverty could not have prevented the earl and countess dressing for dinner, however threadbare their evening clothes. Nor would they appreciate being interrupted, even by the arrival of their son and heir. Felix changed quickly out of his riding coat and breeches and went down to the gallery where the family always gathered before dinner in the summer. Windows opening onto the garden all along the west side made it drafty in winter but delightful on a warm July evening.

"Felix!" Lady Victoria pounced in a flurry of white muslin. A plump, pretty sixteen-year-old, she wore her long blond hair tied back simply with a pink ribbon, to denote her schoolroom status. She hung on his arm, merry blue eyes sparkling. "So you deign to grace us with your noble presence."

"Where did you learn such high-flown language, Vickie?" he drawled.

"She has been reading romances from the lending library. Pay her no mind. Felix, how good it is to see you."

He took Constantia's hands in his and kissed her cheek. At twenty-two she was as beautiful as at eighteen, even in a high-necked, far from modish gown of blue jaconet. Golden ringlets, eyes of a deeper blue than the rest of the family, tender mouth in a heart-shaped face whose usual shy gravity was dispelled now by a joyous smile.

Connie was his favourite sister, though Augusta, now a married matron, was nearer his age. In their youth, Connie had worshipped him and followed him into many a scrape. The chattering tomboy had metamorphosed into a quiet, graceful young lady without lessening the affection between them. Felix knew very well that her retiring, compliant manner hid a will as resolute as Miriam's, a heart as steadfast — and as kind — as Fanny's.

"Connie was afraid you had been killed at Waterloo," said Vickie with a ghoulish relish that reminded him of little Jane Prynne. "Were you there? Was it very horrid?"

"Dreadful. But it brought me a stroke of luck I'll tell you about when Mama and my father come down."

"The vicar and his wife and the curate are dining with us this evening," Connie said doubtfully.

"He can tell us anyway."

Felix shook his head. "No, this is family business. It will have to wait."

"Then I shall have to make sure they leave early," declared Vickie.

Her brother and sister rounded on her with dire threats of retribution if she misbe-

261

haved and put the earl in a tweak on Felix's first evening home.

"I'll fill your favourite reticule with snails," Felix promised.

"Pooh, you are too fine a gentleman to go hunting sn . . ." She choked on the last word as Lord Westwood entered the gallery.

"Too fine to go hunting?" queried the earl with a smile. "Have you joined the dandy set, Felix? I hear Brummell will not go beyond the first field for fear of muddying his boot-tops. My dear boy, it is a pleasure to have you with us again."

"My pleasure, sir." He bowed and shook his father's hand. "I hope I find you well?"

Despite his lined face and grizzled hair, the earl looked very like his heir, tall and broad-shouldered, with a still handsome, patrician countenance. A decade of struggling to stay one step ahead of the bailiffs had not crushed his haughty air, so innate that even his evident pleasure at greeting his only son scarcely softened it. Felix admired his determination to keep up the standards of his class through thick and thin.

Lady Westwood came in, a *grande dame* still though a necklace of pearls and jet gleamed where once diamonds had sparkled. Her pale blonde hair showed no touch of grey, her calm face was almost unlined. Felix bowed and kissed her hand.

"An unexpected pleasure, Felix," she said coolly.

"I beg your pardon, ma'am, for not having advised you of my visit — indeed, for not having written in some time. I have been excessively occupied with business of late." Except for the past fortnight, he thought guiltily, when his friends' company and Fanny's comfort had been his sole concerns. He was glad of the interruption when their guests were announced.

Mr Beneton, the dignified, elderly vicar, had christened Felix, and his wife's toad-eating was too familiar to be offensive. The curate, Enoch Jones, was a stranger, however. A dark, wiry young man with the long, narrow face of a melancholy mule, he never took his worshipful eyes from Lady Constantia's face. Connie was kind to him in an absent way, but Felix observed no sign that she returned his all too obvious affections. Just as well, for if she set her heart on a doubtless penniless cleric, he suspected she'd have him, come hell or high water.

After dinner, when the gentlemen joined the ladies in the perfectly proportioned drawing room, Vickie beckoned Mr Jones to her side with an imperious gesture. He cast a yearning glance at her sister but obeyed. Suspicious, Felix lingered nearby, leaning against the elegant Adam mantelpiece.

"I fear you are unwell, sir," she said with the utmost solicitude as the curate took a seat beside her on a crocodile-legged sofa.

"Unwell?" he asked in alarm. "I assure you, Lady Victoria, apart from the usual touch of dyspepsia, I am very well."

"But you are so pale! Perhaps you are sickening for some horrid illness."

"I confess I felt an unusual palpitation of the heart as we drove up from the village."

"You did? I wonder that you have ventured out. The evenings are monstrous treacherous at this season."

"They are?"

"Why yes. The warmth of the day does not prepare one's constitution for the cool evenings. If I were you, I should . . ."

Lady Westwood called Felix to come and satisfy Mrs Beneton's curiosity about English Society in Brussels. His own curiosity as to what remedy his devilish youngest sister proposed was soon satisfied. Mr Jones crossed the room to speak to the vicar; the vicar came to speak to his wife. With a discontented air, Mrs Beneton turned to the countess and said, "Mr Jones is unwell, I regret to say. We shall have to beg your ladyship's indulgence and take our leave before tea."

As the vicarage party left, Vickie threw a triumphant glance at Felix and Connie. Her triumph was shortlived.

"Victoria, it is time for you to retire," said her mother.

Few were those who dared argue with Lady Westwood. Vickie retired. The eloquent plea in her eyes as she bade her brother goodnight made him grin. He must remember to tell Fanny. Vickie's cunning victory and subsequent defeat would amuse her no end.

"I trust Victoria is not developing a tendre for that young puppy," said the earl with a frown.

"Good Lord, no, sir," Felix exclaimed. "On the contrary, she was . . ." Connie shook her head at him in warning and he realized he had been about to reveal their sister's devious stratagem.

"She was protecting me from his attentions, Papa."

"Has Mr Jones been troubling you, Constantia?" asked Lady Westwood censoriously.

"Oh no, Mama."

It was Felix's turn to rescue her, or rather young Mr Jones. "I daresay Vickie's imagination is run wild." His mother's stare told him that imagination in a young girl was no more acceptable than presumption in a curate. He hurried to change the subject. "Now that we are alone, I can tell you my news. Mr Rothschild has given me a bonus, a very large bonus, as a reward for what he is kind enough to regard as an extraordinary service."

"Felix, that is wonderful," cried Connie, but Lord Westwood's frown returned. He walked restlessly to the window.

Watching him, his wife said, "Constantia, you may leave us. Talk of business is not at all suitable for a young lady's ears."

Felix received another eloquently beseeching glance as Connie swallowed a protest and departed.

The earl turned. "I cannot like to be obliged to a Jew moneylender," he said, vexed. "It is bad enough that the fellow has employed you these past four years. You know my opinion of your decision in that regard."

"With respect, sir, Nathan Rothschild is a highly esteemed banker, and on the friendliest terms with the Duke of Wellington. I am proud to have been his agent, but my reward will, I believe, permit me to leave his employ."

His father was startled. "So much?"

"Nineteen thousand."

"Nineteen thousand pounds?" His father paled and sat down abruptly. "What did you do to earn so much?"

"Nothing to be ashamed of, I promise you, but a confidential matter which I cannot discuss. Sir, am I right in thinking this will allow me to offer for the lady I admire?" His parents both stared at him. "The lady you admire?" repeated his mother warily. "Do we know her?"

"I believe you must be acquainted with her mother, ma'am. She is Lady Sophia Gerrold, the elder daughter of the Marquis of Daventry."

"Daventry's daughter!" Lord Westwood exclaimed. "My dear boy, why did you not tell us you had reached an understanding with the girl? With her fortune, something might have been arranged despite our lack of funds."

"Lady Sophia? A thoroughly suitable choice, Felix. I did not know you had so much common sense. A well-bred young lady of superior family — an excellent match."

"Not a settled one, however! I beg your pardon if I have misled you, but we have no understanding. Though I flatter myself she

267

was uncommonly kind to me just before her family left Brussels, Lady Sophia has rejected many suitors."

The earl and countess were only slightly disappointed. Neither believed that Lady Sophia could possibly reject the heir to Westwood, now that his fortunes were reestablished. Their confidence was contagious, so Felix wasn't sure why he felt a vague dissatisfaction with life as he followed them upstairs later.

As he had assured Fanny, his parents agreed that Lady Sophia would be the perfect wife for him. What more could he ask?

"I shall be able to quit working," he explained to Vickie, leaning against the post of her pink-and white curtained bed. Perhaps that was the trouble — he enjoyed his work. "I'll come home to live and learn to manage the estate."

"Good. Shall I have a Season, Felix? I'll be seventeen next month."

"Yes, if you behave yourself until the spring."

"Impossible," she sighed, "but I shall try."

He didn't tell her about Lady Sophia. She was too young to understand, even if the marbled cover of a Minerva Press novel was poking out from beneath her bedcovers.

Connie was waiting for him, reclining on a chaise longue in her dressing room, a shabby blue Paisley shawl about her shoulders.

"I'll buy you a silk dressing gown," he said, perching on a corner of her dressing table, "and how would you like a cashmire one for winter?"

"Did Mr Rothschild really give you so much money? What did you do to earn it?"

Swearing her to secrecy, he told the story. "Father will be able to make me an allowance suited to my station," he continued, "so I could live in Town but I mean to settle at Westwood, except when you are in London."

"I? Why should I go to London?"

"You and Vickie shall have your Seasons in Town."

"Oh no! I am too old to make my comeout."

"Yes, my dear, you are an ape-leader and an antidote, which is why that callow puppy of a curate never took his languishing eyes off you throughout dinner. You will enjoy the balls and the theatre, Con, and you will meet gentlemen more proper than a country curate to be your husband."

"But Felix, I don't want to go. I have had offers from eligible gentlemen, you know, even here in the country. Two or three times I was quite in disgrace for refusing splendid matches, but I could not bring myself to marry a man I did not respect, only for the sake of the family."

He frowned, unsure why he was more disturbed than her words appeared to warrant. "You did not care for any of them?"

"How could I, when they all seemed to believe they were doing me a favour by offering for my hand? Mama said I must not regard it, that a daughter of the Earl of Westwood, even portionless, is a fit bride for the highest ranking peer in the land."

"So she is, and you, my dear, are a prize beyond compare. I am glad you were strong enough to hold out against the coxcombs who did not appreciate you. But now you'll have a dowry, everything will be quite different."

"I don't want to go," she said stubbornly.

"Even if you had my wife to chaperon you instead of Mama?"

"Your wife! Felix, are you going to marry? Tell me all about her at once!"

"She's known as the Goddess to her admirers, of whom she has many, alas." Felix explained the situation and described Lady Sophia's fair, graceful beauty and cool dignity.

"She sounds very like Mama," murmured Connie. "I expect she will make a superb countess one day."

"I can only hope she will choose to be an English countess, not a Belgian comtesse. One of her suitors in Brussels was an excessively wealthy Belgian count."

"A foreigner, however rich, is surely no competition for you. Who are her other beaux?"

"Mostly officers, with the advantage of showy uniforms. However, some may have met their end at Waterloo," he added somberly. "Believe me, that's not how I would wish to overcome my rivals."

"Those poor soldiers! I wish I could do something to help them. Did you . . . did you lose many friends?"

He told her about Sir Alexander Gordon, and Canning, and De Lancey. "And others were badly wounded. Lord Fitzroy Somerset lost his arm, though he is remarkably cheerful about it! Frank Ingram was blown up by one of his own shells and dashed near kicked the bucket."

"Ingram? I remember you mentioned in one of your all too rare letters that you were sharing lodgings with a young couple called Ingram."

"Brother and sister, not a couple. He's an

artillery officer, as was their father. Miss Ingram has followed the drum all her life. She's an admirable person, Connie. Though she has been through the greatest hardships, she keeps a sense of humour, and she is always kind and hospitable. She and Frank adopted the daughter of a fellow officer who was killed in Spain, an adorable little girl. Fanny could not care for her better if she were her own child."

"I should like to meet Miss Ingram."

"Impossible, I fear. They have no connections and don't move in the first circles. Indeed, when I brought them to England, Fanny was quite overcome by the grandeur of Miriam and Isaac's establishment, and the Cohens live in a simple, unpretentious way, you know."

Connie gave him an odd look. "You brought the Ingrams to England?"

"Frank needed Miriam's care. I've told you how she saved my shoulder in France with her medical skill."

"Yes, of course. And I have wanted to meet Mr and Mrs Cohen this age."

"You're a dear, Con." He crossed to the chaise longue and gave her a hug. If only his parents were like her! "I'd like nothing better than to make them known to you, but it can't be done. Mama would flay me alive with her tongue if I introduced my friends to you."

CHAPTER 15

Summoned to his mother's private sitting room a few days later, Felix entered with a feeling of trepidation, a vestige of his childhood. The formal, if slightly faded, elegance of gilt scrollwork and green striped satin did nothing to set him at ease.

Lady Westwood glanced up from her writing desk. "I am writing to Augusta," she said. "Have you any message for your sister?"

"My compliments will suffice, I thank you." He had no great affection for Gussie, who had been a prim and proper miss — and given to tale-bearing — since earliest youth.

Her ladyship wrote a few words, set down her pen and turned to him. "Much as we enjoy your company, Felix," she said, "I feel you would be wise to pay your addresses to Lady Sophia in the near future. According to the Post, many members of the ton are departing for Paris in the train of Wellington and King Louis."

"If you think it advisable, ma'am, I shall leave in the morning."

"Westwood informs me that you have expressed Radical ideas about farm wages and the Corn Laws." Only a slight curl of the lip indicated her disapproval; her tone remained calm and collected. "You will do well to hold your tongue on such subjects when you speak to Lord Daventry."

"Yes, ma'am." As though he would rattle on about agriculture, especially Isaac's liberal views, when he begged the Goddess's father for permission to pop the question! At most he would assure the marquis that Lord Westwood had not, like many another, let the estate go to rack and ruin to pay for the improvements to the house.

Felix had never taken much interest in the work of the estate. He had been pleasurably surprised, as he rode around the farms with his father's steward the past few days, to discover that the land was in excellent heart. The orchards and fertile fields of the Somerset plain were well-ditched and drained, the upland farm productive, buildings in good repair, woodland cleared of undergrowth and dead limbs.

Mortgages had their disadvantages but,

now that the debt could be paid off, West-wood was able to support tenants and landlord alike in comfort. With Lady Sophia's dowry, the family fortunes would be restored to their former splendour.

"I have discreetly mentioned Lady Sophia's name to one or two of my correspondents," Lady Westwood continued. "Everything I have heard confirms my belief that I could not hope for a more suitable daughter-in-law. Your choice is admirable, my son, and it only remains for me to wish you good fortune in your application for her hand."

She tilted her head in a way that was both dismissal and permission to kiss her cheek. Felix obliged.

At six o'clock of a sunny evening, Felix rode into London. The first thing to be done was to discover Lady Sophia's whereabouts. He could call in St James's Square to enquire, but should the Daventrys be in residence it was an awkward hour to make his bow.

Dinner at Brooks's, he decided — even in July many of his friends were probably in Town.

His thoughts turned involuntarily towards Nettledene. Two or three hours of daylight remained. He could easily ride down there, make sure all was well with Fanny, and return to Town in the morning in good time to call in St James's Square. He had spent so much time in the saddle recently that another twenty-odd miles was nothing.

He arrived at Nettledene just before the dinner hour, left his horse in the stables, and went into the house by the back door. As he reached the front hall, a light step on the stairs made him glance up.

Fanny was coming down. Lost in thought she didn't notice him. Instead of making his presence known, he watched her. She looked like a wood sprite in a leaf-green gown trimmed with knots of brown ribbon, a green ribbon threaded through her shining brown curls. Felix hardly dared breathe lest he startle her into flight.

As she came closer, he saw that she was a melancholy sprite, her pensive face clouded. What was wrong? Dismayed, he was about to step forward and demand an answer when Samuels entered the hall.

"My lord! Welcome back. I'll set another place this instant."

"Felix!" Sun broke through the clouds as Fanny sped down the remaining steps with sparkling eyes and glowing smile. Then she stopped, put her hand to her mouth, and blushed delightfully. "I beg your pardon, my lord. It's just that Miriam and Isaac call you Felix and I . . ."

He took her hands. "And I trust you will, too. We are still friends, are we not?"

"Oh yes." Her flush deepened. "Yes, I hope we are friends. You will call me Fanny?"

"If I may?" he teased. "I don't wish to presume."

"Felix!" Miriam came down the stairs with Isaac behind her. "What a surprise."

He grinned at her. "Is it not always a surprise when I inflict myself upon you?"

"A surprise, but hardly an infliction," said Isaac. "Come and have a glass of sherry before dinner."

"I ought to change out of my dirt."

"That is not necessary," Miriam assured him. "Fanny and I don't object to a little odor of horse with our horseradish, do we?"

She linked arms with Fanny, who smiled and shook her head, still very pink-cheeked.

"Horseradish?" queried Felix. "Roast beef for dinner? Fanny, do you recall Henriette's Yorkshire pudding?"

"How could I forget?" She laughed, her confusion dissipating as she told the Cohens about the Yorkshire soufflé.

They went into the drawing room. A glass

of sherry in his hand, Felix cornered Miriam.

"Has Fanny been unhappy?"

"A little."

Looking towards the French doors, where Fanny stood chatting gaily — almost flirtatiously — with Isaac, he frowned. "She does not seem so."

"Now, she is not!" said Miriam, exasperated.

Puzzled, he asked, "Is she worried about Frank?"

"I hardly think so. He improves daily, and walks in his chamber. He will come downstairs tomorrow."

"I'm glad to hear it. But what is wrong with Fanny?"

"Perhaps she has not enough to do." She seemed evasive. "She is used to a busy life, remember. Here at Nettledene, the housekeeping is out of her hands, Hannah takes care of Anita, and even Frank no longer permits either of us to tend to his wounds. Fanny reads a good deal, but she is accustomed to more activity."

"Does she not walk?"

"In the garden. It is not safe to walk alone beyond at present. We are close to the Dover road and discharged soldiers are beginning to flock back to England. Of necessity they were taught to be aggressive, but without the army's discipline many of them are disorderly, to put it mildly."

"No, she must not go outside the garden alone!"

"If you are staying for a day or two, you might walk or ride with her, or take a carriage and go farther afield."

"I'm on my way to propose to Lady Sophia, but I daresay I can spare a day or two. My mother fears the Daventrys may follow the ton to Paris, but if so I can always go after them. My parents are cock-a-hoop, Miriam, that I have found so eligible a bride — always supposing that she accepts me. She will be an ideal countess one day."

"No doubt," Miriam said dryly. "Fanny has told me something of her."

"Fanny may not have done her justice," Felix protested, discomforted. "Lady Sophia was . . . well, rude, to give you the word without the bark. No blame attaches to her. She was brought up, as I was, to judge people by their status in Society. It was you who taught me how muttonheaded that is."

"Let us hope that you will succeed in passing on the lesson to your wife."

"First, let us hope that she will consent to be my wife," said Felix.

"You don't seem to be in a quake that she

may not."

"Of course I am," he said uncertainly, "though my parents are convinced she will accept. In their eyes, the future Earl of Westwood is good enough for anyone," he explained as Samuels came in to announce dinner.

Over the roast beef, they talked about the children. Spurred by competition, both Anita and Amos were beginning to learn their letters.

"Luckily their names both start with A," Fanny said, laughing. "As it is, Anita brags because hers also ends with an A. Felix, she has taken to calling me Aunt instead of Tía, because Amos does."

He inspected her with mock seriousness. "Believe it or not, you don't look a day older for being called Aunt. Indeed, you could easily pass for eighteen." Only a slight exaggeration, for she was looking particularly pretty with the soft gleam of candlelight on her hair and the merriment returned to her brown eyes.

The compliment brought a touch more colour to her cheeks but she retorted with spirit, "I hope not. To be forever regarded as a naïve young girl would not suit me at all."

"Bravo!" Miriam cried. "Too many men

281

treat women as incompetent children all their lives."

"I shouldn't dare," said Isaac, with a loving smile for his wife. "Amos is learning that lesson early. Anita is a bright child."

"Is she not?" Fanny was delighted. "Felix, you will be amazed at how much better she speaks now than when you left. Hannah corrects her much more consistently than I ever did."

"Does she still claim her papa was in the artirelly?"

"Well, yes, but that's because it's difficult to pronounce, not an error of grammar."

"Her grammar is much better than Amos's now," said Miriam. "Of course he is a little younger, but he tries harder because she is there. Being together is very good for both of them."

"Anita could not be happier," Fanny affirmed.

Nor could she, Felix thought with relief, entranced by her dancing dimples. Whatever the cause of her sadness it seemed to have vanished.

After dinner the ladies withdrew. Felix accepted a glass of a superb Armagnac he himself had discovered in Bordeaux while smuggling gold to Spain. It was as magnificent as ever, worthy of his full attention, but after a few sips he suggested that they should take their glasses and join the ladies.

Miriam was alone in the drawing room. "We were not expecting you so soon," she said. "Fanny stepped out into the garden. There is a full moon, and the flowers' perfume always seems strongest on a warm evening. Call her in, Felix."

He set down his glass and went to the French doors. The fragrance of roses hung heavy in the still air. By the light of the rising moon, Fanny's slight figure was visible at a distance, strolling away from him. He went after her.

Hearing footsteps on the flagstoned path, Fanny turned. Her breath caught in her throat as she recognized Felix's tall, powerful silhouette, his hair gleaming gold in the light from the house. Her determination not to confound friendship with warmer feelings wavered and grew dim.

She wanted to speak to him in private, but what folly to choose such a romantic setting!

With a stern, silent warning to her fluttering heart, she forced herself to speak calmly. "Felix, I can never thank you enough for bringing us here."

Unable to resist laying her hand on his arm, she felt the hard muscle of an active, vigorous man beneath the smooth broad-cloth. He covered her hand with his, warm, strong yet gentle.

She rushed on before she was lost. "Frank is recovering much faster than he would have in Brussels and Anita adores Amos and Hannah, and Leah too. No one could be kinder than Miriam and Isaac. You are fortunate indeed to have such friends."

"I know it."

"Miriam is so very generous. She and I have a great deal in common, having both trailed about the world after our menfolk, but I think she does not quite understand why I refused the new gowns she offered. I accepted this one — an old one of hers, altered — because she had guests." She had noticed Felix's admiration of her dress and she could not bear that he might suppose she was taking advantage of Miriam's generosity. "I did not want her to be ashamed of me."

"Miriam would never be ashamed of anyone because of their dress."

"Perhaps it is just my silly pride. But oh, Felix, I don't wish to be more beholden than I need."

He gazed down at her earnest face. Shadowed, her eyes were full of mystery. Her soft mouth tempted him to gather her in his arms, to press kisses upon those tender lips. Hot desire flooded through his body.

His senses reeled as he fought the assault of moonlight, roses, and the enchanted sprite at his side. To his aid he summoned the image of the Goddess's cool beauty . . .

"Felix, have you found her?" Miriam's voice came from the house.

"We had better go in," said Fanny uncertainly.

Had she guessed at the turmoil within him, read hunger in his eyes? Her trust rebuked his passion. If Miriam's voice had not intervened, he'd have forfeited that precious trust, for at the crucial moment the Goddess's image had deserted him.

He tucked Fanny's little hand beneath his arm and together they returned to the drawing room.

Afraid that desire was writ large on his face, Felix declared his intention of going up to see if Frank was still awake. He took his abandoned glass of brandy, and begged another of Isaac for the patient, with Miriam's doubtful acquiescence. Reaffirming his friendship for the captain was, he felt, a sure way to quell his fancy to seduce the captain's sister.

Frank was awake and glad to see him. Sitting up in bed, he was still pale and very thin, but he no longer appeared to be at death's door. He rolled the Armagnac around his mouth with every evidence of appreciation.

"I haven't tasted anything like this since one of my men snabbled a couple of bottles after we crossed the Pyrenees. Naturally, I was forced to confiscate them to maintain order in the ranks."

"Naturally. Everyone knows Wellington don't stand for looting. Here's to your very good health."

The captain's grin slipped. "And to yours, my lord."

"My lord?" Felix rallied him. "As I recall, Captain, you were wont to use my name."

He made an effort to be cheerful. "My humble apologies, Roworth. I intended no insult, I promise you."

"Then I shan't sink to the infamy of calling out a sick man, though Miriam and Fanny both think you well on the road to recovery. What's wrong?"

"Wrong? What makes you think anything's wrong? They are right, I grow stronger every day."

"If you don't want to tell me, that's your privilege, but perhaps I can help."

"No one can help, or Mrs Cohen would have. I expected too much of her skills.

Look at me." He threw back the covers, pushed himself to the edge of the bed, and stood up, a trifle wobbly. Stripping off his nightshirt, he revealed a body seamed and knotted with countless scars, white and red and purple, from shoulders to thighs. "What woman will want me now?" he asked bitterly.

Felix steeled himself not to show his horror. "You appear to be . . . er . . . intact where it matters."

"Would that I weren't, for then I might not care. Or that at least some sign appeared on my face as a warning of what is below. Better, perhaps, that the blast had blown off my head instead of leaving me like this, a sight to send any female into hysterics."

"Did Fanny and Miriam run screaming at the sight?"

"They are not ordinary females," Frank said roughly. "They saw only the hurt, not the hideousness." Shivering despite the warmth of the night, he reached for his nightshirt.

Unable to deny that Fanny and Miriam were out of the common way, Felix helped him put his arms in the sleeves and return to bed, for his meagre strength was exhausted. Lying back, he closed his eyes. "It's bloody humiliating being so weak," he said, trying for wryness.

"Are you too weak to lift a glass? It would be a pity to waste the Armagnac."

"True. That much I think I can manage." He sat up and took the glass from Felix.

Sipping the amber nectar, they talked of indifferent matters until Felix decided it was time to leave him to sleep. He delved into his mind for words of comfort.

"The scars are bound to fade over time, you know. And one day you'll find a woman as exceptional as your sister, who loves you and doesn't give a damn."

"Then Lord help her, for I'm not likely ever to be in a position to marry. Roworth, thank you. You've been devilish good to us — don't think I don't appreciate it."

Both embarrassed, they clasped hands briefly and Felix left.

The following day, Felix begged a picnic from Mrs Samuels, borrowed a carriage from the Cohens, and took Fanny, Anita, and Amos to Ightham.

With a promise of bixits at the end of the climb, the children's short legs willingly stumped up Oldbury Hill. At the top a brisk breeze cooled them after their exertions. Fanny took off her daisy-wreathed straw hat before turning with tousled hair and rosy, laughing face to admire the view.

Somehow she managed to look enchanting even in a dishevelment that would have horrified Lady Sophia — or his mother.

Deciding it was too windy at the summit for the picnic, they returned to the shelter of some bushes half way down. Food restored the children's energy and they spent the next quarter of an hour running down the steep slope into Felix's arms.

What a marvellous father he would be, Fanny thought, not for the first time. Would Lady Sophia let him play with his children, or would they be confined to nursery and schoolroom, as she knew happened in many great families? Hair ruffled, neckcloth awry, he was enjoying himself as much as they were.

Nonetheless, he tired of the fun before they did. "Now we'll go to feed the swans," he announced, adding in a lower voice to Fanny, "We could have gone first, but I remembered Anita's propensity to give hungry birds all available sustenance, and I didn't want to risk the picnic."

"Very wise," she agreed with a smile.

"What's swans?" asked Amos.

"Great big white ducks wiv long necks," said Anita, glowing with excitement. "There's swans in the park in Brussels. They be . . . they are always hungry."

The swans on the moat of the ancient fortified manor were almost as delighted with the remains of the picnic as Anita was to feed them. Amos was nervous at first and clung to Fanny's hand. He lost his wariness all too soon. Felix caught his jacket just in time to stop him tumbling into the moat. Then he tried to feed a swan from his hand instead of throwing the crust. The swan pecked his fingers and he sent up a howl, more of shock than of pain.

He sobbed into Fanny's shoulder as they walked back to the carriage. Anita, her hand in Felix's, kept stopping on tiptoe to peer into his face and ask anxiously, "Are you awright, Amos? Did it hurt? He's only crying 'cos he's liccle, Uncle Felix," she explained. "He's brave, really."

Half a sticky bun from a confectioner's cheered Amos. Sticky-faced and sticky-fingered, he and Anita both fell fast asleep as soon as the carriage began to move.

"Not an entirely successful outing, I fear," said Felix wryly.

"Oh, but it was." And all too easy to pretend they were just an ordinary family. "I have not had so much fun in an age. There is bound to be some contretemps or other when one takes two small children out, and Amos is perfectly all right. Thank heaven you caught him before he fell in. If you ever plan to go near water again, warn me so that I can take dry clothes, in case." Only she must not assume that there would ever be another outing. She wished the words unsaid.

But he laughed and said, as if he took it for granted, "I will. I wanted it to be a surprise. Next time I shall ask your advice beforehand."

"The house was a charming surprise and I should like to see more of it some day. Felix, I want to ask your advice, or rather your opinion. Miriam gave me a book to read and I don't quite understand all of it." Sighing, she rearranged Anita more comfortably against her side, ignoring the stickiness. "I am woefully ignorant, you know. Mama taught us what she could, but books were always difficult to come by."

"What book did Miriam lend you?" Felix asked cautiously. "I've never pretended to be inclined to book-learning."

"Mary Wollstonecraft's *A Vindication of the Rights of Women*."

"I might have guessed," he groaned. "Can you not ask Miriam — or even Isaac — to explain?"

"Isaac confuses me with philosophy, and

Miriam's explanations tend to turn into harangues. She feels very strongly on the subject."

"You don't need to tell me! All right, what is it you want to know?"

All the way back to Nettledene, they discussed Mary Wollstonecraft's ideas. Felix had never read the book, nor heard it mentioned by anyone but Miriam except in tones of anathema. He was surprised at how much sense her arguments made, at least as propounded by Fanny. Because of her lack of experience with English society, Fanny was confused by a few points. He did his best to elucidate.

"Thank you," she said as they drove up to Nettledene. "Now I understand. You explained very clearly."

Pleased, he told her, "So clearly I almost convinced myself."

Her laugh rang out and Anita stirred. "What's funny, Tía?" she asked sleepily.

"Uncle Felix, love."

"Uncle Felix makes you laugh a lot." She bestowed an approving look on him.

Amos woke as Felix carried him into the house. Set on his feet, he ran to hug Miriam, who came from the drawing room to greet them.

"Mama, a great big swan did bite me."

"A great big swan bited you," Anita corrected.

Felix's eyes met Fanny's, brimming with mirth, and they both burst into laughter. His outing, he decided, had been not merely successful but utterly delightful.

It was a damned shame her noble grandfather had cast off her mother, thus exiling her from the world she should have belonged to, from his family's world. As it was, his parents would consider her and Frank, and especially Anita, almost as unacceptable as his Jewish friends.

CHAPTER 16

"Felix, I wish you will stop flirting with Fanny." Miriam frowned at him over the gold-rimmed glasses she had taken to wearing for reading.

"Flirting! I am simply enjoying her company," he protested, indignant.

"I believe flirtation comes so naturally to you that you don't even notice what you are about," she said dryly. "From the outside it looks like flirting, though I cannot be sure what Fanny thinks. You are about to propose to Lady Sophia — indeed you meant to do so a week ago! — and it is shockingly unfair to her."

"I suppose so," he conceded, "but she need never know."

Taking off her spectacles, Miriam gave him an exasperated look. "While you and Fanny are both guests in my house, I hope you will respect my wishes."

"Of course, m'dear." Twice before she had

objected to his gallantries, with a peasant girl in the Pyrenees, and with a sophisticated lady who happened to be the wife of his host in Bordeaux. She had probably been right both times, so she could be right now. This case was quite different, though, because Fanny was his friend. He had never enjoyed so delightful a flirtation, if that was what it was.

Suddenly Miriam's words sank in. "A week ago? Have I really been here so long? Good gad, she may be in Paris by now. And it's also time I was reporting to Rothschild. I must go up to Town."

"Isaac has business in London tomorrow. You can travel with him." She set aside her book as Isaac and Fanny, dressed for dinner, came into the drawing room. "Felix goes with you tomorrow morning, my love. His leave from Mr Rothschild is at an end."

Fanny's face fell. Even as he discussed travel arrangements with Isaac, Felix reinterpreted Miriam's declaration: "It is shockingly unfair to her."

Unfair to the Goddess, he had assumed. Had she meant, to Fanny? Impossible! Fanny knew very well that he hoped to marry Lady Sophia. He had kept her, as a trusted friend, apprised of every phase of his courtship. She understood that his family's rank made it necessary for him to take a noble bride, while their condition made a wealthy wife advisable.

As Fanny had pointed out herself, she was not a naïve young girl. She had had enough suitors not to be misled by a pleasant flirtation between friends. No, Miriam had meant he was being unfair to Lady Sophia, and she was right, as usual. When he was married, he resolved reluctantly, he'd foreswear dalliance with any but his wife.

Fanny's cheerfulness that evening was a trifle forced, and she retired early. When he bade her goodnight, Felix renewed his assurances that she and Frank could count on him in any difficulties.

She smiled up at him sadly. "You are so very . . . kind."

He thought he heard Miriam mutter to her husband: "Blind!" but it made no sense so he must have misheard. He asked Fanny to give Anita a farewell kiss from him.

She nodded, whispered a strangled "Goodnight, and goodbye," and left the room.

Treading slowly up the stairs, Fanny castigated herself. Would she never learn? Every time he arrived after an absence, her spirits soared. Every time he departed she plunged into the slough of despond. Her mind knew he was not for her; if only she could persuade her heart of that truth.

She went to her chamber and sat in a chair by the window, gazing out over the gardens, dimly lit by a waning moon, shadowed as a future without Felix. Once married, Lady Sophia would never let him consort with the likes of the Ingrams, and indeed, once he was married, Fanny didn't think she could endure to see him. Her throat ached, but no tears came.

At last, still dry-eyed, she went to see that Frank was settled for the night. He had been carried down for an hour or two every afternoon these past few days, but he was still weak. He was her future, he and Anita. She loved them. In time, perhaps, in caring for them, she'd escape the pain of her love for Felix.

In the morning, Felix and Isaac departed before the ladies came down. Felix offered to take the ribbons.

"You expect me to trust you with my horses?"

"I taught you to drive!" said Felix in mock outrage, taking the reins from the groom and mounting into the phaeton.

Laughing, Isaac joined him. "Unwillingly! Only because Miriam insisted it was necessary if we were ever to reach Spain. As I recall, the prospect of teaching a Jew appalled you."

"What an arrogant numskull I was." He gave the pair of sorrels the office to start. "I didn't precisely live up to my principles, hating you simply because of the blue blood in your veins. What we'd have done without Miriam to keep us in order, I cannot for the life of me imagine."

"Wellington would have had to whistle for his gold. How right Jakob Rothschild was to send her with us."

As they turned out of the stable yard and trotted down the drive, Isaac asked, "Have you decided whether you are going to give Rothschild your notice?"

"If Lady Sophia accepts me, certainly. If not, probably. I've enjoyed working for him and shall be sorry to give it up, but I ought to be learning how to run Westwood. My father isn't growing any younger, as you pointed out, and duty calls."

"Then you mean to call on Lady Sophia first? To throw yourself at her feet, as you once advised me! My first errand is to Mr Rothschild. If you wish, I shall tell him you are on your way."

"I'll come with you. The Daventrys may not be in Town, and in any case we'll probably arrive too early to call, since you dragged me out at dawn." The longer he could put off the evil hour, the better — no, not the evil hour! The difficult task. Offering for a young lady's hand in marriage was a notoriously arduous affair.

He had practice, of course. Proposing to Miriam had been awkward enough, especially when he discovered in the middle of his heartfelt offer that she was an heiress. That had come as a shock! This time he'd be sure to sort out the financial business with Lord Daventry first. A properly brought up female like Lady Sophia would want nothing to do with settlements.

Perhaps she'd be in Northamptonshire, or Paris.

He drove straight to New Court. He and Isaac went into the bank and asked for Mr Rothschild.

"He's at the Bank of England," said the clerk in a voice of nervous awe. In fact, the whole establishment seemed to be in a state of breathless anticipation.

"What's going on?" Isaac asked.

The man drew them aside. "It started the day before yesterday, with a draft from Mr Amschel in Frankfurt. Mr Nathan sent me to the Bank of England to cash it, and they told me they cashed only their own notes, not those of private individuals. When I told Mr Nathan — well, I never thought to see him lose his temper, cool as he usually is."

"What did he do?" Felix demanded.

" 'Rothschilds are not private individuals!' he roared. Next morning he gave nine of us clerks purses stuffed to bursting with ten-pound Bank of England notes, and he took another, and we all went round to Thread-needle Street and started cashing them. Nearly £100,000 in gold we had by the end of the day."

Felix and Isaac began to laugh. "And then?"

"He went back this morning, with nine more fellows. We're waiting to hear."

"Devil take it, I wouldn't miss this for the world," said Felix. "How can I bear not to work for a man with such colossal nerve?"

Provided with newspapers, he and Isaac sat down to wait. The hour arrived when it would be perfectly proper to call on the Marquis of Daventry. Felix glanced at the clock and shook his head.

Not long after, Nathan Rothschild strolled into the bank, followed by nine grinning clerks. He nodded to Felix and Isaac with an air of grim satisfaction. "I'll be with you in a moment, gentlemen," he said, continuing to his private office.

The entire staff converged on his hench-men.

"Soon after we arrived," the most senior began the story, "one of the bigwigs came in. Lord, was he in high fidgets, but he tried to hide it with a laugh."

" 'How long do you mean to keep up this jest?' he asked," broke in another clerk, snig-gering.

"And Mr Rothschild, in that placid way of his, he said, 'Rothschild will continue to doubt the Bank of England's notes as long as the Bank of England doubts Rothschild notes.' "

A roar of approval arose.

"So this chap goes off, and we go on cash-ing notes, until pretty soon he comes back and says they called an emergency meeting of the directors. The upshot is, in future they'll cash any draft of any Rothschild."

There was a murmur of gratification, but no one had doubted that their employer was going to win. Through the murmur cut Mr Rothschild's voice and the clerks hurriedly scattered about their business.

"I cannot wait to tell Fanny and Miriam that story," said Felix, laughing, as he and Isaac went into the inner office.

The banker received their congratulations with a grunt. "Well, my lord, you have returned to work? How do you fancy Paris again?"

"Very much, sir, but I hesitate to commit myself. You see, sooner or later I must learn to manage my father's estate."

"Naturally. Your duty to your family comes first."

"However, the earl is in excellent health, so there is no urgency. On the other hand, I am hoping to win a young lady's hand in marriage, and if I do, I shall have to give up my employment, with deep regret, I assure you, sir. So my future course rather depends on the lady's answer."

"Take another fortnight. But if you decide sooner to quit, let me know."

"Of course, sir. Isaac, I'll see you later?"

"When I've finished my business for the day, I'll go to my father-in-law's. You can contact me there."

A few minutes later, Felix was walking along Cheapside towards St James's. He ought to be preparing a speech for Lord Daventry, and another for Lady Sophia, but his mind kept returning to Nathan Rothschild's triumph. Fanny would admire such masterly tactics. Even Wellington must approve the neat way the banker had turned the enemy's flanks and defeated him with his own guns, yet left him with no possible legitimate cause for complaint.

He reached Pall Mall with no idea what he was going to say to the marquis. Passing the magnificent façade of Carlton House without a glance, he turned into St James's Square and came face to face with an old friend.

"Roworth! Where the devil have you been hiding?"

"Here and there, Gardner, here and there."

"Haven't seen you in years, my dear fellow. Buy you a drink."

The Honorable Aloysius Gardner did not have to insist, though in view of his afternoon's quest Felix stuck to ale. The first sip suggested to him that the hollow sensation in his middle was hunger not, as he had supposed, sheer terror at the prospect of jumping with both feet into parson's mousetrap.

Gardner had just breakfasted, but he lingered, reminiscing about the escapades of their youth, while Felix consumed pickled oysters, followed by a large beefsteak with mushrooms. In the end it was the Honorable Aloysius who regretfully had to take his leave, recalling an engagement.

No further excuse for delay presenting itself, Felix made his way to the Daventrys' front door. The knocker had not been taken down; the ground floor curtains were open. The family was at home.

On asking for a private word with the marquis, he was shown into his lordship's study. Feverishly considering possible openings, he paced the room, wending his way between deep, luxurious leather chairs and pausing before the half dozen books that graced the single bookshelf. The Peerage, the Baronetage, the Turf Register, and three volumes on agriculture, he noted absently.

The only other item of note in the "study" was a sideboard bearing several decanters. To this Lord Daventry immediately repaired when he entered after what seemed to Felix an age but was actually only two or three minutes. "You'll take a drop of something, Roworth?"

"Just a little Madeira, thank you, sir."

"Here you go. It's good to see you, my boy. Sit down, sit down. You were lucky to catch us in Town. We're just passing through, on our way to Paris. Everyone's there now, the ladies tell me, since we put paid to Bonaparte for good. A splendid victory! Here's to Wellington."

He raised his glass in a toast and Felix followed suit. He was sorely tempted to embark upon a discussion of the Battle of Waterloo but the marquis was made of sterner stuff.

"We left Brussels in a bit of a hurry," he said. "Lady Daventry was nervous, and who can blame her. M'daughter was sorry to leave her . . . hmm . . . friends."

So obvious a hint could not be ignored. "I was sorry for your absence, sir, but glad that Lady Sophia was safe. You know, I believe, why I did not . . . er . . . speak to you before your removal."

"Yes, indeed, my boy, and very proper of you. Am I to understand that the . . . hmm . . . obstacle is a thing of the past?"

"It is, sir. My . . . er . . . financial situation is much improved. I can give you details."

"No sense in wasting time on that yet. Wait until you have . . . hmm . . . addressed Sophie. I don't scruple to tell you that she's been a worry to her mother and me, and I make no guarantees, mind."

"I admire your reluctance to force her into an unwanted match, sir."

"Finicky, that's what she is." Lord Daventry grew confidential. "But she may be . . . hmm . . . changing her tune. Her little sister's just wed, you know, and a girl don't care for that. Then poor Garforth was killed at Waterloo, and Bissell maimed. Those two lads in the Guards came through unscathed, but they're no more than boys. And the count, well, a foreigner, you know. A fine fellow, to be sure, but after all he's in Belgium and we are not."

So he was now head of the list, Felix thought, a peculiarly cold feeling invading his chest. "Then may I take it you approve my . . . er . . . suit?"

"Gad, yes! One of the finest families in the country, after all. Can't think of anyone I'd rather . . . hmm . . . entrust her to, now that your little . . . er . . . difficulty is out of the way. She's in the drawing room now, if you want to get the business over with."

Felix drew a deep breath. "Yes, I daresay I had best . . . hmm . . . strike while the iron's hot."

As the marquis led him across the hall, he felt dismayingly as if he were walking in dead men's shoes. Both Garforth and Bissell knocked out of the race by the fortunes of war! Fanny was right, glory was a poor substitute for life and health.

Lord Daventry ushered him into a large, light room decorated in the chilly perfection of the Classical style.

"Someone to see you, Sophie," he announced.

Lady Sophia sat by the window, a book in her hand. Her pale blonde ringlets gleamed as she turned her head and said in her usual calm way, "Good day, Lord Roworth." The perfection of her beauty stunned him anew.

Her mother dropped the fringe she was knotting. "How delightful to see you!"

"I believe your housekeeper wishes to have a word with you, m'dear," Lord Daventry said to his wife in voice heavy with significance.

"Oh yes, I'm so sorry, Roworth, I must have a word with my housekeeper. You will excuse me, I know."

Felix bowed, murmuring "Of course, ma'am," while in his head a little voice screamed, "Don't go, don't go!" Silently he admonished it: "No more pluck than a dunghill cock. Fanny would be ashamed of such faint-heartedness." He marched across the room to the Goddess's side.

"I trust I see you well, Lady Sophia?"

"Very well, I thank you, sir. Pray be seated." The awkwardness of their situation had no visible effect on her composure. She must be aware he had come to make her an offer, for otherwise her mother would never have left them alone together.

Felix sat down in a chair with a curved, inlaid back on which Grecian ladies in flowing draperies posed in unlikely attitudes. It was as uncomfortable as it looked. "I understand I am fortunate to find you at home," he said. "You are on your way to Paris?"

"Yes. You know the city, do you not?"

"I was there last year, before I had the honour to make your acquaintance at the Congress of Vienna." In Paris he had acted as liaison between Wellington, then ambassador to France, and the Rothschilds — could he mention his work, now that he had as good as resigned the position? Better not, he decided, recalling his parents' bitter opposition. He went on to describe the city to her.

"Whatever his faults, the Emperor has made many improvements to his capital," he finished.

"It sounds charming, even pleasanter than Brussels. Such splendid balls we had there, especially the Duchess of Richmond's, and so many other entertainments. Do you recall the Cavalry Review?"

Felix remembered it well, and also the picnic where he had pleaded Fanny's cause and been given the cold shoulder. And the Horse Artillery picnic where Fanny had so effectively deterred an over-ardent suitor. He wondered whether the unfortunate Barnstaple had survived the battle. Fanny might have heard, from Mercer or Prynne. He'd ask her; she'd understand that he felt a sympathetic interest in the lieutenant.

"You are very grave, sir," said Lady Sophia in a questioning tone.

He called his wandering thoughts to attention. Neither Fanny nor bloodshed and death were suitable subjects for polite conversation. Seizing the first topic that came to mind, he asked what she was reading.

"An essay on St Paul, by Mrs Hannah More." She handed him her book. "Her writings are excessively edifying."

"No doubt." He glanced at the title page and hastily set it down. "Have you by any chance read Mary Wollstonecraft Godwin's *Vindication of the Rights of Women?*"

"Certainly not," she said coolly. "It is a most pernicious book, written by a wicked woman. I assure you, sir, my mama would never permit such a work in the house."

"Nor, I daresay, would mine," said Felix, and she looked gratified. Connie was right. Lady Sophia was very like his mother, his patterncard of what a countess should be. "It's a great pity," he added, "for Mrs Godwin presents a number of ideas worthy of serious consideration. I suppose Lady Daventry does not allow you to read novels, either."

Inadvertently he had succeeded in disconcerting her. Caution vied with confusion in her lovely face as she responded, "Some novels are unexceptionable."

Not the ones Vickie sneaked under her bedcovers, he'd wager. While he was in London, he must go by Leadenhall Street and buy her the latest volumes from the Minerva Press. And he'd borrow the *Vindication of the Rights of Women* from Miriam, if Fanny had finished with it, and smuggle it into Westwood for Connie to read. Perhaps she'd like to correspond with Fanny and Miriam about it, though they could never meet.

"It has been a pleasure to see you again, Lady Sophia," he found himself saying. He rose and bowed over her hand. "I wish you a very enjoyable sojourn in Paris. Pray make my excuses to Lady Daventry for not taking my leave of her, but I have an urgent engagement elsewhere."

And he strolled from the room. In the hall, the butler handed him hat and gloves with a sympathetic air. No doubt he thought Lady Sophia had rejected one more suitor.

But she hadn't. Felix descended the front steps in a daze as he absorbed the realization that he had failed to come up to scratch. Much as he admired the Goddess, he did not like her. He positively disliked her intolerance, especially the way she had snubbed Fanny.

It was devilish lucky he had come to his senses in time, for once he had proposed, honour forbade a gentleman to cry off.

He wanted something more in a wife than a perfect countess. He wanted Miriam's warmth, and generosity, and open-mindedness. He wanted a sense of humour, and a sense of passion, and he wanted a friend. How could anyone who had once loved Miriam be satisfied with the cool, calm, and always collected Lady Sophia Gerrold?

Had her composure survived his departure, he wondered guiltily. He had raised her expectations, then shattered them. He consoled himself with the thought that she might not have planned to accept him anyway. Besides, within a week in Paris she'd have collected another court. She had never suffered any shortage of admirers.

And he *had* admired her, yet now he could not understand why he had ever wanted to make her his wife. Felix was not an introspective man, but as he walked he searched his soul.

He had never loved her, he realized. Pride came into it, a need to feel his birth made him worthy of courting a marquis's daughter, despite his slender means, his employment, his civilian status among those magnificent uniforms. And that was another reason for his pursuit: the determination to triumph over his rivals. Most of all, he had chosen her because his parents would consider Lady Sophia the ideal bride, and he wanted to please his parents.

Connie had had the pluck to reject the suitors pressed upon her by their parents.

Without conscious volition, his rapid, agitated strides had carried him back towards the City. He had no particular destination in mind. Indeed, he was at a loss as to what to do next. He ought to go home and tell his mother and father that he was not going to marry Lady Sophia. Once again they would be bitterly disappointed in him, and they would not understand why he had not made his offer.

Fanny would understand, and sympathize. He'd go back to Nettledene first, to talk over his decision with her. She was bound to tease him, but he didn't mind that.

As Felix reached Charing Cross, he suddenly stopped and stood staring blankly at the statue of King Charles I on his horse.

Good gad, he wanted Fanny!

CHAPTER 17

"So the lady accepted you," grunted Nathan Rothschild.

Feeling like a proper nodcock, Felix confessed, "Well, no, as a matter of fact I didn't offer in the end. I realized I want to marry a different lady. The thing is, my parents aren't going to be exactly cock-a-hoop over this." But he had weathered their disapproval over his employment. Whatever he had felt in his mother's sitting room, he was no longer a child. It was his life, and life without Fanny didn't bear thinking of. "She'll need all my support. How much notice will you require, sir?"

"A month." He looked sardonically amused at Felix's dismay. "You may work it off persuading Lord Westwood to accept your ineligible young lady as a daughter-in-law. If you succeed, perhaps the practice will enable you to convince his lordship that a Jewish banker is not the Devil incarnate."

Felix grinned. "I'll do my best."

"Then all that remains is for me to work out how much I owe you, my lord." He pulled a heavy ledger towards him and opened it.

"Sir, that's not at all necessary! You have been more than generous and it has been a privilege to . . ."

He was interrupted by the eruption into the private office of a stout, grey-whiskered gentleman he recognized as the Duke of Oxshott. His grace's face was crimson with fury.

"Do you know what your whippersnapper of a chief clerk has done?" he bellowed. "He has the unmitigated gall to tell me . . ."

"Take a chair," Rothschild invited, perusing his ledger.

"Do you know who I am, sir, do you know who I am?" Purpling, the duke tossed his card on the desk and began reciting his noble lineage in a roar that must have been heard on the other side of New Court.

The banker glanced briefly at the card. "Take two chairs," he suggested, entering figures in the account book in his neat hand.

As the duke, eyes popping, opened and closed his mouth in flabbergasted silence, Mr Rothschild took a sheet of paper, wrote, signed, and handed it to Felix. "Take that to my whippersnapper of a chief clerk," he said blandly. "A month of paid leave, and the coming month, which I daresay will tax your abilities to the utmost. However, I rate your abilities highly. Good day, my lord."

Felix shook his hand heartily. He was tempted to stay, but he wasn't sure whether he'd be called upon to rescue the banker from the duke or, more likely, the duke from the banker. He made good his escape.

His only desire now was to rush back to Nettledene and tell Fanny he loved her. When a small man in a battered hat accosted him in the courtyard, he brushed him off, scarcely noticing, and hurried on. A plaintive "Oy, guv, just a word . . ." faded behind him.

He made for Bedford Square, hoping that Isaac would already be at his father-in-law's, ready to leave. The revolution in his feelings was going to come as a great surprise to the Cohens, but he was sure they would be pleased. They had grown amazingly fond of Fanny, as did everyone who knew her.

With the probable exception of his parents, he admitted, his euphoria fading. His love for Fanny did not change the fact that she was a penniless nobody with a decidedly unconventional upbringing. He'd have to go down to Westwood and prevail upon them to receive her with complaisance, if not joy, because he was going to wed her with or without their consent. But first to Nettledene, to offer her his heart and his hand.

A tiny doubt crept in. He wanted to spend the rest of his life with Fanny, but would she want to marry him?

To his relief he reached Bedford Square and was forced to abandon that discouraging line of thought. He rang the Jacobsons' doorbell. The door opened promptly.

"I'm to meet Mr Cohen here," he told the footman. "Has he arrived yet?"

"Come and gone, sir, not half an hour since. You'll be Lord Roworth? Mr Isaac left a message to tell your lordship he had to go fetch Miss Miriam — Mrs Cohen, that is. The master's been took ill."

"Oh Lord, now of all times!" Felix recollected his manners. "Please convey my sympathy and best wishes to Mr and Mrs Jacobson. Where are the nearest livery stables?"

Directed to Caroline Mews, he hired a mount and set off for Nettledene.

His horse was a powerful but skittish grey. Even after they left the city streets, the busy traffic on the Dover road kept Felix on the alert. He had no chance to reflect until he turned off into a country lane, by which time the brute was tired enough to behave. Then, the niggling doubt returned.

Fanny had refused as many suitors as had Lady Sophia, or more, according to Lieutenant Barnstaple. Of course, none of them had been heir to an earldom, but he doubted she set any store by that. On the other hand, all had been soldiers. He recalled with delight the fiery vehemence of her declaration: "I shall never marry a soldier!"

For the first time in ten years, Felix was absolutely and without qualification content to have been unable to buy a pair of colours.

That gave him a fighting chance, but by no means guaranteed that she would accept him. Ruefully he acknowledged that he was not a perceptive man, and he had no notion if her feelings for him went any deeper than sincere friendship. He wanted her love, yet he knew he'd marry her without it and hope to win it. What he did not know was whether he was prepared to take a bride who would marry him just to provide security for her brother and the child.

She was too honest not to tell him if that were the case, too proud to accept his help if she chose to refuse him. All he could do was wait and see.

He caught up with Isaac in the village and rode beside the phaeton to the house. They found Fanny and Miriam on the terrace, seated on a bench with the baby. Frank had been helped out to lie on a chaise longue in the sun; on the steps down to the garden, the children were absorbed in some game with sticks and stones.

Fanny looked up with a smile as Isaac stepped through the French doors. He looked even graver than usual but before she could ask if aught was amiss, Felix followed him. She stared at him, incredulous, possibilities racing through her mind: Lady Sophia was in Paris and he was going after her; she had rejected him; she had accepted him and he had rushed to Nettledene to inform his friends of his success.

An air of suppressed elation about him suggested to Fanny that she was going to have to congratulate him.

Then Miriam turned and caught sight of her husband's face and at once demanded, "What is wrong?"

Isaac went to take her hand. "Your father, my love. He has suffered some kind of seizure."

"Oh, poor Papa." Her voice shook. "I must go at once. Can we leave this evening, Isaac?"

"Of course, if you can be ready. I'll send to the inn for fresh horses."

"Yes. There are a hundred things to be done before we can go." Absently, she handed Leah to Fanny and stood up.

"I'd be happy to take care of the children for you," Fanny offered, disentangling her hair from Leah's fist. Felix's news would have to wait, as he obviously realized.

Miriam turned to her. "Thank you, Fanny dear, but I shall take them with me. I cannot tell how long I shall be gone." She glanced at Isaac, who nodded. "Fanny, Frank, we had not meant to speak so soon, but Isaac and I have decided we should very much like to adopt Anita."

"No!" cried Fanny instantly, horrified. "No, it is excessively generous of you, but I cannot give her up."

"It would make your lives much simpler," Isaac pointed out in his sober way, "and I believe she would be happy here. Take some time to consider and talk it over."

"I don't need to." Fanny cast a look of frantic appeal at her brother. Surely he must agree!

With a somewhat rueful grimace, Frank came staunchly to her support. "It's not that we don't think she'd be happy, but her father was my friend and she's been part of our family pretty much since she was born. It wouldn't be right to hand her over, even to you, as if she were a foundling."

"Bravo!" Felix exclaimed, with such heartfelt relief that Fanny felt he had shared her trepidation.

"We expected you to choose to keep her," said Miriam with approval. "Fanny, Hannah will go with us to London, but you are accustomed to taking care of Anita yourself. If you wish to have a truckle bed for her moved into your chamber, just tell Samuels."

"But we ought not to remain here when you are gone," Fanny protested. "I cannot believe it is proper to stay on in one's hosts' absence."

"My dear, pray do not be nonsensical. Where else should you go?"

"I don't know." She bit her lip, suddenly longing for the uncomplicated support of her military "family."

"It doesn't seem right," her brother again seconded her.

She looked from him, still an invalid though much recovered, to Anita and back. "We have no real choice, Frank."

"Yes, you do," said Felix nonchalantly. "I'll take you to Westwood."

Fanny was not the only one stunned

into silence.

After a moment, Miriam said calmly, "An excellent solution. Now I really must go and make arrangements for our departure." She went into the house.

Following her, Isaac turned on the threshold and said, "If you don't mind waiting until tomorrow, I shall send back our carriage to take you to Somerset. It's more comfortable than anything you can hire around here."

Felix thanked him, just as Fanny found her voice. "But your family!" She envisioned a house filled with Lady Sophias, cold, haughty, aloof, contemptuous of the lowly Ingrams.

"I told Connie about you and she's eager to meet you," he said evasively.

"And your parents?"

"Any family in England should be proud to welcome a wounded hero of Waterloo."

"Quite a hero!" said Frank. "Blown up by his own shell." He grinned suddenly. "Come on, Fan, I'm sure Lord and Lady Westwood are too polite to throw us out on our respective ears. Let's take our chance to see how the nobility lives."

Felix forestalled her protest. "Good, that's settled then. Frank, let me help you in. You'll want to be rested for tomorrow."

They left her on the terrace with the baby and the children, still engrossed by their sticks and stones.

Already servants were running about, making preparations for the Cohens' journey. Felix assisted Frank to his chamber, then returned to the terrace. Fanny was gone, no doubt having taken the children to the nursery. He desperately wanted to talk to her, but not surrounded by listening ears.

He had not intended to take her to Westwood before they were betrothed. Even then, he'd planned to go down in advance to persuade his parents to accept her before she had to face them. Fate had intervened. Now, his need to declare his love was urgent, so that he'd have the right to protect her against his parents' disfavour.

A private conversation was obviously impossible until the Cohens left and peace returned to the household. He went in search of Miriam to see if there was anything he could do to help.

She was in her stillroom, directing the packing in straw of the potions she expected to need in Town. When he arrived, she dismissed the maid and set him to work in her place.

"Make sure glass does not touch glass. I take it Lady Sophia refused you?"

"No, I never asked her."

Miriam looked worried. "She was not in Town?"

"Oh yes, on her way to Paris. I made all right and tight with the marquis, and then I sat with the Goddess for twenty minutes, alone together, discussing Paris and Brussels and Mary Wollstonecraft."

"Felix, you didn't! The poor girl must have thought you fit for Bedlam. So you simply ran shy."

"No, I simply realized I didn't want to marry her after all. I want to marry Fanny."

"You have come to your senses at last!"

He stared, nonplussed. That wasn't at all the reaction he had expected to his blunt announcement. "What the deuce do you mean?"

"Gudgeon," she said affectionately. "You have been in love with Fanny this age. I was afraid you would discover it too late."

"It was a near-run thing. You might have told me!"

"I would have. Isaac stopped me. He said one simply cannot go around telling people whom they love, especially if they are under the impression they love someone else."

"I suppose not," he admitted, grinning. "Oh, Miriam, I can't wait to show her how I adore her."

"You must. Don't rush your fences, Felix. Wait a while before you propose."

"Why? I want her to know at once that I love her."

She sighed, shaking her head. "You are such a very straightforward person. Remember that only this morning you went up to London to make Lady Sophia your wife! Tell Fanny you have changed your mind, but give her time to adjust. Besides, if she chooses not to accept your offer, she will feel unable to accept your invitation to Westwood."

His heart sank. "Will she have me, Miriam?"

"Now, how can I answer for her? Whether she does or no, your parents are less likely to take the Ingrams' arrival amiss if you are not betrothed, are they not?"

"Probably," he said grudgingly.

"Let them become acquainted with her first. Let them find out what a dear she is."

"She is, isn't she? A darling!" Restored to euphoria, he agreed to wait and finished packing her jars and bottles.

He went up to the nursery. Amos and Anita, in their nightgowns, were eating their supper under Fanny's eye while Hannah and the nursery maid packed.

"Uncle Felix, I'm going to London," said

Amos importantly.

"I been to Brussels and lots and lots of places," Anita reminded him.

"I'm going to see Grammama an' Grampapa."

Anita's mouth drooped. "I don't . . . haven't got a Grammama."

Felix wanted to tell her that she soon would have, as soon as he married her Tía Fanny and legally adopted her. On the other hand, he couldn't guarantee a warm reception from her adopted grandparents. "You'll soon have two new aunts," he promised, "Aunt Connie and Aunt Vickie, when we reach Westwood."

"What's Westwood?"

"My home. We are going there tomorrow, you and me and Aunt Fanny and Uncle Frank."

"Felix, I must talk to you about that," said Fanny with a hint of desperation. "You and Frank seem to think it's all settled but . . . Amos, careful!" She swooped on his cup as a wild gesture with a spoon missed it by a fraction of an inch. "Drink your milk before you spill it."

"We'll talk at dinner," said Felix, retreating. By then, he'd have had time to marshal his rebuttals to the difficulties she was going to raise.

Retiring to the library to cogitate, he found Isaac packing books into a faded red leather box. In the general confusion, he had not told him yet about his change of heart. It wasn't quite as easy as confiding in Miriam.

Idly he picked up a book from the table and opened it at random, as if it might suggest the right words to him. The pages were filled with unreadable squiggles.

"Can you really understand this stuff?" he asked.

"Hebrew? I'd hardly take the book up to London with me if I couldn't," said Isaac dryly. "How did your business in Town go?"

"I gave Rothschild my resignation this afternoon. You should have been there. It was almost as good as when he grassed the Old Lady of Threadneedle Street." Felix described the banker's set-down of the choleric Duke of Oxshott.

Isaac laughed, but then said with a frown, "You resigned. Does that mean Lady Sophia accepted you?"

"As a matter of fact, I realized just in time that she is not at all the sort of wife I want."

"So you have come to your senses at last!" he echoed his wife.

"I have been blind, have I not?" he said ruefully. "I thought I had learned from Miriam not to judge people by their station. I've been pleased with myself for my democratic notions, yet my parents' pride still influenced me, made me unable to conceive of Fanny as more than a friend. I had no right to blame Lady Sophia for her arrogance. She behaves as she was taught, according to her upbringing as a nobleman's daughter."

"Ever since you first told us about her, I've wondered whether you were just reacting against having fallen in love with Miriam. Lady Sophia is so obviously suitable as a bride for the heir to an earldom, whereas Miriam would not have suited you at all."

"If she had accepted me, I'd have persuaded my parents to overlook the Christian-Jew nonsense in the end."

"I doubt it. For one thing, it's not nonsense. But quite apart from that, Miriam is too strong-willed for you."

"Are you claiming to be stronger than I?" Felix demanded indignantly.

"God forbid!" Isaac said, grinning. "No, the difference is that I'm willing to bend a little, whereas you would be irked beyond bearing by a wife who — let's face it — is in many ways stronger than either of us. Besides, she does have some respect for my book-learning, to which you cannot lay claim."

With a rueful laugh, Felix set down the Hebrew book. "True. It's just as well she turned me down. Do you think Fanny will have me?"

"My dear fellow, I refuse to answer that. Most young women in her situation would jump at the chance, but Fanny is not like most young women."

"If she was, I'd not love her as I do. You don't think I have lost my senses again? You believe I love Fanny?"

"Oh yes, it's been obvious for weeks." He laughed at Felix's grimace. "I doubt, however, that it is equally obvious to her, so don't be in too much of a hurry to fling yourself at her feet."

"That's what Miriam said," Felix grumbled to hide his pleasure at their affectionate concern. If he'd married Lady Sophia, she'd have tried to make him relinquish the friendship that meant so much to him. "Don't the two of you have anything better to do than discuss my affairs?"

"At this moment, plenty. That's the last book." Isaac closed the chest and fastened the brass catch. "It's time we were off."

Ten minutes later, Felix, Fanny, and Anita waved goodbye from the front steps. Then

Felix carried Anita up to the truckle bed set up in Fanny's chamber and told her his own version of Jack the Giant Killer. As he talked he looked around the light, airy room, hung with white-sprigged blue muslin, and compared it with the cramped, dingy chamber Fanny and Anita had shared in Brussels.

Despite her initial misgivings, Fanny had quickly adapted to life at Nettledene. He trusted her to adjust equally fast to the ceremonious formality of Westwood, though it would not suit her as well. Once they were married, he'd insist on setting up a separate household in one of the wings, where she could be herself.

If she would marry him. The uncertainty daunted him as his doubts of Lady Sophia's acceptance never had. How easily he had deceived himself!

First he had to get Fanny to Westwood, and he had had no chance to prepare his arguments. The best was that he loved her, and Miriam had advised against using that. He went down to dinner in a mood of considerable trepidation.

Mrs Samuels provided her usual excellent meal in spite of the disruption of the household. Samuels served them with green pea soup and withdrew.

"It's all very well Frank saying your

parents will not throw us out," said Fanny at once, "but I cannot suppose they will welcome us, for all your talk of wounded heroes. Frank is no titled Guards officer."

"I don't want to mislead you, Fanny," he said soberly. "They will not welcome you with open arms. But Westwood is my home, too, and they cannot choose my friends. I've kept my friendship with the Cohens from them for far too long."

"To be forced upon people who don't wish to know me!" she said in a stifled voice. "I had rather stay here."

"Connie truly wishes to know you."

Her eyes met his in a plea for reassurance. "Truly?"

"Yes, and she said she has longed this age to meet Miriam and Isaac, though she is a shy creature. What's more, now I come to think of it, she said something about wishing she could help wounded soldiers, even before I told her about Frank and you and Anita."

"Anita is another problem," Fanny pointed out, agitated fingers pleating her napkin. "Lord and Lady Westwood will have every right to take offence at her presence, indeed, to refuse to receive a love-child in their house."

Felix blenched. "No need to tell them,"

he said hurriedly. "All we need say is that she is your ward. You have always been surrounded by people who know her history, so there has been no point in trying to conceal it, but for her sake you ought not to bruit it abroad."

"You told Miriam and Isaac."

"I would not deceive my friends. Parents are another matter."

At that she smiled, shaking her head, and he looked relieved. "Oh, Felix, what an unprincipled rogue you sound, but it's true, alas. One does not wish to worry one's parents unnecessarily."

"Don't turn sanctimonious on me! One does not wish to be hauled over the coals for every little scrape one falls into. You will not feel obliged to reveal that Anita was born on the wrong side of the blanket?"

"Not unless I am asked, which, I own, is unlikely."

"Then you will come to Westwood?"

He had an answer for each obstacle. She had given him every chance to withdraw his impulsive invitation and still he seemed genuinely eager, determined even, that they should go with him. But there was one more hurdle to cross, the highest of all.

"I . . . Oh, it is such an awkward situation!" Blushing, she stirred her cooling soup.

331

"What is?"

"Lady Sophia. If you are betrothed, surely she will visit Westwood and . . ."

"I am not betrothed." He spoke quietly, without emphasis, without apparent chagrin, yet with an intensity Fanny could not interpret. "I am not going to marry Lady Sophia."

So the Goddess had refused him. Fanny should have been elated but her euphoria evaporated in an instant. She ached for his disappointment, however well hidden. And Lady Sophia had never been a real rival, simply because Fanny herself had never had any real hope of winning his love.

Nothing had changed. She was still not nobly born, not wealthy, not gently bred, not fashionable, not even beautiful. All she had to offer was her love, and that he must never guess. His pity would be unendurable.

Was she run mad, then, to accept his invitation after all? Could the joy of his company possibly compensate for the torment? She had no strength to resist the temptation.

Avoiding his eyes, she said hesitantly, "We will come to Westwood."

Chapter 18

Flooded fields gleamed on either side of the raised road from Wells to Westwood and a grey haze of drizzle hid the steep wall of the Mendips. Felix was pleased. Poor visibility would mute the impressive effect of the mansion's façade. He did not want Fanny to be overawed by his home.

He had carefully planned their arrival. They had dined early at an inn in Wells, and now Anita was fast asleep between him and Fanny while Frank drowsed on the opposite seat. Fanny sat upright, tense as a hare in its form when the greyhounds approach. Irate landladies and amorous lieutenants she took in her stride; even Lady Sophia's cut direct in the park had annoyed, not cowed her; yet the prospect of meeting the Earl and Countess of Westwood had her shaking in her shoes.

If Felix had his way, she would not have to face that meeting until the morning, when she was rested from the journey. If he was lucky and his parents had guests, nor would he.

As the Cohens' coachman drew up in front of the house, Felix consulted his watch. Dinner should have been served fifteen minutes ago — perfect timing. He opened the door and let down the step.

"Wait here while I organize umbrellas."

He ran up the steps to the shelter of the portico and opened one leaf of the wide oak front door. A footman was crossing the great hall bearing a platter that looked too large for the family alone. Catching sight of Felix, he almost dropped the dish, then gave a helpless, apologetic shrug and rushed on into the dining room. A moment later the butler came out, stately as ever.

"Good evening, my lord."

Felix swiftly explained the situation. The man permitted a harried expression to pass across his face. Nonetheless, within a few minutes Frank had been carried up to Felix's chamber, kept always prepared, and Fanny was sipping tea in the small saloon while a chamber was readied for her and Anita. Anita, fast asleep, lay sprawled on a sofa with Felix close beside her. When he carried her in she had clung to his sleeve and it was still grasped in her little fist.

"She will not wake if you untangle your-self," said Fanny with a tired smile. "She will crease your sleeve."

"No matter, I'll have to change into evening dress tonight and Trevor should be here tomorrow. I promised the poor chap faithfully he'd never have to travel on the Mail again."

"I must change into my evening gown to meet your parents?" she asked, dismayed. He had warned her of the ceremony observed at Westwood, but to expect a weary guest to change just to make her bows to the earl and countess seemed excessive!

"You need not meet them this evening, especially as they have guests. The journey is excuse enough for you to retire as soon as your room is ready."

"Are you certain?" Once again, the fear swept over her of so offending Felix's parents by her gaucherie that he'd feel obliged to disown her friendship. "I'd hate to be remiss in any way."

"I'm quite certain. But if you don't object, I'll catch Connie when the ladies withdraw and send her to see you."

"Oh yes, please. I shall have much more confidence in the morning if I have already met one of your family."

At that moment the door opened and a

girl in white came in. Her inelegant, bouncing gait and the fair hair flowing loose down her back suggested that this was not Lady Constantia but her younger sister. Her attention on Felix, she did not notice Fanny.

"Felix, is it true you . . ."

"Sshhhh!" he hissed.

"Oh!" She tiptoed over to the sofa and gazed down at Anita's rosy cheeks, long black lashes, and tumbled curls. "Oh, she's just like a doll. A beautiful porcelain doll."

"If you will turn around, Vickie, I shall introduce you to Miss Ingram."

Horrified hand to her mouth, Lady Victoria swung round and curtsied. "Miss Ingram, I beg your pardon, I did not see you. You must think me horridly ill-mannered. Is it true your brother was injured at Waterloo? And is that little girl his ward? May I play with her? Will she sleep in the nursery? My chamber is right next door because I am still in the schoolroom, which is why I wasn't allowed to dine downstairs tonight. We have guests, you know, tonnish people, not just the vicar."

Fanny smiled at her. "How do you do, Lady Victoria." She was perfectly able to deal with an enthusiastic schoolroom miss, even if she was titled. "I think Anita had best sleep in my chamber tonight, but tomorrow you shall play with her, if your governess permits."

"She will." Vickie glanced warily at the door. "All the same, I'd better go now or I shall be in the suds. Good night, ma'am. I'm glad you have come to stay."

As she dashed out, the housekeeper came in to show Fanny to her chamber. Felix carried Anita up, but transferred her to Fanny's arms outside the door. At Westwood, the proprieties must be carefully observed.

"Good night, Miss Ingram. I'll make sure your brother is all right."

"Thank you, Lord Roworth." She copied his formality, an intangible barrier between them. "Good night."

She carried Anita into the room. The housekeeper followed and shut the door, another barrier. Sighing, Felix went to check on Frank, who was deep in exhausted sleep, then changed into his evening clothes and descended to the great hall.

Lurking behind the magnificent marble staircase with gilded wrought-iron rail, he waited for the ladies to come out of the dining room. He had not long to wait. His mother led the way with a lady he did not recognize, followed by the wives of two local gentlemen, and lastly, on her own, Connie.

"Pssst!" He beckoned to her.

"Felix!" she exclaimed in a whisper, joining him. "I wondered what all the commotion was about. Mama did not say and everyone was much too polite to ask."

"I've brought guests." He raised his voice to normal as the drawing-room door closed behind the last of the visiting ladies. "The Ingrams."

"Oh Felix, how delightful!" Her smile turned to a frown. "But you told me I should never meet them because they are . . . not precisely common but . . ."

"Not at all common!" he said indignantly.

"No, that is not what I meant. You said they have no connexions and do not move in the first circles, if I remember correctly. Yet you have brought them to Westwood! What will Mama and Papa say?"

"I hate to think," he admitted, "and Fanny is terrified. You wouldn't think someone who has been through innumerable battle campaigns would be afraid of a mere earl and countess. Con, will you go up now and talk to her, try to put her at her ease? She has met Vickie already, but Vickie is far too scatterbrained to be any comfort."

"Of course, but I must be in the drawing room before the gentlemen come in or Mama will put me on bread and water."

338

"Figuratively, I trust. Don't worry, I'll go and keep 'em circulating the port for at least half an hour."

He was not surprised to find the after-dinner conversation revolving around Waterloo and Napoleon, now a prisoner aboard HMS Bellerophon. His personal closeness to the battle still allowed him to claim a certain expertise. He easily kept his father's guests sitting for close to an hour while they in turn, however unwittingly, prevented his father's interrogating him about his guests.

When they repaired to the drawing room, he managed to snatch a brief tête-à-tête with Connie.

"Did you see her?"

"Yes, and I like her prodigiously. We talked about her brother — you did not mention that he is still an invalid. I shall do all I can to help the poor, brave young man recover his strength," she said earnestly.

"You are a sweetheart, Con. That will give me more chance to have Fanny to myself."

"Oh, Felix, you are in love with her! I half suspected as much when you first told me about her. But what about Lady . . . ?" She cut herself short as one of the visitors approached them with a request for music. Obligingly she went to the pianoforte.

Feeling he had done his duty by his

parents' guests, Felix slipped out of the room, retired to his temporary quarters, and went to bed.

In the morning he rose early. The housekeeper would have explained breakfast arrangements to Fanny, but he had no intention of letting her meet the earl and countess without his support. Three of last night's party were staying at Westwood, too, so she would face a terrifying battery of well-bred inquisitiveness.

The first to arrive in the breakfast room, he was half way through a plateful of ham and eggs when Fanny and Connie came in together. His sister's beauty failed to divert his gaze from Fanny's fresh prettiness in her sprig muslin gown. He stood up, smiling in response to her warm, dimpled smile and the dancing light in her brown eyes.

"Lord Roworth, how is it you never told me what jewels you have for sisters? Lady Victoria has taken Anita to the nursery for breakfast, while Lady Constantia lent me her abigail and would not let me come down alone."

"I was prepared to make my breakfast last until you appeared, Miss Ingram," he assured her.

"I did not know you would be here already," Connie said, giving him a look that demanded last night's postponed explanations at no very distant time. "The customs of a strange house can be sadly confusing. Do sit down and eat. Your eggs are growing cold. Miss Ingram, come and help yourself from the sideboard. We are informal at breakfast."

"Informal? Do Lord and Lady Westwood not come down to breakfast?" she asked hopefully.

"In general Mama does not, but today they both will because we have guests who do not care to breakfast in their rooms. Will you have some kedgeree?"

"Thank you, just bread and butter. I am not very hungry this morning."

"Nonsense." Felix was well acquainted with her appetite and he'd be damned if he'd let it be destroyed by apprehension. It had taken her a month at Miriam's to make up for the weight she had lost after Frank was wounded. He jumped up and filled her plate with a little of everything, then seated her beside him and set about distracting her.

He succeeded so well that she and Connie were laughing over the Duke of Oxshott's discomfiture when Lord Westwood came in.

"Good morning, sir." Felix rose. "I'd like to present Miss Ingram."

She started to stand up to make her

curtsy, but he put his hand on her arm. She was a lady, no schoolroom miss to rise when an older gentleman, however distinguished, entered the room.

"Miss Ingram." The earl nodded, his aristocratic face expressionless.

"How do you do, my lord," she said, pale but composed.

"Pray do not let me interrupt your meal, ma'am. I trust you have been made comfortable?"

"Thank you, sir, very comfortable." Fanny toyed with the remains of her breakfast while Lord Westwood helped himself at the sideboard.

Tea, the universal remedy, thought Felix, and refilled her cup as he spoke. "I hope to make Miss Ingram's brother known to you later, sir, if he is well enough to come down. Their little ward, Anita, is in the nursery."

The earl's lips tightened, but before he could speak, Connie put in boldly, "Captain Ingram fought at Waterloo, Papa."

"Indeed. Which regiment, Miss Ingram?" The earl joined them at the table.

"The Artillery, sir."

His eyebrows rose and he cast a piercing glance at Felix. The sons of noblemen did not enter the Artillery.

There had been a time when his father's

piercing glance had made him shudder. Since then he had become accustomed to facing the penetrating gazes of Nathan Rothschild and the Duke of Wellington. As piercing glances go, the earl's came in a poor third.

"Frank Ingram was wounded at Quatre Bras, sir," he said calmly. "Shall I ring for fresh coffee?"

The butler and a footman were replenishing coffee, tea, and chocolate pots when Lady Westwood entered with her noble guests. Felix presented Fanny, who was received with cool courtesy. In the confusion as the new arrivals were served and seated, he abstracted her from the room, along with Connie, but not before his father had demanded his presence in his study in half an hour.

"I must see Anita and Frank," said Fanny as the breakfast room door closed behind them.

"I am looking forward prodigiously to making the captain's acquaintance," Connie said eagerly.

"Not in his chamber — or mine, rather," her brother warned as they started up the stairs. "You'll have to wait until he comes down."

"As to that, I have a splendid notion.

Felix, you know the little room that opens off the gallery? If we turn that into a bed-chamber for Captain Ingram, he will not have to go up and down stairs, and he can exercise in the gallery or easily walk into the garden."

"That is a wonderful idea, Lady Constantia." Fanny turned on Felix the appealing gaze he was incapable of resisting. "I am afraid that he might not continue his exercises without Miriam to coerce him. He is more likely to walk, at least, if it is easy to leave his chamber. Do you think it possible?"

"Consider it done."

They went first to the nursery, where Anita was exercising an aged rocking horse under Vickie's watchful eye.

"Look!" she cried. "I'm galloping. Look at me galloping, Aunt Fanny. Uncle Felix, 'member when you were my horse? This horse gallops."

"And I never even managed a trot," said Felix, shaking his head.

Fanny and Connie laughed. Vickie looked disbelieving. "You let her ride on your back, Felix? An out-and-outer like you? You are a complete hand!"

"Lady Victoria!" Her governess called her to order for her language. A tall, grey-haired woman with a warm smile, she told Fanny she was delighted to take charge of Anita. "I am in hopes that caring for Miss Anita will impart to Lady Victoria a sense of responsibility, a quality in which she is sadly lacking," she confided.

They stayed awhile until Fanny was quite sure that Anita was happy. Then Fanny went to see her brother, Connie to order the room by the gallery made up as a bedchamber, and Felix to his interview with his father. His reluctance had vanished. He was determined to be Fanny's knight in shining armour, and if the ogres happened to be his parents, so be it.

Both Lord and Lady Westwood awaited him in the study with its superb plasterwork ceiling and shabby furniture. The earl broke off what he was saying and invited his son to sit down. Felix declined, choosing rather to lean casually against the carved marble fireplace.

"Who are the Ingrams?" asked his mother, with more mistrust than curiosity.

"My friends."

"You mean nobodies, I collect," said the earl. "An obscure artillery captain and his sister! I do not pretend to regulate your friendships when you are abroad on your 'business', but I had expected you to have more sense of propriety than to bring home common acquaintances."

"It is the outside of enough, Felix, to introduce such people to your sisters."

He kept his temper on a tight rein. "Such people as Captain Ingram saved you from Bonaparte, ma'am. Nor is there anything common about Miss Ingram. She is uncommonly kind-hearted, uncommonly courageous, uncommonly . . ."

"Enough!" said his father impatiently. "I am prepared to accept that the young woman is possessed of many virtues. Nevertheless, she does not belong at Westwood, especially when you are trying to fix your interest with Daventry's daughter."

"But I am not, sir." With a sardonic smile at their consternation, he continued, "I have decided that Lady Sophia and I shall not suit."

"Not suit?" snapped Lady Westwood. "You cannot hope to find a more suitable bride."

"And not a fortnight since you informed us of your admiration for the girl, your intention to pay your addresses," the earl reminded him. "Such fickleness is inexcusable."

"I know what it is, that female has entrapped you with her wiles!"

He stared at his mother. "Fanny?" he said, incredulous. "On the contrary, she didn't want to come here, and I'm not at all certain that she will have me."

"You admit that she has bewitched you," the countess declared with a triumphant air.

"Oh yes, I cannot deny it." Now his smile was tender.

"My dear boy," said his father, abandoning tact in his irritation, "one may be enamoured but one does not marry females of her condition. No family, no fortune, not even great beauty, and she already has a child of questionable provenance. Marriage is not only unnecessary, it is unthinkable."

Felix rounded on him in a cold fury. "Sir, if you dare to speak in that fashion of the woman I love and hope to wed, you will never see my face again. Miss Ingram is above reproach. If she will be my wife, I shall be the happiest man alive, and I shall marry her with or without your approval."

Not waiting for a response, he stalked from the room.

He found Connie supervising the rearrangement of the room for Frank. Drawing her aside, he recounted all that had passed.

She listened wide-eyed to the tale of his defiance, but when he finished she clapped her hands. "So you did not propose to Lady Sophia? I am glad. When you described her and Miss Ingram to me, I thought at once that Miss Ingram sounded much more amiable."

"Amiable, adorable, but not eligible. I don't give a tinker's curse for eligibility! It's not as if she were a butcher's daughter, let alone an opera dancer."

"If they cannot change your mind, Mama and Papa will try to convince Miss Ingram that an artillery officer's daughter is as unfit as a butcher's daughter to join the family," she said, worried.

"They may well succeed," he said grimly, "though they may not need to. I have no assurance that Fanny wants to marry me. I thought, when I told her I wasn't going to marry Lady Sophia, that she'd be pleased if only because she has a low opinion of her. I even hoped her delight at being rid of a rival might tell me she cared for me. But she seemed indifferent. What am I to do next, Con?"

"I don't know. You will think of something, but keep her away from Mama and Papa until you do. Why not take her riding? Luckily it has stopped raining. I shall keep Captain Ingram company while you are out."

With Connie's promise to try not to let Frank overtax his strength, Fanny willingly agreed to go riding. The sight of her in her brown habit on the small, sluggish mare his sisters shared reminded Felix of the review in the Allée Verte when her mount had been a huge troop horse. He recalled his wrath at her imagined danger, and his irritable reaction to her warm friendship with Frank's fellow officers. He had been jealous! He had loved Fanny far longer than he knew.

If only he had not wasted so much time pursuing Lady Sophia, he might already be married to Fanny instead of just beginning to woo her.

Followed by a groom, they rode up the hill behind the house. The brisk breeze that was clearing away the clouds brought roses to Fanny's cheeks and her eyes sparkled like the sunlit raindrops on the meadow flowers. Yet new, dark clouds gathered in the west, and her brightness dimmed as they returned to the stables an hour or two later. Lifting her down from the mare's back, Felix ached to hold her close and knew he didn't dare risk his parents cowing her into submission to their will.

Miriam had advised him to wait, but for once he was not going to follow Miriam's advice.

As they went into the house, Fanny still felt his hands at her waist. If she were truly ill-bred, she'd have given in to her burning desire to throw her arms about his neck in defiance of all propriety and decorum. She was betwixt and between, neither refined enough to be his wife, nor so lost to decency as to become his mistress. She should not have come.

In the great hall, they met Lord Westwood. He stared with contempt at the posy of scabious and ox eye daisies Felix had picked and stuck in Fanny's hat band. "A word with you, if you please, Miss Ingram," he said coldly.

For Felix's sake as much as her own, she refused to be intimidated. On his behalf, she resented the earl's disdain for his son's guest. She raised her chin and looked him straight in the eyes, blue as Felix's but icy where Felix's were warm. "Certainly, my lord," she said graciously, "as soon as I have changed out of my riding dress."

As the earl turned away, Felix grasped her arm, put his finger to his lips, and pulled her in the opposite direction. "A word with you, if you please, Miss Ingram," he said. "Come into the library, it should be unoccupied." He closed the door behind them.

"Lord Westwood looks at me as if I were a

snail!" Her voice shook with anger.

Felix was disconcerted, as if he'd expected to have to comfort her. Instead, as with Lady Sophia in the Brussels park, he had to make excuses. "My father's haughty air is not deliberate, Fanny. It's part of him. I was like that until Miriam taught me modesty."

Amusement edged out anger. "You, modest!"

"Am I arrogant?" he asked, mortified.

"No, not arrogant, Felix — or only rarely!" Despite the teasing qualification, she hadn't meant to hurt him. She laid her hand on his arm and looked up at him, earnest now. "You have a sort of self-assurance that I daresay stems from an inbred belief in your own worth."

"Pompous?" he groaned.

"Oh no, that's not what I mean at all." Afraid he might read her feelings in her face, she busied herself taking off her gloves. "It is . . . it is a very attractive quality."

The gloves dropped to the floor unnoticed as he seized her hands. "Fanny, will you marry me?"

Startled, afraid — no, certain — she must have misheard, she stammered, "But . . . but your parents . . . and what about Anita?"

"We'll adopt her, and I don't care two figs for my parents' notion of consequence."

The dear, dear man, from the chivalry of his heart, was offering her and Anita a home. She had every reason to refuse: a pride that shrank from accepting charity; a fear that he would come to hate her for disrupting his relationship with his parents, for being an inadequate viscountess. . . . She had every reason to accept: Anita's future; love, love, love. . . .

Her head in a whirl, she cried, "Oh, Felix, I cannot. . . ."

A discreet tapping at the door interrupted her. She tore her hands from his and moved hastily to pretend to scan the bookshelves as the butler came in.

"My lord, a person demanding to speak to your lordship."

"A person?" asked Felix irritably.

"A Cockney person, my lord, in a catskin waistcoat and a hat that appears to have been sat upon," said the butler, his voice resonant with disapproval. "He enquired whether Captain and Miss Ingram were in residence. I did not feel it my place to enlighten him but I put him in the small anteroom."

"The man from Brussels! Fan . . . Miss Ingram, it must be the man who asked those impertinent questions about you and Frank. How the deuce did he track us down?" He turned back to the butler. "Have him thrown out on his ear."

"No!" Fanny protested. Sooner or later the man must be dealt with, and besides, she needed time to think, to decide between the promptings of heart and self-respect. "If he has found us at Westwood, he will find us wherever we go. Lord Roworth, please, will you try to find out what he wants, without admitting to him that we are here?"

"Never fear, I shall not let him cut up your peace." Felix strode out.

And as he left, Fanny knew that when he returned she would want to fling herself into his arms, and that she must not. He must be given a chance to withdraw his impulsive offer, even if it broke her heart.

CHAPTER 19

Cannot what? Felix thought. Cannot marry an arrogant man she doesn't love, even to give Anita a home?

Furious at the interruption, he stormed into the anteroom. "What the devil do you want?" he snapped at the seedy little man.

"Well, now, m'lord, that's no way to talk to summun as 'as come to do your friends a favour. And a devil of a time I've 'ad of it a-follerin' yer backards and forrards cross the Channel. I ain't stirrin' till I've 'ad me say."

"A favour?" The word penetrated Felix's distraction. "What sort of favour? And why did you not say so when first I talked to you?"

"Acos I din't know for sure if they was the right Ingrams, did I?" he said indignantly. "Tell 'em there's summat in it for 'em and you'll get pretenders popping out o' the woodwork. Jist makes it 'arder for a cove as all 'e wants is to make a honest living. It's no good tellin' them lawyers 'this cully 'ere says 'e's the right 'un.' Gotta 'ave proof, don't I, or near as makes no odds."

"You work for a lawyer? And you have proof that my friends are the Ingrams you are looking for?" If Fanny refused to marry him, a bit of a legacy would make a world of difference to her.

"I don't s'pose, m'lord, as you 'appen to know their ma's maiden name?"

A sudden suspicion dawned on him. Had the mysterious, disregarded, titled grandfather decided to put in an appearance in their lives? He racked his brains for the requested information. "I don't believe I know it. Not her surname. I know her Christian name was Frances."

"That'll 'ave to do."

"And Frank was accidentally given her middle name, which is a deadly secret," he added with a grin.

"Lady Frances Cynthia Kerridge," said the little man stolidly, "daughter of the Duke of Oxshott." He stared, affronted, as Felix collapsed onto a chair in a fit of laughter.

"Oxshott!" he gasped. "That pompous sapskull! But wait a minute, Oxshott's not old enough to be Miss Ingram's grand-father."

"The late duke, I oughter 've said. It ain't no joke, m'lord. I'm a discreet sorta cove or no lawyer'd hire me, but seeing I knows you're their friend I'll tell yer. It's a matter o' two estates and a plum apiece, or there-abouts."

"A hundred thousand apiece!" Felix sat up and began to take serious notice.

A few minutes later, he returned to the library, to tell Fanny the news and to judge by her reaction whether to renew his pro-posal at once. He wanted her too much to stand aside, proudly noble, because she was suddenly wealthy. If she accepted him now, he'd be sure it was not just for the sake of a home for herself and Anita.

All the same, he was glad he had already offered, before she knew of her changed fortunes. Now she'd not think he had been too high-and-mighty to pay his addresses to a simple soldier's daughter, nor that he cared a pin for her money.

Fanny was standing at the window with her back to him, bare-headed, a sunbeam gleaming on her brown curls. Hearing his step she turned, the train of her habit looped over her arm. Her face was in shadow, but he saw she was holding the nosegay he had fixed on her hat.

"What did he want?" she asked anxiously, coming to meet him.

"What was your mother's maiden name?" he countered.

"He is still asking about that? I don't know. She did not like to talk about her past."

"Then you are going to have to tell me Frank's middle name."

"Oh, Felix, need I? I swore I would never reveal it."

"I'm afraid to ask him," he confessed, "and though I suspect I already know, I must be certain. Can you not trust me?"

She managed not to smile but her dimples gave her away. "He was christened Francis Cynthia," she choked out. "He will kill me if you ever breathe a word of this. What is all this about?"

He took her hand, led her to a chair, and made her sit down. Fanny was not given to fainting, but the news was enough to make anyone swoon. "Your maternal grandfather died eleven months ago," he began.

"Well, I cannot be sorry," she said candidly, "for he treated Mama disgracefully. Who was he?"

"The Duke of Oxshott."

"A duke!" Fanny looked puzzled. "The

name seems familiar, but I cannot think where I have heard it. Certainly not from Mama. I know, it was from you, and just this morning. Are you saying I am related to the horrid man you saw at Mr Rothschild's? So that is why you made me sit down! How dreadful, he must be Mama's brother, my uncle."

"I'm afraid so. It seems your grandfather, too, had a low opinion of his son and heir. Taggle, the fellow who tracked you down, caught a glimpse of the will and claims he was described in that legal document as a nincompoop. However, the late duke was an equally irascible gentleman — a cantankerous old curmudgeon, according to Taggle — who quarrelled constantly with all his relatives. The only exception was your mother, because, having banished her, he had not seen her in nearly thirty years."

"He came to regret casting her off?"

"I suspect it would be more accurate to say that time and distance diminished his anger at her disobedience. Be that as it may, he left to her, or in equal parts between her legitimate offspring, all his unentailed possessions." Pausing, he met her questioning brown eyes and steeled himself. She didn't need his protection now, didn't need the security he could offer her and Anita. His only hope was that she needed his love. "You are a very wealthy woman, Fanny."

"Wealthy?" she whispered, turning very pale. For a moment he thought she was going to faint, but before he could move towards her she sprang to her feet. "I must tell Frank."

He watched her run from the room, his heart twisting painfully within him.

No doubt his parents would be delighted to hear that the woman their son wanted to marry was an heiress and the niece of a duke — until they discovered that Miss Fanny Ingram's only concern was her brother. Felix strode out to the stables, shouted for a horse, and galloped off across the fields, indifferent to the drenching rain.

Cold and famished, he returned to the house just in time to change for dinner. During his absence, Trevor had arrived. With his usual long-suffering air, the valet called for hot water and helped his master out of his sodden clothes. Felix was sinking into the luxurious warmth of his bath when his father's man brought a summons to the earl's dressing room.

Sighing, he washed quickly and climbed out again. With Trevor's assistance, he was soon dressed in his austere, elegant black, his cravat arranged to a nicety, his shoes polished to a shine that only Trevor could achieve. He went and knocked on the earl's door.

"Come in." Dismissing his valet with a gesture, Lord Westwood attacked. "Your inamorata is both discourteous and impertinent. She kept me waiting for over an hour."

Felix was astonished. He had been prepared for permission to court Fanny with all assiduity. "She had an unforeseen visitor, sir," he said cautiously.

"So I understand: a vulgar, disreputable fellow such as one would expect her to consort with."

Why had she not revealed her visitor's business? Pride, he thought. She would not stoop to bargain for respect that was not freely offered.

The earl continued. "I attempted to impress upon her — for her own good — the discomfort the difference in station must cause her if she were to remain at Westwood. She had the impudence to respond that she would take my opinion into consideration!"

His admiration for Fanny redoubled, Felix grinned. "No doubt she will do just that," he observed. "Miss Ingram is no fool."

"No, you are the fool!"

"If you will excuse me, sir," said Felix with

dignity, "I want a word with Captain Ingram before dinner."

Frank was settled in the room off the gallery, with his dinner on a tray. Not surprisingly, he was in high spirits. "I understand you have been protecting us from good fortune these several months," he said, grinning.

"Yes, and when I think you might have avoided Quatre Bras . . ."

"Ah, I wager that's why Fanny isn't as pleased as she ought to be. She wouldn't tell me. I'd never have sold out just before the battle, though."

"No, I suppose not."

"You haven't told anyone else, have you? Fanny and I have decided to keep mum until we've finished with the legal formalities, though it seems that's all that's needed. She found our baptismal certificates among our mother's papers and they settle the matter, according to Taggle. He thinks the lawyer will post down here at once as it's a substantial estate."

"Very substantial. My congratulations. You will stay here for the present, then?"

"If it is not inconvenient," Frank said guardedly.

"Of course not. You ought not to undertake another journey so soon."

"I'd just as soon not, especially as your sister has taken up Miriam's good work. Lady Constantia is the loveliest, gentlest ministering angel a man could dream of. I've persuaded Fanny it would be bad for Anita to be moved, too. The poor child hated being parted from Amos, and here she already adores Lady Victoria. You are lucky in your sisters."

"So are you," said Felix with heartfelt sincerity, but his emotions were in a whirl. Fanny wished to leave Westwood. Was his parents' coldness responsible, or was she afraid he would press an unwanted suit? She must know he would not persecute her with his attentions. He could not bear to see her unhappy.

"Fanny is very unhappy," Connie accused her brother. She had run him to earth in the stable yard, where he had just returned from a solitary ride. "How can you treat her so? I had not thought you so weak-willed as to crawl like a worm at Mama's and Papa's bidding."

"A worm!" Felix noticed a stable boy smirking nearby and drew his militant sister through a brick archway into the English garden. "Their disapproval has nothing to do with it."

"They have nothing to disapprove of any more, since you have been treating Fanny like a stranger for three days. This morning, Mama went so far as to commend her neat stitches. Have you changed your mind, Felix, as you did with Lady Sophia?"

He groaned. "I am deeper in love than ever. When I see her I want to . . . well, that's not the sort of thing a fellow can discuss with his sister."

Connie blushed and hid her face in a mass of pink and yellow honeysuckle. "Is that why you are avoiding her? You are afraid of . . . of losing control?"

"Good Lord, no! I hope I have more command over myself than that."

"Then why?"

"Because she doesn't need me any more, Con. I'm telling you this in confidence, mind. It turns out that she and Frank are closely related to the Duke of Oxshott and they have come into a fortune."

"A fortune? And a noble family? Then what has she to be miserable about except your determination to avoid her?"

"Perhaps I have been too aloof," he conceded warily. "After all, we are good friends."

"Felix, you dear, blind idiot, she loves you. Why do you suppose she was in a quake at meeting Mama and Papa, when you have told me how intrepid she is? Why did she come to Westwood despite her fears, when she might have stayed comfortably at Nettledene?"

"Why did she say 'I cannot' when I asked her to marry me?"

"Did you tell her you love her?"

He thought back. "No," he admitted. "I told her I'd adopt Anita and that I don't care a fig for my parents' opinion. And we were interrupted."

"There you are, then. It is all a stupid misunderstanding, I vow. Perhaps she was going to say, 'I cannot refuse though I feel I ought.' You wait here in the honeysuckle bower and I shall send her to you."

It seemed to Felix he waited forever, pacing between fragrant, overgrown beds of clove pinks and candytuft. Could Connie possibly be right? Was that what Miriam had meant when she called him blind — blind to Fanny's feelings as well as his own? Was that why she had warned him against flirting with Fanny? Had he hurt her?

He'd rather die than hurt her. He dared not hope she could love such a crass, insensitive brute.

Fanny was in the nursery, watching Anita

and Vickie walking about with books balanced on their heads. The governess made Vickie do it to improve her carriage. As far as Anita was concerned, anything Vickie did, she did, too. With a natural grace, she excelled at book-balancing.

When Connie came in, both girls lost their concentration and their books at once. They fell into a fit of giggles and Fanny summoned up a smile.

Smiling took a tremendous effort. Everything took an effort. Nothing seemed worth doing since Felix had made it so very plain that he didn't really want to marry her. Now that she was wealthy, his chivalrous generosity was unneeded, but he didn't have to avoid her. Did he think she'd pursue him, insist on holding him to his offer?

Why, oh why, did Frank insist on staying at Westwood when all she wanted was to flee?

"Fanny, may I have a word with you?" Connie's voice broke in upon her misery. She sounded agitated, determined yet a trifle unsure of herself.

"Of course." Fanny dragged herself from her chair and followed Connie out into the passage. A sudden alarm disrupted her lethargy. "Is Frank . . . ?"

"Captain Ingram is better every day. I'm

sure he is too much recovered to have a sudden relapse. Fanny, I feel like a horrid busybody but I must speak. My brother . . . You and Felix . . . Oh, dear, I am making a dreadful muddle of this."

Fanny turned hot all over, then cold. "Felix?" she faltered.

"You and he have unfinished business, do you not? He is waiting for you in the English garden. Will you go to him?" Connie begged.

"The English garden?" she repeated stupidly. "Waiting for me?"

Connie gave her a little push. "Go on."

She started towards the stairs at a sedate pace, then suddenly her feet sprouted wings. Felix waiting for her? How long would he wait? In time with her racing pulse, she ran down the stairs, across the hall, oblivious of startled servants and Lady Westwood's scandalized stare.

Approaching the garden, her footsteps slowed. Unfinished business, Connie had said. Perhaps she had persuaded her brother that he must explain his coolness. Perhaps he simply wanted to be quite certain that she had not misunderstood his reasons for offering his hand. Daunted, she hesitated as she reached the end of the laurel hedge.

She wished she had stopped to put on her

hat and gloves. At least she could have preserved her dignity instead of letting him see how desperately she wanted him.

Pride drove her on, pride and an unquenchable hope. Her heart fluttered in her breast as she turned the corner into the English garden.

It seemed to Felix that he waited forever, pacing as he considered and discarded openings. Yet Fanny must have hurried for when at last she appeared she was hatless and out of breath. The sun gilded her curls as she approached along the gravel path, her footsteps tentative. He still had not found the words he needed.

So he simply said, "I love you."

"Oh, Felix!" She ran the last few steps and then her arms were about his waist, her head against his chest. A little sob escaped her as he hugged her closer. "I thought you were just being kind."

Attempting to kiss her, he got a mouthful of curls, so he picked her up and carried her into the arbour. Seated on the bench with her nestled in his lap, kissing was so much easier that he went on doing it for some time. Her mouth was warm and sweet, irresistible, and her slender body was well-nigh irresistible too. She didn't appear to mind his roving hands, but at last he called himself sternly to order and moved her to the seat beside him — close beside him, with his arm round her in case she took it into her head to move away, though he didn't believe there was much likelihood of that.

"Kind?" he asked dreamily.

"I thought you were being kind, offering Anita and me a home because you had given up hope of Lady Sophia. Then suddenly Frank and I were rich so we didn't need a home any longer, but I was very tempted to accept anyway, so I ran away to avoid temptation. And you began to ignore us, so I was certain that your offer was just made out of kindness."

"My darling widgeon, I ignored you because you ran away. I didn't want to harass you. And where did you get the idea that I had given up hope of Lady Sophia? Some people may call me a fool but . . ."

"How dare they! Who?"

"Miriam, because I didn't realize that I love you; my father, because I told him I love you; and Connie, because I didn't guess that you love me."

"Oh, that's all right, then."

"Aren't you going to avenge me?" he teased, his heart swelling with tenderness.

"No, Lord Westwood is entitled to his opinion and Miriam and Connie were right, my darling slowtop," she said lovingly. He couldn't let her insult him so he stopped her speaking the best way he knew how. When she surfaced from the kiss, she accused him, "You told me you had given up hope of Lady Sophia. Wait, no, I assumed you had been refused but all you said was that you were not going to marry her."

"That was careless of me. As I was saying, I am not such a slowtop that I didn't realize in time, before I proposed, that Lady Sophia was not at all the sort of wife I wanted. I admit it was a few minutes later that I realized what sort of wife I did want."

"What sort was that?" she asked provocatively.

"I decided I simply could not live without dimples, one here —" he kissed it "— and one here." And he kissed that one, too. "So, you see, I was thinking of my own survival, not being kind at all. But now you are much richer than I am, so it's your turn to be kind. Fortunately I know you are the kindest-hearted person in Christendom."

It was up to her to prove him right, so she kissed him, very kindly indeed.

We hope you have enjoyed this Large Print book. Other Thorndike, Wheeler, Kennebec, and Chivers Press Large Print books are available at your library or directly from the publishers.

For information about current and upcoming titles, please call or write, without obligation, to:

Publisher
Thorndike Press
295 Kennedy Memorial Drive
Waterville, ME 04901
Tel. (800) 223-1244

or visit our Web site at:

http://gale.cengage.com/thorndike

OR

Chivers Large Print
published by AudioGO Ltd
St James House, The Square
Lower Bristol Road
Bath BA2 3BH
England
Tel. +44(0) 800 136919
email: info@audiogo.co.uk
www.audiogo.co.uk

All our Large Print titles are designed for easy reading, and all our books are made to last.